LESLIE O'SULLIVAN

PRESS RELEASE

BEHIND THE SCENES ❤ BOOK 2

PRESS RELEASE

LESLIE O'SULLIVAN

CITY OWL
PRESS

PRESS RELEASE
Behind the Scenes, Book 2

CITY OWL PRESS
www.cityowlpress.com

Cover Design by MiblArt. All stock photos licensed appropriately.

Edited by Theresa Cole & Lisa Green.

For information on subsidiary rights, please contact the publisher at info@cityowlpress.com.

Print Edition ISBN: 978-1-64898-315-3

Digital Edition ISBN: 978-1-64898-316-0

Printed in the United States of America

ALSO BY LESLIE O'SULLIVAN

Rockin Fairy Tales:

Pink Guitars and Falling Stars

Gilded Butterfly

Wild Azure Waves

Crimson Melodies

Emerald Spire (Winter 2024)

***

Behind the Scenes:

Hot Set

Press Release

Not to Scale

PRAISE FOR LESLIE O'SULLIVAN

"*Hot Set,* by Leslie O'Sullivan, is a contemporary love story that creatively infuses modern concerns with the nostalgia generated by a period television show. The Irish setting was fantastically romantic, and I thought the cast of characters was refreshingly practical for a group involved in show business." — *Reader's Favorite 5-star review*

"As full of heart and soul as the music it describes, *Crimson Melodies* drew me in with a fresh take on a classic tale, masterfully combining celebrity and monster romance vibes to give me everything I wanted and more!" — S.C. Grayson, author of *Beauty and the Blade*

"Submerging readers into a fantastical world, *Wild Azure Waves* is a love story swimming with music, mysticism, and magic." — *InD'tale*

"*Pink Guitars and Falling Stars* is a fast paced and very engaging read, with a constantly evolving main character and a colorful cast. The adventure wraps up nicely, and ends with a hint of what is next in the Rockin' Fairy Tales series. This is a great read if you are looking for an action-packed modern fairy tale with aspiring rock stars who fall from the sky." — *Paranormal Romance Guild*

"*Gilded Butterfly* is a unique and magical mashup of fairy tales, Shakespeare, and lore, unlike anything I've read before. At its heart, is a beautiful story about family, the destructive power of chasing fame and money, and the healing power of love. The twists, turns, and magic sprinkled throughout create an engaging story that brings a new kind of fairy tale to modern Hollywood." — *Megan Van Dyke, author of Second Star to the Left*

This book is written with love for everyone who proudly dons the title of geek or nerd and goes bonkers over their favorite fandoms. You are my people.

CHAPTER I

ULTIMATUM

The weekly call from my boss is overdue. Every Wednesday, this phone chat with L.A. guarantees loss of appetite and teeth grinding. I regress into a secondary schooler summoned to the principal's office instead of the thirty-two-year-old head of P.R. for a brilliant TV period drama that's currently rocketing in popularity.

I beat samba, waltz, and tarantella rhythms around the phone on my desk to summon the call with no result. Perhaps tapping out "Bohemian Rhapsody," best rock song ever written, will do the trick. Better yet, here in the land where the blood of druids and pagans still flows through my fellow Irish locals, a ritualistic *"ring damn you"* chant may be the wisest choice.

If only I knew one.

The glint of an overhead light catches my new coat of nail polish. I chose a perfect tonal match to my plum-colored skirt and suit jacket. My reflection in the glass office wall is a study in plum. My suit and nails are the exact shade of my leather desk chair. Except for the pale skin of my face, I'd disappear completely into my surroundings, a carnivore poised to pounce on the unaware. Here in my personal jungle of plum, steel, and glass, I am the alpha predator.

Or am I?

I glare at the non-ringing phone on my desk. This call is my weekly judgement, shifting my position to more prey than predator. Och! I'm being as dramatic as a scene in our television show, *The Chieftain's Son*. My overly loud exhale falls somewhere between ironic chuckle and frustrated huff. I prefer to initiate calls instead of being shackled to the receiving end. Control is my goddess, and I gladly worship at her bejeweled sandals.

A backwards shove of the chair gives me freedom to pace between door and desk. My feet pinch from a day in heels. I can't decide if I'd rather down a generous pour of the red blend waiting at home or soak my feet in it.

"Ring, you bloody bastard."

The alarm on my cell trills half-six, day's end for most everyone else here at The Clan, production headquarters of *The Chieftain's Son*. It's my daily reminder to catch people before they leave for the day if I've got a bit of news or instructions for them. My frustration ebbs a bit at the thought of the accolades for our brilliant show. In our first season out of the gate, we scored ten Crystal nominations, the most prestigious U.S. television award, along with additional smatterings of European honors. Everyone on our team in the FYC, For Your Consideration, campaign across multiple awards made final cuts. That's an entire bird's worth of feathers in my cap for the backbreaking work to coordinate the publicity and marketing chores between here in Ireland and Hollywood. Truth is, the challenge lights me up as bright as a Beltane bonfire.

So, why does my gut ping like radar detecting an imminent attack while I wait for the damnable L.A. phone call?

Through the glass wall of my office, I return waves from folks leaving for the day. When I deal with Hollywood, the time difference between here in County Kerry, Ireland, and the land of palm trees and over-priced sunglasses makes their quitting time the beginning of my workday.

Collin, one of our senior writers, pops his head in. "Pub call, Meg. You in?"

"Waiting to chat with L.A. Maybe after."

He flips a strand of black hair out of his eyes. "Bobby's standing the first round."

I hate to turn down a fresh drawn Guinness, mother's milk. "Can't commit, Coll, but thanks."

"Anyone ever tell you, Ms. McGrath, it's no crime to ease up now and then?"

"Every day." Easing up is a non-negotiable for me. High standards make the world go 'round. "If luck is with me, I will walk through the pub door before the second round."

"Here's hoping." He tosses me a parting smile and heads out. From a side view, I notice Collin's belly has shifted from paunch to trim. The once-a-day walk and weekly round of golf Gillian Bettencourt O'Leary, our newest staff writer and wife of our star, instigated with the writing staff is paying off.

Ten more minutes plod along as slow as cattle blocking the lane, and I drop back onto my desk chair. This isn't the first time Dashell Everett, my boss at the True Time Network, ranked a call to his on-site publicist for *The Chieftain's Son* television program a lower priority than morning espresso. With *The Chieftain's Son* debut at San Diego Cali Con, the celebration of the popular arts chock-full of celebrities and high-octane fans, less than a month away, Dash and I have a laundry list of logistics to button up. Or rather, I'll fill him in on everything I've inked in. He'll respond with a few inane questions, one or two ludicrous suggestions, and then sign off with his signature morning yawn.

Maureen, the most manic of our writing staff, swings in on my door like a kid on a playground. Her kinky red hair frizzes in an impressive nimbus to frame her face. It must be a nightmare to run a comb through that maze. She balances a small dessert plate on her palm, maneuvering a flat figure eight with it through the air.

"Megsie, I've brought deliciousness."

I slash an X with my hand. "We agreed to bury the 'Megsie' thing."

She dances around my desk, tempting me with the pastry on her plate. "How about Megalith? Megawatt?" Maureen cuddles up to my chair and waves the goodie under my nose. "Dulce de leche Napoleon with your name stamped in the icing."

I accept the offering of my favorite dessert and set it next to my computer. "Did you think to bring a fork?" Maureen's fiancé is the pastry chef at our fanciest hotel in Waterville, the closest town to The Clan production complex. The man is a god with his sweeties. "Or are you withholding utensils until you explain the conditions of this blatant bribe?"

She spins my chair so we're face-to-face and clasps both hands over her heart as if suffering a mortal wound. "Can't I gift one of my bridesmaids with something to put a smile on her face and crumbs on the lapel of her tailored suit jacket?"

I defy anyone not to crack a smile in the wake of Maureen's Maureen-ness.

"I want your opinion on the sweetie. Grady's thinking to make our wedding cake a three-tiered version of this Napoleon."

I cock my head. "The groom's baking his own wedding cake?"

"You think he'd trust anyone else to do it?"

There's something Maureen's Grady and I share. If you want a thing done the way it should be, you do it yourself.

Her livewire locks tickle my nose as she darts in to give me a peck on the cheek. "You caught me on the bribe. Nothing in life comes without an angle, Megsie." She rests elbows on my desk. "Here's my ask. I know you planned for the two of us to room together at Cali Con, but will you die of loneliness if I have my own digs?"

"Bringing Grady to San Diego, are you?"

"He begged the week off from the hotel, and we thought it would be lovely to tool around California with Jack and Gilly a bit after the convention." Her eyes take on a wicked glint. "You're very welcome to share the room with the both of us, it could be interesting."

The needle on my danger meter bounces into the red at the mention of our star and his hush-hush missus. "Tool around where with Jack and Gilly?" I'm at my wits end trying to keep news of Jack O'Leary's marriage on lockdown. How can those eejits think prancing around together in the land of Paparazzi-on-every-corner is anything but image suicide for Jack? It's vital his female fans continue stoking their fantasies about him being available.

"Stand down, Warden. Bobby'll be with us as well." She crosses fingers on both hands and makes circles in the air. "We'll make sure to keep at least two bodies between the happy couple wherever we go. You have my word not to make your job any harder than it already is."

Truth be told, toolin' around on adventures with the person who shares your dreams sounds grand. Seeing Jack and Gilly together pokes at the fingertip-sized scar on my heart from the few times in the past I'd thought such a connection was possible. Part of me pulls to support the two publicly, but the stronger force says to sit them down and warn: what are rainbows now will disappear when the sun shines bright enough to illuminate fan backlash.

I mentally count our reserved rooms. Our senior writer, Danna, bugged out of Cali Con in favor of staying here and cracking the whip so Collin, Benj, and Benny, the rest of our writing staff, will polish their scripts for the second half of season two. Gilly, Bobby, and Maureen will carve out writing time while we're in San Diego. "You and Grady can take Danna's room."

Maureen bows. "You're a love, Meg."

Before the door closes, I call after her. "Bring me a fork." I jot a quick note to schedule a meeting to discuss "toolin' around" with all parties involved.

My eyes flick to my wrist. The watch I set to Hollywood time is nearing half-ten.

These calls with Dashell Everett make me a dog on a leash. They're infuriating and irksome. It rankles I'm required to pass every business move I make through him. The end of my probationary period with the True Time Network is almost up. Surely, with the splash I've planned for *The Chieftain's Son* at Cali Con, on top of all I've done for the show, Dash will finally sign off and give me free reign and full authority to run things on my own without his constant gatekeeping. To kill time, I adjust room assignments on my spreadsheet.

"Meg, got a minute?"

I almost squeak with surprise when the man himself, Jack O'Leary, star of *The Chieftain's Son* and the face voted most likely to set female hearts aflame, pokes his head in my door. The advantage of glass walls is to see someone coming, which only works if you're looking in the first place.

I'm tempted to lock my door until I get the business with my boss done, but blowing off my lead actor isn't good policy. "Always. Come in."

I wave him in. His new bride, Gillian Bettencourt O'Leary, follows as close as a shadow in his wake. Here's the very pair making my job harder than it needs to be.

"I've got a call coming in, but I'm yours 'til then."

I rub my lips together. I'm not being charitable or fair. Gilly is a rare talent, one of our ten Crystal Award nominees for writing a truly beautiful season-one finale. She didn't scheme to slip between Jack's sheets as so many would. The two fools fell in love.

They plop into my guest chairs, never releasing the hold on each other's hand. Gilly smiles at me. I've got to give her credit. Even after I tried to warn her off Jack, she's been kind to me. It's me having trouble warming up.

"I've got news I thought you should know," says Gilly as Jack trains a loose strand of strawberry blond hair behind her ear. "I've signed with Jack's agency."

I nod my head. "I know, your agent called me."

"Great. Then he told you about the panel he booked for me at The Con?"

I lean forward. "The Con?"

"Sorry, Meg, I mean Cali Con. My parents used to go all the time. They always called it The Con."

I hold up a finger. "Hold on. Did you say 'booked'?"

My tone is harsh enough to make Gilly sit back in her chair. Jack's features harden, a male of the species defending his mate.

I compose myself. "Go on."

Gilly lays a hand on Jack's arm, clearly sensing the protective waves jumping off his skin. "It's the *Pages to Screen* panel on Friday morning."

"Her award noms give my woman wicked clout," says Jack, beaming at Gilly.

"And you didn't think to check with me first?" I regret the snap in my voice. We're not adversaries here. Same team. Same goals.

Then why is the burn in my chest getting hotter? The goddess of control sits at the edge of my desk, crossing her legs and throwing me an over-the-top-of-the-glasses look. *The Chieftain's Son's* presence at Cali Con is my domain. My plans for our show's involvement at the event are flawless. Wrinkles, alterations, or hiccups of any kind take a swing at my perfection.

Jack's blue eyes shift from crystal to storm-cloud gray. He and I got along brilliantly before Gilly showed up. Now, I'm afraid he sees me as the witch who insists on keeping his marriage secret while I force him to play kissy-face with his co-star, Niks Tellefson. It's Jack's dedication to the show, not any loyalty to me, driving him to act out the fauxmance with Niks. I wonder if Gilly and Jack have a voodoo doll of me at their place. That would explain my constant headaches.

"We're checking with you now, Meg," says Jack, his tone confirmation of the diminished warm fuzzies between us.

I've got to fix that. Not just for the sake of the show. I miss the easiness we used to enjoy with each other.

Gilly is so flustered, a stab of guilt pricks at me. For the love of God, she tears up, and I feel like a first-class shit.

"I'm really sorry, Meg," says Gilly in a six-inch voice. "I thought you'd be happy the show increased its representation at the Con."

I take a deep breath and wave my hands. "I am." I manage a smile. "It's grand. I'll blast it out on social straight away so the fans will know where to find you."

Gilly's made every effort to warm to me. The barrier between us is my doing. Our showrunner, Bobby Provost, is close with Jack and Gilly. He's also one of the few people on the show, besides Maureen, that I count as a real friend. I don't want to damage our long-standing friendship by ruffling Jack's feathers and making the new Mrs. O'Leary cry. In truth, I'm frustrated with myself for not scouring the Cali Con schedule for more potential exposure for anyone involved with the show.

My push was for Deidre LaRochelle, author of *The Chieftain's Son* book series and permanent fixture here at The Clan, to represent in a big way at Cali Con. Deidre had slammed the door on that idea. I get it.

Deidre's been paying her appearance dues on the convention circuit for over a decade. She's paid up.

I adjust my bruised ego over Gilly's news and initiate damage control. "What do you golf nuts say? Give me a Mulligan. I truly appreciate *Chieftain's Son* scoring another panel seat." I use my pinkie to flick a mascara flake out of the corner of my eye. "I'm wound a bit tight with Cali Con so close."

Gilly reaches across the desk and pats my hand. She doesn't mean to condescend, but that's how my nerves translate the contact. "You're amazing, Meg. Cali Con is going to be killer."

"Amen," I say, rising from my seat. "Now, off with you both. I'm due"—I frown at the phone—"overdue for a call from L.A."

Jack regains the friendly attitude I appreciate and waves a business card at me. "I hired the assistant you recommended."

I recognize the card of Cam Stephens, the latest in a line of assistants I tried out who didn't live up to my standards. After a bit of a struggle, we'd mutually agreed it was a bad fit. I truly believe Cam will do fine for Jack.

"Will Cam be joining us in California?"

"Naw. He'll be coming on board when we get back."

"Fine." I smile at Gilly. "Your appearance news is brilliant, Gillian. I'll update your schedule."

Jack smiles as they slide out the door. "We promise to print it out, save it to our phones, and write it in Sharpie on our arms."

It takes me a second to register his tease. There's the good-natured Jack O'Leary impossible not to like. I should hire him as my life coach.

Arms wrapped around each other, Gilly and Jack glide down the hall. Before they're out of sight, Gilly turns to drink in a long look at me. I expect agitation, but instead, softness unnervingly close to sympathy shows through the glass. There's no call for me to be the object of such an expression.

The two lean their heads together and whisper. Whatever the exchange, it ends in a kiss not intended for an audience.

"Glass walls," I hiss under my breath and look away from them. A flurry of emotions spins through my head, wedges on a wheel of fortune. Unwelcome and unexpected spikes of what I'm loathed to admit is jealousy hit me. What those two have, many would call enviable. I dig thumbs into my temples. I refuse to be envious of Jack O'Leary and Gillian Bettencourt O'Leary. It's a bad investment of energy for me right now. I don't have the time or desire to be on the hunt for what they have. I owe *The Chieftain's Son* my all. It's made a strong showing in its first season, and I'm charged to keep it at a gallop.

I sneak a glance in their direction. The last remnant of jealousy melts into a puddle of wistfulness. Even I admit there is genuine sweetness in their relationship. They are so easy with one another. It's hard to believe it's only been months since they first met. The two seem like an old couple who've already shared a lifetime of love and memories. I lay a hand to my cheek, surprised to find a bit of moisture at my fingertip. The half formed tear sends the skeptic in me on a mini break. How must it feel to be so sure of a partner?

I dismiss the unwelcome sliver of loneliness attempting to sneak into my psyche. There's logic they fell hard for one another. They're an equation of proximity plus the fusion of artistic personalities. The real question here is: how much has love diluted their own individual identities? Ah, there's the peril of love. It takes two people and sloughs off enough of who they are to snug their puzzle piece into someone else's. I never want to be stuck to another person to create a single shadow. "*Me*" has power. "*We*," signifies a proportional loss of self.

The phone finally rings. I wake the agenda on my laptop as I check my hair. What am I doing? This isn't a video chat. I could be in bathrobe and slippers. Dash would never know.

Snatching the receiver, I commence the meeting. "Meg McGrath."

A sleepy California accent answers. "Mornin', Meg. It's Dashell."

He speaks as if caller ID doesn't exist. "Your mornin', my evenin'." Damn it. There was too much unintended edge to my tone. "You're on speaker so I can type. Are you looking at the agenda doc?"

I hear Dash gulp whatever his liquid morning fuel might be. "Give me a sec to bring it up."

While Dash retrieves the agenda, my computer pings with a message. My heart skitters when I click on the attachment. A gorgeous color graphic rendering of a towering wall of Southern Cal Stadium, the baseball complex across from the Diego Bay Events Center, home of Cali Con, graces my screen. Adorning the massive structure is a building wrap featuring the signature portrait of Jack and Niks as their characters from the show, Donal Cam and Nieve. Letters spelling out *The Chieftain's Son on the True Time Network* shimmer in gold. It's dazzling. It's perfect. The jewel in my Cali Con crown.

"Dash, the final version of the building wrap for Southern Cal Stadium is in. It's grand. I'm forwarding you the latest rendering with the changes we asked for." I hear keys clicking at his end as I read the rest of the message. "According to schedule, it'll be up less than two weeks before the convention starts."

Dash's hum of pleasure flows from the speaker. "It is a beaut'. Nice work, Meg."

I glow with accomplishment.

"We're placing the *Star's Shadow* wrap next to yours. True Time's two hottest shows, lording over the event," says Dash.

Thank goodness we're not on video chat, so I'm not forced to temper the bitterness tugging down the corners of my mouth. I worked blazing hard to secure that prime location. My cutthroat negotiations knocked a show from one of the three big U.S. networks off Southern Cal Stadium to make room for *The Chieftain's Son*. Dash tosses off the building wrap placement for his bit of Sci-fi fluff, *Star's Shadow*, like it happened with no more effort than ordering a sandwich with salt and vinegar crisps.

"Another update, Gillian Bettencourt is slated for an additional panel." I share the addition, feeling my scorecard needs another tick even if her agent is the one who pulled off the booking. "*Pages to Screen*."

"Fine, fine," says Dash. "Add it to your Cali Con playbook."

"Already done." As if I need telling to keep the game plan up to date.

"About that playbook..." Dash clears his throat. "There's a question I must put to you, Meghan. Is it enough?"

I bite my bottom lip to prevent going on the defensive. How can he be asking me this now, less than a month before go time? I've bled, securing panels, press events, party appearances, autograph sessions, hotels, security, transportation, media blitz, appearance fees, and fecking building wraps. What the hell can he mean?

My mind flashes on the possible comebacks my boss expects and settle on a good one. "Is it ever enough? I'll continue to work full-tilt once I hit the ground in San Diego to make sure I grab up any additional opportunities for *The Chieftain's Son*."

"Let me be up front with you, Meghan."

Well, crap. That's two Meghans in one conversation. I am in the principal's office and not for anything good.

"Please."

"You've done quite the admirable job with *The Chieftain's Son*. I know your probationary period with True Time is flashing red, so I owe you clarity about my end of things. I've got a full plate. It's time I step away from my involvement in *Chieftain's Son* so I can focus on upcoming projects and network expansion."

Step away? I do my best not to choke on the adrenaline surging up my middle. Is this the happy news I'm to be trusted to captain the publicity and marketing for *The Chieftain's Son* without requiring Dash to sign off on every bit of minutiae?

"We're prepared to offer you the permanent number two position on the publicity/marketing team for the show."

I did not hear him right. "Excuse me, did you say number two?"

"Yes, you'll stay on board with *The Chieftain's Son*, but I'll put a more seasoned player to head up the department. Like I said, Meg, you've done a fine job with an untested show, but our baby hit the stratosphere. You're still a newbie in the overall game, so I think it's best to move forward with a number one who has a proven track record. Together, you two will keep the show's climb meteoric."

My hands shake. "This isn't fair. I've been instrumental in the rise of *The Chieftain's Son*. Ten award nominations in the U.S. and more if you add in Europe, Dash."

"*Star's Shadow* grabbed ten Crystal noms as well. If you'd beat them, I might be inclined to overlook the P.R. mess between your star and his alleged mystery woman that whipped fans into a social media uproar. I know you've been teasing an offscreen Jack O'Leary/Niks Tellefson pairing, but so far, the impact of your hints is a Band-Aid on a broken arm. Jack is our publicity brass ring. We've got to avoid the fallout and potential ratings drop if the public catches a whiff that your fabricated romance is a ploy to dupe them."

My stomach curls in on itself. If Dash knew about Jack and Gilly's marriage, he may fly over here to push me off the Cliffs of Moher. "I've got a game plan."

"I'm sure you do, but there remains the question of your experience and expertise to pull it off. Placing a head of P.R./Marketing in Ireland that isn't as green as your local countryside will head off a disaster."

"I've been pulling it off."

There are a few false starts on his end before he lets loose. The pulse on my throat bangs like it's trying to split my skin.

"You didn't pull off Jack's offshoot project."

"Hold on, Dash. *Secrets of My Ireland* is supposed to be a between-seasons filler to give the fans a steady dose of Jack. You greenlighted the concept and tentative production calendar for the space between seasons two and three. *The Chieftain's Son* shooting schedule was too tight to fit it in between seasons one and two. We can't burn out our biggest draw."

"Timing isn't the issue. Jack hasn't signed a multi-season contract for *Secrets*. I know for a fact piles of movie scripts are landing on his doorstep. If he lands a sweeter between-seasons deal, we're screwed with a one-off."

Shit, I should've pushed Jack harder to sign on for more than a single go of the companion project. I counted on his loyalty to stay on for more. Dash is right. I've committed a classic rookie error. Jack will do what's best for his career, not mine.

I squeeze my eyes shut, searching for a clear thought path. A single question for Dash rises above the static. "What can I do to prove to you the number one spot belongs to me? Give me a challenge, a goal. I guarantee I am as capable as your Hollywood pro."

He's silent for too long. Is he figuring out the cleanest way to fire me or taking my request seriously?

"Dash, it's humiliating and unfair to be demoted to number two given where I've taken the show already. If you won't consider keeping me in the lead position, I may have to bow out."

Holy Mother. Did I just give one of the chief executives at the True Time Network an ultimatum? No denying I'm green, but I do believe I am capable and talented enough to foster an even steeper rise in *The Chieftain's Son* popularity and ratings.

There's an edge of panic in Dash's voice I find gratifying. "Let's back up a little here, Meghan. I need you to stay with the show."

One more Meghan and I'll scream.

"The plan is to marry your *Chieftain's Son* expertise with a proven hand in the overall publicity playing field. I'm drafting a winning team."

Now it's my turn to be silent. Grunts and hums from the other end of the line give me hope. They need me. I'm important enough not to be shoved off Ireland's sea cliffs.

"The offer wasn't meant as an insult. I thought you'd appreciate a mentor."

Is he kidding? Does he expect me to lap up a blatant demotion?

My throat tightens. I will not cry. My mother's *I'm not surprised* expression vaults into my psyche. She believes my job on the show is a lark, a temporary fling. The script my parents wish I'd follow is to take a slight taste of a bigger world, then choose to live small. Settle in my home village and market local businesses, marry a man I've known since primary school, and be a loyal daughter. Their script, not mine. I want to be a Jack O'Leary, the kid from a small Irish town who succeeds in a big way. Accepting the life my family perceives for me is the definition of failure.

"I'll be frank with you, Meg. It isn't solely my call. Given *Chieftain's Son* splash and potential for longevity, True Time wants a heavier hitter to take lead on the show. Personally, I feel I owe you the shot you're asking for."

A shot, a chance. I'll take whatever he offers. My knee-jerk ultimatum gains traction. There's some gratification the network doesn't want to lose me altogether.

"Here's what I can offer. First, fill every *Chieftain's Son* panel, autograph session, and other events to bursting. I want lines of fans

salivating at the chance to be in the same room as our people. I want to
see Jack O'Leary's and Niks Tellefson's faces plastered all over the news
coverage of Cali Con. Make *The Chieftain's Son* San Diego's hottest
ticket."

"Done." Sounding confident is the first step to being confident.

"Next, I want a twenty percent increase in trial subscribers to the
True Time streaming app credited to *The Chieftain's Son* by Sunday night
of The Con."

Twenty fucking percent! Dash might as well have asked me to perform
the labors of Hercules.

"And a signed contract from Jack O'Leary for three seasons minimum
of *Secrets of My Ireland*. You pull all that off, and I'll go to bat for you at
True Time."

"Anything else?" I say it as if he's asked me to do something as
simple as washing his electric car.

"All right then. I wish you luck, Meghan McGrath." His tone is
brittle. We both know his checklist is virtually impossible. We both
know he's dangling this sweetie so, in the end, I'll accept the number
two position under a fool from L.A. The click of Dash's Hollywood
phone is a mouse trap snapping on my future.

I let my head fall onto my hands. I've stepped in it now.

CHAPTER 2
POOLSIDE

I do my grandest thinking underwater where survival equates to lung capacity. Every morning, thirty-five laps allow me to shed tension and the pressures taxing both my dreams and waking days.

Today, I consider staying under an option.

How the hell am I going to pull off Dash's laundry list? The smart play is to call him back with an *"I've seen the light"* admission and accept the number two position. I'd still be on the show and in the game. I'll acquiesce to whatever Hollywood wanker he banishes to Ireland to take over the number one P.R. spot and pretend the fool has something to teach me.

That call would be the death of my dreams and the first step on the road to marrying Deacon O'Connell or Owen Mulrooney, popping out ten kids, and stagnating in Cahersiveen for the rest of my life. My parents would light a thousand candles in triumph as I marched my row of children to their house for family dinner each Sunday after mass.

Ten kids, good God. It takes me thirty-five laps a day to maintain plump. After double digit pregnancies, I'd displace enough pool water to flood the deck.

I'll never make that call to Dash. I'm not a second-place person. If I can't fill the top spot, I'll burn in the fires trying. I should tell Bobby, the showrunner of *The Chieftain's Son*, what I'm up against. In every duel, combatants have the right to a second.

I gulp air on the next stroke. No, I won't put another divot in my pride by admitting to Bobby that True Time's confidence in me has unfairly become threadbare. Bobby is a passionate sort. He'd be red-hot angry and might say something to Dash intended to help that only succeeds in landing me on shakier ground.

My ground is shaking enough.

If I'm going to climb my personal Everest without oxygen, it'll be a solo act. Solo is my forte. My string of successes has been planned, orchestrated, and carried out by me alone on my own terms. This may be an ungodly challenge, but it's mine. I am a team of one. I'll choreograph a win. I will not fail.

A flip turn sends me into lap thirty. Today's watery workout is a preemptive strike against seventeen hours in the air between Shannon Airport and San Diego. At least I'll layover long enough at Heathrow to grab lunch with my college roommate, Julie. I was hoping she'd be the flight attendant on my jump over the Atlantic for a lengthier life chat, but she's coming in as I'm going out. She promises to have a generous pour of cabernet waiting for me. There's no taboo on day drinking when the day is spent skirting the clouds.

Dash's insane list of what I need to accomplish turns my nerves into a quivering mass. Hopefully, flying in a day ahead of the rest of my crew will give me time to hone those willies into an outer layer of confidence.

Blue tile-crosses mark the wall at the far end of the pool. Are they an intentional cue for good Irish Catholics to think of God as we swim laps?

The closest thing to God in the pool with me is a ghostly image of Father Connery wagging a finger. By vowing to check every box of Dashell Everett's list of demands, have I committed the sin of ambition? Och, there are worse sins. If I am sinning, Father C. will get an earful at my next confession. I'll do years of penance to keep my job.

On my penultimate lap, I catch sight of the line of life preservers along the wall. Beneath them is a *How to Save a Life* poster. As far as signs or portents go, it's not fancy, but I'll take it. I will save my own life.

I'm so preoccupied with sin and redemption, I nearly crash into the pair of legs dangling in the water. Pulling up short, I sputter out a mouthful of pool water.

"Sweet Maker, Taryn. Must you plant yourself in my way?"

My sister kicks her legs, spraying me in the face. "You set my alarm for godawful o'clock to unlock the gym for you. Out you go. We're off to the airport at half-six."

I breathe in the chlorinated air trapped above the indoor pool and check the clock on the wall. Six o'clock. Time enough to shower and get on the road.

Taryn bends so her face is even with mine. "You should've bunked off your laps this morning to give yourself an easy go getting ready."

I cluck my tongue. "No reason to break routine, and you know what Mommy says. As long as you don't go past curvy and chunky, God'll forgive you." I slap the surface of the water.

My sister rocks her head back and forth as I watch our mother's voice play through her thoughts. "This swim obsession of yours is not as thick as the time you gave being a vegan a go."

My love of Irish beef, butter, and cheese made my stab at the vegan lifestyle a point of hilarity with my family. I'm not in a relationship with kale and quinoa, but I do try and give my cholesterol levels a fighting chance with the greens. Taryn and I were both born with Mommy's pear-shaped silhouette. We three McGrath women will cast a fruit shaped shadow 'til we're in our graves.

Taryn swings her legs out of the pool and dries them with a towel. She tosses me a fresh one off the stack behind her as I climb out of the pool. This place is her pride and joy, the Cahersiveen Swim and Gym. She's the shiny red apple of my parents' eyes. The daughter content to stay at home and open a local business as they did. My folks' tiny art gallery started with watercolors by local artists around the Ring of Kerry. Now they've expanded to include photographers.

I created an online presence for the gallery and tripled their income, which turned out to be a fatal error. My parents believe doing the same for the local businesses in small towns and villages that dot the Iveragh Peninsula is the life work I'm meant to do.

It's not the scenario I paint for myself.

"Have you made up your mind on your fool's errand?" says Taryn, giving me squint-eye.

"If you're asking if I've changed my mind to fight for my job, the answer is no." I flip my hair forward and give it a rub before twisting it up in the towel.

"Can I say something?"

"Not if you're still campaigning for me to take my boss's offer of number two."

Taryn grabs my upper arms to hold me in place. "Did it ever occur to you bellyaching over being stuck here in Kerry is a gut punch to the family?"

I shiver despite the muggy air. "You know I don't mean it to be."

"You're tone deaf, Meg, spouting negativity about a small life and dreams to paint on a bigger canvas. That small life is what is dear to me, to Mommy and Daddy."

I cover her hands with mine. "I'm not devaluing what's a perfect fit for you."

The weight of disappointing my family turns my stomach into a hunk of lead. If I fell into the pool, I'd sink to the bottom. *Me* alone is the skin I live in. Sometimes it's a friend, sometimes it burns the life from me, carrying the weight of full responsibility, but the times I've given the *we* scenario a go, it's blown up in my face. People disappoint. Levels of investment differ. I'm best as a solo pilot for my own life. I choose the course, the expectations, and create success.

Guilt from family pressure can't knock my hands off the controls.

She gives me a little shove and turns her back. "But you are." Arms crossed, she turns to face me. "We live in the most beautiful place in the world. Cahersiveen's given me a gorgeous, hard-working husband who adores me and my own place here." She windmills her arms to take in the pool and gym beyond. "I want you close to be auntie when I have my babies."

I wrap a second towel around my body, anxious to shower and get going.

"Taryn, you know my heart'll always be with our town and family." Kicking off my swim shoes, I make a puddle on the concrete. "More than half the people we went to school with already left with no intention to come back. I don't see you spooning guilt their way."

"They're not my only sister."

We both stand our ground, shooting stubborn from our eyes. The battle lasts half a minute before we're clutching one another.

"I love you, Tary, but I want to play beyond Ireland. See if my talents and working my fingers to the bone can take me to America, to Hollywood."

She rubs her nose in my hair. "As I see it, you've one foot in Hollywood already with the show."

"I want both feet in. Can you understand, Sissy?"

Her pout reminds me of my first day heading off to primary school. Taryn was having none of being left behind. I came home to the arms and legs pulled off my dollies.

"I can understand, Megs, but I hate it. I don't want my big sis off far and away."

I swipe pool water and maybe a tear or two from my face. "I'm going to win this fight and keep my job. With the way *Chieftain's Son* is going, it'll probably keep me here a good ten years."

"Taking the number two will definitely keep you here for ten years. I promise to make you an auntie several times over by then."

I shake my head.

"I know you, Meg. You're set on leaving before the full ten no matter if you're number one or two. You've got American stars in your eyes." Just as I think she's going to let off and at least pretend to support my big picture, Taryn's expression turns mean. "Think of what you can do for local businesses with your marketing wizardry. It's giving back, Meg. Why can't you give back and be happy?"

"It's not the path I see for myself."

Taryn snorts. "The solitary path. That's why you're fighting the number two spot. Meg McGrath barrels along and gets the job done alone. It's clear what your 'why' is, but where's your 'we,' sister?"

My shoulders crack as I roll them to chase the tension of Taryn's pressure. "You know, apart from family, I've not had success with the 'we' model."

Taryn's groan ricochets off the tile walls. "If you go on about that fucker Dominic betraying you back at the end of secondary school, I'll shove you into the water."

"You know it was more than that. He used our relationship to sabotage my Trinity scholarship project."

"As I said, fucker. Not everyone is out to get you, Meg. You can't let a decade-old *kiss-and-steal* dictate the rest of your life."

"But it's okay for my family to do the dictating?" Truthfully, I love the idea of expanding local Irish businesses, but it's not a path the persistent voice in my mind calls out for me to follow right now. Someday, I hope to dabble in what Taryn's egging me on to do, in addition to a future brilliant job that takes me away from Ireland to Los Angeles, the heart of the entertainment industry. I will carve my place in that world. If I'm given the chance to bring *Chieftain's Son* to where I know it can go, then I'll have the clout to move up.

"You're breaking my heart, Megs."

It's my turn to wear the McGrath mean face. "Stop, Taryn. My mind's made up, and a mountain of guilt isn't going twist it into the shape you and Mommy want." The towel drops from my body. I snatch the end and snap it at Taryn. She's quick, and soon, I'm on the receiving end of her wicked towel crack. "Ouch."

"That's for making your mother cry," she shouts. We launch into a full-fledged towel flicking battle until we're laughing like fools.

CHAPTER 3

THE BLUFF

I enjoy a bit of fun and don the aloof attitude of a celebrity as I saunter over to the driver holding up a sign with my name under the True Time Network logo at the San Diego Airport. Plenty of stares fly my way only to shift the focus of their hunt once they decide I'm nothing to dwell on. Here on the eve of the eve of Cali Con, lots of folks are on high alert to spot the pretty and famous.

My driver, Chip, gushes over *The Chieftain's Son*, quoting line after line. His high cheekbones and rapid-fire delivery make it impossible to believe he's not named for the hyperactive woodland critter from my kiddie books. "I work for True Time, so it's cool to give me scoop on Jack and Niks. How serious are they? Do you think they'll get married like Donal Cam and Nieve on the show?"

Ha to you, Dash. Even this lackey behind the wheel of a company car buys my finely honed fauxmance between the stars of my show. My confidence recovers a jot after the bruising it's suffered from Dashell Everett's threat of demotion.

"So, Chipper, how long have you been working for Mr. Everett?"

"It's not Chipper, just Chip."

"Apologies." That was a slip on my part. He reminds me of the kid who works at the chipper down the street from my folks where they get their Friday dinner fish and chips.

"I don't work for Mr. Everett." He barks out a laugh. "Technically, I guess I kind of do. I work for Mr. Malley, and he works for Mr. Everett."

Chip's chattering wears me out, making me keenly aware I've been on a plane for nearly twenty hours.

"Mr. Malley's the greatest. You know him, of course, since you both work for Mr. Everett."

"Can't say I've met your Mr. Malley."

Chip looks momentarily baffled but then launches into a soliloquy about the Cali Con panels he's dying to see. As we come in range of the Diego Bay Events Center, he points out every hotel towering above the harbor. The kid squeals as he calls out the name of any show on the building wraps that peer down at us. We jerk to a stop at a red light as he flails an arm toward the side of the street opposite the water.

"Oh my God. Look at the façade 'Vertigo Redux' slapped on the library. I'm totally going to be first in line when the *Redux Experience* opens on Wednesday." He leans so far over the wheel to stare up at the next hotel, I'm afraid he's going to jump the curb.

It's unnerving being on the wrong side of a car that's on the wrong side of the road. I silently wish for a steering wheel to materialize in front of me so I can take control of Chip's mad ride.

"I'm guessing it's your first Cali Con, Chip?" I want to call him California Chip. He could be on a tourism advert with his sun-bleached hair and tan.

"Yep. I'm like so grateful Mr. Malley brought me down here to help him out. I like totally owe him. He got me a P.A. job on *Star's Shadow* when I had no experience. He keeps telling me I have the personality to go into P.R., but my sights are on being a producer."

Mr. Malley must possess endless reserves of patience to put up with Chip, the ball of hyper, and his likes.

The zingy tone of an alarm wails from his pocket. Chip's face loses its tan. "Oh crap. You're late to the True Time meeting."

I grab the edge of the seat when he screeches up to the curb in front of the events center. In a frantic blur, he reaches into the back seat to retrieve a large manila envelope. The package sails onto my lap.

"Whoops. Sorry. Your badge, press kit, and the other stuff Mr. Malley says you'll need is in there." He points to the events center. "Go to those double glass doors, and they'll let you in. The meeting is on the second level, room 28A." He looks panicked. "I think it's 28A, it might be 28D. Crap."

I push open the door, anxious to get free of Chip's mania. "I'll find it. You've done a grand job getting me here. Thanks, Mr. Chip."

"I'll make sure your stuff gets to your hotel room." He nods to a huge bridge that spans above the highway and ends at a steel and glass building blocking the morning sun. "Bayview Grand. True Time snagged an entire floor for the *Chieftain's Son* and *Star's Shadow* people."

I can't fault Chip in either the enthusiasm or abundance-of-information departments, but another minute with him and my blood pressure will burst my eyeballs. I slam the car door a bit too hard to be considered friendly, so I counteract with a tight smile and wave.

Chip salutes and goes on his merry way to deliver my luggage. For an awkward moment, I wonder if I should have tipped him. There's a ridiculous notion. He's a True Time Network employee, not a bellhop.

After five thousand miles, I step onto true California soil. I don't count the airport since that's more like neutral ground instead of a destination and doesn't truly commit you to a place. My new pair of heels aren't touching soil exactly, rather the sidewalk in front of the Diego Bay Events Center. I'm about to enter a room with heavy hitters that, before now, existed as nothing more than CCs on emails to me. The only network people I've met in person are the small team of suits who pop over for table reads and meetings with Bobby. Even Dash and I are only a pair of faces on our rare video chats to one another. He and his cronies will get their first glimpse of the small-town Irish girl steering one of their hottest properties.

I infuse confidence into my soul. I will go head-to-head with True Time players. I will impress. I will overcome the smallest niggle of doubts any of these network types harbor for me.

There is no other option.

I pause, taking in the calm before the storm of Cali Con. Every light post down the way wears banners with a pair of wide eyes, the logo of Cali Con International. Above the logo, superheroes and super villains watch me from the banners, flapping in the rising wind. Next year, I'll plaster Jack O'Leary as Donal Cam staring down from those banners.

I tap the notes icon and mic on my cell. "Light pole banners."

Across the busy city street from where I stand, a train rattles to a stop at an open-air station. My jaw falls to the vicinity of my shoes. Every car of the train is wrapped in a magnificent panorama of *Star's Shadow*. A pastiche of the cast floats above the signature fortress the lead character in the show, *Starry Night*, calls home. Even the lettering of the title and True Time's logo seem to sparkle in three dimensions from the side of the train car.

As if mocking me, a bus sails down the street wearing its own version of the *Star's Shadow* images. Trains, buses, and building wraps... I'm staring at the holy trinity of P.R. *The Chieftain's Son* boasts a mere one out of the three. A sick feeling of letting my people down slithers through my middle.

Dash's voice pokes holes in my faltering composure. *"Is it enough?"*

The answer smacks me across the face. As much as I've done to scream *The Chieftain's Son's* presence here at Cali Con, I could have done more. So much more.

"Train and bus wraps..." I make another tap on my notes icon.

I scan the cityscape before me. Near the train stop, a giant arch announces the *Gaslamp Quarter – Historic Heart of San Diego*. Surrounding the arch are buildings stretching into the primary blue California sky. My heart stops quivering and begins to sing when I catch sight of Southern Cal Stadium. There, towering above the soon-to-be nexus of nerds and pinnacle of popular culture is the building wrap for *The Chieftain's Son*. The chiseled Celtic warrior, Donal Cam, stands majestically beside the ethereal goddess, his beloved Nieve. The couple gazes over the harbor behind the events center as if it's a sacred pool belonging to them alone.

The shadow of dread recedes. God bless Jack O'Leary's parents for creating such a gorgeous example of humankind. Every female heart at the convention will beat faster or stop beating all together when they catch sight of my fabulous star. I'd place money the visage of Niks will be featured in more than a few fanboy and fangirl fantasies as well.

I take a dozen pictures of the wrap and send the best to Bobby. I'll wander after the True Time meeting to find a brilliant angle to grab a shot stunning enough to post on our social media feeds.

Right now, my ass is due at the meeting. I text Dash to let him know I'm close.

An escalator ride inside the curved glass domes of the events center has me believing I'm the star of my own futuristic fairy tale. My path stretches up to the sky and then sends me on a trek down endless carpeted hallways alongside floor-to-ceiling glass windows that overlook docks full of posh boats, nothing like those of the fishing variety I'm used to at home. Here and there, food vendors stock cases with sodas. Menus of pizzas, sandwiches, and something called a chili pie are being slipped into metal stands. I rethink my heels as a hike three-city-blocks long leaves me panting. I check the map to find room 28D. Of course, it's at the very end of the building.

When I hit a dead end, a long black curtain blocks a series of rooms marked 28A through 28E. If not for the buzz of voices coming from behind the shiny fabric, I might spend the entire weekend circling the place to find the bloody meeting.

One voice rises above the rest as I finally locate the open door for room 28A. "The *Top of the Mawrnin' Clan* should be riding in on their donkey cart any second."

I stop dead. There's nothing else remotely Irish on the True Time Network, so no doubt, the rudely stereotypical comment is about me. Worse, the dig might have come from Dashell Everett, the man I'm bound and determine to impress. Who else would know I'm enroute?

Pausing long enough so the crowd doesn't suspect the slur reached my ears, I steel myself and step through the door.

Everywhere I look are backdrops with the Cali Con eyes staring at me. Partitions between rooms are pushed aside, and twenty plus round tables are scattered throughout the space. Along one wall is a dais with a podium and a mic. A tall woman in a burgundy suit I'd kill for climbs the steps to the podium.

It's not a solo True Time meeting. Reps from every heavy-hitting network and streaming service claim tables at this party.

"Meg." A warm hand rests on my elbow. When I turn, I'm face-to-face with Dashell Everett for the first time. "Welcome to California." He gives me a perfunctory handshake and gestures to a round table with a *True Time Network* sign in a Lucite frame gracing its center. "We're over here."

I approach a table with a half-dozen men in suits. My laughable imaginings of the True Time California executives fade to black. No Hawaiian shirts and cargo shorts here. I'm the lone female at this party and probably the only one of these True Time players in jeopardy of losing their position.

As I approach, the man next to the single empty chair stands and pulls it out for me.

"Everyone, meet Meg McGrath, our P.R. on the ground for *The Chieftain's Son*," says Dash as he takes the seat to my left.

There are a few nods, welcomes, and applauses. I'd like a voice print analysis to track the *"Top of the Mawrnin' Clan"* crack to its owner. I don't want it to be Dash, but the voice I heard wasn't far off from his.

I twist to my right to thank the gentleman who'd pulled out my chair, and I'm met by a pair of ice blue eyes that sparkle like water swirling around the bottom of a glacier. It's a color you'd expect in a reflection. My "thank you" freezes to match his eyes.

A stylish amount of Henna brown stubble dusts sharp cheekbones on the lean face tapering to a dimpled chin. "I'm Cian Malley with *Star's Shadow*. Nice to meet you." His hand hovers between us.

I'm about to grasp it when Dash leans across me, low-talking to Cian. "Meg here is a Cali Con virgin. I'm counting on you to show her the ropes."

There are light chuckles around the table as I do a horrible job keeping annoyance off my face.

"I'm sure I'll do fine on my own, if it's all the same to you, Mr. Malley."

Malley. This must be Chip's Mr. Malley. The one who took a chance on a green kid. Is Dash seeing a common theme here? Is Cian Malley True Time's designated wrangler for the new kids in the Cali Con game? I'm not flattered to be lumped in with Chip.

Cian reaches forward to grab the top magazine on a stack in the center of the table. He presents it to me as if it's the first course of a fancy meal. I beam with pride and then tone it down a bit, not wanting to bust out a rookie reaction. There in front of me is the most provocative shot from the recent photo shoot *Entertaining for You* did on set of the season one wedding night scene between Donal Cam and Nieve.

While Dash chats up a pair of the suits across the table, Cian bows his head and speaks in low tones intended for my ears alone. "Dash has it backwards. Anyone who scores a cover in the Cali Con special edition of *Entertaining for You* could probably give me tips."

After darting a glance at Dash, I copy Cian's secretive position. "There are bodies I stepped over to nab that cover." In a moment of horror, I realize Cian is one of those bodies. His show, *Star's Shadow,* was my final hurdle in securing the prime placement.

He scratches his stubble. "And I've got the bruises to show for it."

"Kudos on the Crystal Award noms, Meg," calls a middle-aged man across the table with salt-and-pepper hair and a forties-movie-star jaw nestled above several chins.

"Thank—"

Dash cuts me off. "True Time's Award cup runneth over. We're proud of our matching set of ten." He hikes a thumb at Cian. "Ten for *The Chieftain's Son* and ten for *Star's Shadow*. Cian's the wizard behind the Crystal Award campaign for the network."

He catches sight of the magazine in front on me and hoists it for all to see. "Here's another True Time shot over the bow. The little network that could."

I wait for my slice of the praise pie.

Salt and Pepper, whom I make note no one bothered to introduce me to, bangs on the table. "I'm tooting the horn for *Best and Boggs*. We managed six nominations again this year. That's a three-year streak of more than five. Who says the cop procedural is dead?"

Dash leans on his forearm, staring across the table as if he's decided to up the ante or call on a hand of poker. "Not gonna lie, our front and center, side-by-side building wraps on Southern Cal Stadium landed me on a couple of hit lists." He reaches behind my chair to clap Cian on the shoulder. "The True Time Network is swinging for the fences, gentlemen."

Am I invisible? Is this how the game is played? I do the work and local boy, Dash, sops up the credit like brown bread at the bottom of a bowl of stew.

Stewing is exactly what I'm doing as the woman in the burgundy jacket and pencil skirt runs down her list of Cali Con "housekeeping" details, which include golf carts, wrist bands, and security. I take notes on my tablet even though the information is a rehash from emails and press packets. If I don't channel my negative energy into doing something, it'll hit a target I'll surely regret.

Someone on Dash's other side whispers about "latest numbers." The tension in my shoulders sends an ache up the back of my neck. I've got a dozen strategies using *The Chieftain's Son* as bait for new streaming subscribers ready to go. As soon as I'm free of this meeting, I'll release them like doves at a celebrity wedding.

As the Q & A from the podium ends, a buzzing cell on the table steals Dash's attention. Cian's phone goes off at the same time. I swear the room temperature rises as waves of heat jump off both men. It's comic the way they gape at their cells, raise their heads at the same time, and lock eyes.

Dash's knee bumps mine as he swivels in my direction. The grip on his cell turns his fingers bloodless-white. "Fucking unbelievable." I might as well be a window as he looks right through me to address Cian. "Tell me your showrunner did not just walk."

Cian presses his lips together. "Donaldson led me to believe he had to miss the *Star's Shadow* panel because of trouble at home. No idea the bastard planned to jump ship."

Dash runs a hand through his hair and huffs out a breath, bathing me in gale of fish he's clearly eaten in the very recent past. "I've got a high-profile panel in three days with a non-existent showrunner."

Instead of clenching into a ball of angry flame the way Dash does, Cian seems to shed any sign of stress. He flashes a smile at our boss. "Name his replacement."

"Who can you get down here today?"

Cian relaxes against the chair back and crosses his legs. I half expect him to lace his hands behind his head and yawn.

"Anyone you want."

I catch myself staring. I'm sitting next to either the most confident or conceited man on the planet.

"Ortega or Loring. Set up a video meeting in an hour to hash out the turnover." Dash uses his suit jacket as a fan. "Talk to legal. I want every penny of Donaldson's goddamn appearance fee returned by sundown."

I'm stung in the ass. Cian clearly has shorthand with Dash I lack. I deserve the same level of trust, membership in their club. I haven't taken a single professional misstep with *The Chieftain's Son*, and this network bully boy is trying to give away my position. He can't fault me for Jack and Gilly getting caught together back home and starting the mystery girl rumor. I've mopped up that mess with my Jack/Niks offscreen pairing ruse.

Cian bobs his head. "Take it off your plate, Boss."

Dash grunts again and shoves his chair back. It's a disgruntled side of the man that's new to me. Without warning, Dash aims his super-heated mood straight between my eyes. "While we're talking panels, I have to say *The Chieftain's Son* celebrity presence is too thin for my liking."

This is a moment I didn't expect. I feel his accusation from the knot in my neck to my cramped toes. I'm sensing my ultimatum about leaving the show instead of accepting the number two slot is a larger pain in Dash's big-shot ass than I reckoned.

"Text me when you've expanded *The Chieftain's Son's* visibility, Meghan." He unleashes the first live volley in the showdown over my future as the number one.

The gravity of my inexperience sends jolts of panic through me. Dash is angry and angling for a fight. He knows I've already got a target painted on my ass, so he's pressing his advantage. I wonder if anyone has ever turned him down the way I turned down his offer to be number two.

Accepting less than I deserve is a threat to my future. I won't do it. Meg McGrath does not melt willingly into the shadows. If that ticks Dashell Everett off, then so be it. I'll leave before being demoted. I don't give a red-assed damn if the replacement he's planned for me is in for a tough go of it without being able to rely on my special knowledge of all things *Chieftain's Son*.

I've never shied from a challenge, but this goes beyond. I'm out of my element into one where the other players know not only their strengths, but the tricks of the game. If I'm going to make it out alive, I must hit hard without mercy, maybe even stab a back or two. This very little fish can sprout rows of shark teeth.

I turn to look Dash in the eye. I'm as poised as a queen on royal progress. "There hasn't been a moment to share the good news. Deidre LaRochelle and I worked it out for her to join us here at Cali Con."

I've caught Dash off guard. He didn't see a victory in my column coming so soon. Deidre made it clear to Dash she's done her time at cons. He'd given up on her.

"She's agreed to a panel appearance and two limited autograph signings."

Dash's eyes dig into me for a loaded second before he crinkles his lips and nods. One point Meg.

He stands. "Set up drinks for me with Deidre as soon as she gets to town."

"Will do."

He joins a trio of the other suits and heads out of the room. Others around the table drift over to mingle with colleagues. I should network, insinuate myself in the pack. This group is my end game. I'm determined to find a place in the Hollywood hierarchy.

Cian slow claps. "Magnificent bluff."

I whip around to face him. His smirk and self-satisfied laugh make me wish I had one of Taryn's damp pool towels to snap him with.

"I'm sure I have no idea what you're on about."

He smacks his palms on the table and laughs even harder. "I've never seen anyone shut Dashell Everett up so quickly."

The corner of my lip quirks up without permission. I pull it back into a serious line. "Why in the name of St. Brigid would I want to nick the boss? I've been on a plane for the better part of forever. It was my first chance to catch him up."

His smile is approving. "You're dangerous."

I slip my tablet into my bag. "Hardly."

"Formidable then."

How can glacial blue eyes be so warm? I send him my stock end-of-conversation smile and stand to leave. "Comes with the job, eh?"

He stands when I do, a gentlemanly move. I was so busy to take my place at the table, I didn't notice his height. I wager he'd look Jack O'Leary eye to eye.

"Even though Dash was an ass in the way he offered me up to lend you a hand, I'm happy to give a first timer some pointers. Been there myself."

Common sense tells me I should pick his brain over the particulars of scoring bus and train wraps, but Dash's comment about Cian supervising my Cali Con virgin status chafes.

"I'm grand. Thanks."

He flicks his business card in my direction. "For nothing in particular."

I want to wave it off, but I'm not an eejit. Snatching it from his hand, I give him a curt nod and turn to leave.

"Best view of our building wraps is from the second story of the events center."

"I'll go and take a look." I raise a hand and wave. I'd come in on the bayside of the building and not had the chance to see the work from the city side vantage point. It's the perfect chance to grab pictures for social media.

"And good luck with Deidre LaRochelle."

The lining of my stomach turns to ice as I walk away from Cian

Malley. How does the fool know I'm bluffing? Dash bought the news easily enough.

I fold his card in my palm, ready to toss it into the first bin I see. Sense overrides brewing resentment. This Cian fellow may prove an asset I shouldn't dismiss without more thought. Ass or asset, he'll be crossing my path again at True Time events throughout the weekend. I shove his crumpled business card into the pocket of my suit jacket.

Damn. I'm the instigator of making my own life a hell. Flying Deidre's name to Dash would be the perfect solution if there was a sinner's chance in purgatory I could get her to agree to come to Cali Con.

Like the sun cracking through the worst of a dreary day, *The Chieftain's Son* building wrap shines in the San Diego morning. It's there because of my sweat. I've accepted Dash's conditions because I have every intention of fulfilling them. I won't drop tears into a healthy pour of cabernet. I'll upend the damn glass and warm my insides with its content. It's time to get on with the battle of Cali Con.

Before I do anything else, I've got to get Deidre to come to San Diego. She's in L.A. doing press and having a fine holiday with Doolin, her man and the Irish language teacher for our show. She vowed to avoid Cali Con come hell or high water.

A thought as blistery as a midge sting makes itself known. There's a certain person who will require me to crawl over burning embers before she'll help me convince our esteemed authoress to join us.

Gillian Bettencourt O'Leary.

The woman whose life I've scratched and poked into a misery may be the one person who can change Deidre's mind. Our grand dame holds a soft spot for the new writer.

The look Gilly shot me after she told me she'd signed with Jack's agency and secured her own spot on a Cali Con panel returns to me. She's got a softness I've written off as weakness. If I'm damn lucky, I can mine that bit of her to my benefit. A brighter thought lightens my mood. Maureen will be here with Bobby. Gilly and Maureen are thick. Maureen can be an avenue to enlist Gilly's help.

I grab more pictures of the building wrap. My favorite shot gives a hint of the beautiful blue sky over the sports stadium as well as our show's portrait of perfection. I blast it out on social media with the message:

> *Blue skies for The Chieftain's Son at Cali Con. Share the experience with us.* *#ChieftainsSonOfficial   #SDCaliCon   #TrueTimeNetwork   #DonalCamfans* *#Nievefans #ChieftainsSonCastCrew #ChieftainsSonWriters #JustJackO'Leary* *#TheRealNiksTellefson   #ThePenofDeidreLaRochelle   #ChieftainsSoninBooks* *#DeidreDreaming #BProvost #IrelandLovesDonalCam.*

And then add the dozen other hashtags that drive our fan base.

I send up a quick prayer that enthusiasm for the show will sway Gilly to help me. Mommy always told Taryn and I sometimes you've got to eat crow to get to dessert. A fat, juicy plate of squawking bird waits for me.

CHAPTER 4
WHISKEY FLIGHT

"*Come quickly, I am tasting the stars.*" – *Dom Perignon*
The bright white letters of the quote painted on the wall of windows are a bold contrast to the inky night beyond the glass. It's an apt sentiment for a bar atop one of the vertigo-inducing hotels near the Diego Bay Events Center in, what I've learned is called, The Harborside District.

The evening sky is so clear it's easy to see stars spilling overhead to match the white lights tracing pathways through the harbor front city a dizzying forty stories below. Bobby suggested we all meet up in this skyscraping pub. It's breathtaking and intimate at the same time. Padded couches scatter throughout the space with smaller tables lining the windows. Near the back, away from the bar proper, is a semi-sheltered nook I reserved for the next few hours.

Bobby assured me star-stalking snoopers won't seep onto the scene until tomorrow, the so-called "Night Before the Night" of Cali Con. We should be free of prying eyes tonight as we taste the stars.

I'm early. I'm always early. It prevents surprises. Early means I'll be sitting here in my niche for quite a spell before folks start arriving. Jack and Gilly are driving down from her parents' house in L.A. where he's helping her pack up properly for her move to Ireland. Bobby and

Maureen landed at the airport at half-seven, about an hour ago. The four are meeting up at the hotel before they trot over here. I rub my neck where a loose strand of hair tickles. Ah, not four, the five. Grady, Maureen's pastry chef, will be with them as well. All the better. The more in the group, the less likely roving glances will pick out Jack and Gilly as a couple.

I stretch my legs, feeling cramps and strains from traveling. A hearty glass of red will not go unappreciated.

After overseeing the *Reserved* signs on the pair of tables I've pushed together, I make my way to the far end of the room. Behind the bar, a collection of white, glowing rectangles over a shiny black counter gives the place a cold, futuristic feel. I was weaned on polished wood and the all-are-welcome vibe of Irish pubs. This place is aloof, sterile, and alienating.

I'm not used to a bartender who shows his back more than his front. When I lean over the counter and snap my fingers, I spot a familiar profile at the end seat, Cian Malley. Odd he's alone, staring into what may or may not be a glass of whiskey. The man didn't strike me as the alone type. I've pegged him as the any-moment-a-beguiling-woman-worthy-of-a-Hollywood-magazine-cover-will-sidle-in-close-to-him type.

The bartender hovers near Cian's end of things. My road to wine nips into my erstwhile colleague's territory. I tug my clothes into a tidy fit. Here's a chance to be a bit friendlier than I left off with him this morning. My sister loves to remind me folks'll always choose a hearth fire over an ice storm when she thinks I'm being too tight-assed. Chances may be opportunities. It's not wise to let them slip away when they present themselves easily. I may need Mr. Hollywood Malley for an answer or two about Con goings-on.

I resist the urge to check my hair and face before I say hello. It's dim enough in here to be forgiving of any smudges under my eyes from the long day.

Cian's attention is so riveted on his empty glass, my approach goes unnoticed. The bartender tips a bottle of Jack Daniels to remedy the void. Before Cian brings the rim to his lips, I lay a hand over the glass.

"What's this swill you're drinking?"

His startled look is comical. I truly took him by surprise. My fingers wrap around his glass and remove it from his grasp. Dipping my nose over the caramel-colored liquid, I take a sniff before smacking the glass onto the counter. "Cough syrup."

The corners of his lips curve into a smile. "It certainly keeps me from coughing."

The combination of those crystalline eyes and his smile crash into me. He is a very pretty man—one I'm not adverse to looking at while I kill time networking.

"If it's whiskey you're after, Jameson is the ticket."

"That so?" He leans an elbow on the bar, resting his chin on a hand.

"It's sharp and crisp, distilled three times." I flick the side of his glass, making a tiny *ping* with my nail. "Old Jack here is distilled once." I nod to the backlit bottles behind the bar. "See Mr. Johnnie Walker up there? Twice distilled. Better than Jack, but not up to our Jameson."

"So says you."

"So says facts." I motion to the bartender. "Hello there. Will you kindly give me a pour of Jameson, Johnny Walker, and—" I peer into his glass, satisfied there's enough whiskey in it for my purpose. "That'll do."

Cian watches me, assessing. It hits me he's only met down-to-business Meg. Strung-tight Meg. I'm-not-your-project Meg. Without any preamble to explain the shift, here I am schooling him on whiskey with a bit of a flirt in my tone.

I'm enjoying this. It's a muscle I haven't exercised in a while, one my daily swimming doesn't touch. Flexing it should prove interesting.

The bartender, Sam, according to his pin tag, taps down two glasses of ice, and I shake my head. "No, not in these old-fashioned glasses. They won't do the tasting justice. Are you hiding a trio of Glencairn whiskey glasses or at least something with round bottoms?"

I catch the quick glance Cian sneaks at my own round bottom. Instead of feeling offended as I probably should, the attention sends a little thrill through me. It's been a while since a nice-looking fellow, especially one with the lean and lithe body of a swimmer, my preferred physique, took notice of my ass.

I'm caught off guard with a memory of the last swimmer's body I enjoyed full access to. Luke McGill, my former co-worker in Killarney at the *Toolin' Around the Isle* travel company was a nice distraction. Sadly, he was a Peter Pan, the boy who never grew up. I'd managed to keep an emotional distance while enjoying our time playing together as a couple. Playing, not investing. I think I broke his tender little-boy heart.

Sam's teeth glow white from the low-hanging light globes above the bar as he sweeps away the old-fashioned glass with Cian's Jack Daniels. "Nice to meet someone who knows how to respect their whiskey." He digs beneath the bar and comes up with three real whisky glasses, bulbous at the bottom for the swirling with tapered tops to gather the aroma.

Sam fills each Glencairn glass with three different versions of golden amber liquid for our impromptu whiskey tasting. A twinge of homesickness tickles my ribs. That's mad. I've not been away enough time to count, and here I am, close to the place I'm gunning for, Hollywood. I chalk the twinge up to jet lag and line up the whiskeys. Sam is kind enough to leave the three bottles on the counter for my whisky lesson. "Now, Mr. Malley, you're going to taste in order, Jack, Johnny, and James."

Cian laughs. "I never realized a requirement of whisky is to be named with a J. Shouldn't we allow a Robert, Bruce, or Seamus into the club?"

"It so happens Seamus is Irish for James. So, he's already in the club."

Cian wraps his hand around his fresh glass of Jack Daniels and prepares to throw it back like he's drinking shots.

I cover his hand with mine to stop him. The moment our hands touch, we're both suspending in that lovely place when skin meets skin for the first time. He'd held out his hand for me to shake at the meeting, but I avoided contact. There's no avoiding now. I'm reluctant to leave the warmth of his fingers trapped beneath my own. A mingling of surprise and curiosity flares as our gazes meet.

I guide his hand to set the glass on the bar. "Here's how it's going to go. Are you paying attention?"

A low chuckle escapes his lips. "Bossy, aren't you?"

I return his smile. "I prefer to control my scenarios."

Cian flips his hands over, palms up, giving over control. "I'm all yours."

"First, observe." I lift the glass of Jack Daniels to the light. "As a rule, the darker it is, the more concentrated the flavor. What do you see?"

He tilts his head to look through the glass. "Dark caramel?"

"We'll work with that." I nod. "Now, smell." I hold up a finger. "It's not wine. Don't take a gulp with your nose. You'll drown in the alcohol. Ease down. Dip in. Dip out. Let the aroma find you." I raise and lower the glass, letting the sweetness of the Jack Daniels tease my senses.

Cian watches me intently. He's moved closer. "And then," he says in almost a whisper.

"We sip and savor." With my eyes never leaving his, I touch the glass to my mouth and tilt so the tiniest bit of liquid slides over my lips.

"Cough syrup?"

My laugh nearly makes me choke on the drops of whiskey sliding down my throat. I recover and lean in. "Cough syrup."

"My turn," he says, reaching for his glass.

Sliding it out of reach, I meet his hungry eyes. "Not yet. There's the last of it. The finish." I close my eyes. "Savor the taste. Is it honeyed? Smoky? What lingers behind for a moment before it disappears?"

The side of a hand brushes mine and settles into the touch. I open my eyes to see Cian inches away. The finish lingering on my tongue is desire. I see an echo of the same in his expression. This is a place I haven't been in a while. I'd forgotten how pleasant it can be.

More reliable senses return to me as I thrust the glass into his hand. "Give it a go."

His glass remains poised over the bar, but he doesn't taste. "I have a wondering..."

"A whiskey wondering?"

He half closes his eyes, but I see his gaze skirt the ring finger of my left hand. "A Meg McGrath wondering."

Sweet Jesus, I let my guard down for a tick, and look where it led me. He didn't see a wedding band, so question answered. I'm having a nice go with him at our current level of cordiality. I'm not keen to start in on more personal stuff.

Cian narrows his eyes. "What's with the nice? You sent a much different message my way after the meeting the morning."

I wave a hand through the air to erase the past. "First time meeting Mr. Everett in person had my nerves jangled."

"First time meeting and the fact he was a raging asshole to you?"

A flush of embarrassment warms my cheeks. Hopefully, the low lighting hides it from Cian. "Caught that did you?"

"Hard to miss."

"Is it his usual way then?"

His tongue plays over his lip. "Not always."

I drop my gaze to the top of the bar. "Not a friendly lot overall, the True Time bunch."

"A competitive lot. You're the new kid with the blockbuster. That puts them on the defensive."

I muffle a snort. The new kid who's in danger of being ousted despite *The Chieftain's Son* blockbuster status.

"They're not all dicks once you get to know them."

"Not all?"

"Make no mistake, some are real dicks."

The earnest look on his face coupled with the irreverence of his statement makes it impossible not to laugh.

His laugh joins mine, burning a trail of heat through my body.

"Back to business," he says and lifts his glass. "Color. Aroma. Taste. Finish." He repeats the words as he navigates each of the three glasses. "Dark amber. Golden. Tangy. Yummy, but not crossing the line to delicious."

An ochre droplet glistens on his bottom lip. It would be so easy to dab my pinkie fingertip on the spot and then bring the ambrosia to my own lips. His tongue darts out to claim the escapee and my chance is gone.

Cian gives the Jameson another go. "Smooth and sharp at the same time." He turns the glass in his hand to just the right angle for the pale gold whiskey to glow. "I'm a little in love."

Thank merciful heaven, scrutinizing the whisky occupies him while I will my body temperature down to human level. It isn't easy to do as I watch his elegant movements. Each time his eyes close to savor, long, nut-brown lashes rest on sun-kissed skin.

"How did I do?" he asks as he sets down the glass of Jameson.

Our knees touch. If I rise to my feet, I'd be standing between his legs, the perfect position to fall into a kiss. This is lunacy. I'm having waking fantasies about my competition. *The Chieftain's Son* and *Star's Shadow* are in a skirmish. I've got to bring in an ungodly amount of new streaming subscribers credited to my show, not his. The smart play would be to lock Cian away for the next three days so he can't boost his show in any way. Instead, I'm stoking lust I'd forgotten I was capable of. Now that it's back, I'm not eager to squelch it. Maybe a nice weekend fling with a handsome swimmer type is not completely mad.

I was first to paint Jack and Gilly's lightning strike connection as frivolous. Here I am suffering the same electric blow to my common sense. At the moment, I can't come up with a single coherent reason for deprivation. I'm not dead from the waist down. It's those damn sparkling eyes.

The corner of my lip quirks up. "It depends. Which whiskey have you decided is the best?"

"Which is your favorite?"

Staring at Cian, I feel no loyalty to my Irish Jameson whiskey. I'm ready to grab all three bottles and disappear somewhere dark and shadowy with him.

"I prefer Jameson, but—" A hand rests on my shoulder. Bobby Provost, the showrunner of *The Chieftain's Son* appears next to me.

He sniffs at one of the Glencairn glasses. "I've been transported by the to-die-for steak drowning in Jack Daniel's glaze I had for dinner." Bobby bumps my shoulder with his. "The cafe is just inside the Gaslamp. We're going back tomorrow. Everyone must experience such culinary bliss."

Bobby's touch grounds me. All notions of indulgence skitter beneath the gray tone carpet on the dark wood floor of the bar. Behind him Jack, Gilly, Maureen, and Grady form our *Chieftain's Son* team.

Jack reaches between Cian and me to tap the bar. Gilly's already got him clad in a UCLA Bruin's T-shirt. "Are we whiskey tasting then? Count me in as long as there's a Jameson Black Barrel with my name on it."

I'm on my feet, turned away from Cian. "I've got reserved tables for us back there."

Jack, ever the gentlemen, thrusts his hand out to Cian. "Jack O'Leary. Pleasure."

I swivel to include Cian in the group. "Sorry. Introductions. Everyone, this is Cian Malley, the *Star's Shadow* P.R. guy." A spike of fear runs through me. Jack is here without Niks. If the two are purported to be an item, it doesn't make sense she's not in the mix. Damn oversight on my part.

Memory of Dash's voice sucks a piece of my soul. *Is it enough, Meghan?*

Cian shoots me an amused look. "P.R. guy, that's me."

Maureen nods to Cian. "I see you've met our P.R. gal. I'm Maureen O'Donnell, writer at large, and here's our Crystal-nominated writer, Gillian Bettencourt."

"Gilly is fine."

Gilly is not fine. She's mortified by Maureen's announcement of her pedigree. Panic constricts my chest when an embarrassed Gilly looks to Jack for support. I settle between them and gesture to Bobby. "Cian, Bobby Provost, our showrunner."

Jack takes in the couches and tables in the bar. "Where's my Niks? She bet me she'd be first here."

I could kiss him. Dread that Cian would read something into Niks's absence dissolves. As soon as handshakes run their course, I herd my group toward the table.

Grady raises a hand in parting. "I'm Grady. Nothing to do with the show."

Maureen threads an arm through his. "But he makes a mean Napoleon."

Bobby, the kind and affable, waves Cian over. "Join us. We all play for True Time's Team."

Bobby's more-the-merrier philosophy doesn't work for me tonight. There are things to discuss without Cian's ear in the mix.

Cian gives me a warm smile as if he reads my distress. "Appreciate the offer, but I've got a few more things to do on the clock." He raises his unfinished glass of Jameson to me. "Thanks for the education, Meg. I'm inclined to go with the Irish."

"Smart man," I say and follow my team. To my horror, Jack has his hand resting on the small of Gilly's back. I quickly scan the bar for any undue attention. I'm being paranoid. Jack's hand is as likely to be on the small of Maureen's back or mine. His reputation includes his inclination for touching and hugging in interviews and appearances.

Leaving Cian behind, I jerk my head to indicate Bobby needs to sit between Jack and Gilly. He takes the cue.

"First round's on me," says Bobby as the server comes to take our order.

I catch Cian lingering in the archway leading from the bar to the lift. Our gazes meet. He throws me a two-fingered salute.

Most of the group stares out the windows, ooo-ing and ahh-ing over the view, the black liquid ocean on one side, pinpricks of blazing white light outlining the Gaslamp District below. Bobby clamps hands to his knees and leans forward. "Sorry I couldn't make the meeting this morning, Meg. How'd it go?"

"Grand," I say. "With one notable wrinkle."

His brows crease. "Which is?"

"Dashell Everett wants Deidre on the show panel."

Bobby's shoulders sag. "You've been round the bend with him on the subject of Deidre. She's a firm no."

I press a thumbnail into my palm. "I might have told him she's swapped a firm no for a firm yes. I'm hoping to persuade her an appearance could be a pivotal move to get the second five-year pick up for the show from True Time."

Gilly, who is pointing out the quotes painted on the glass to Jack, catches our exchange. "Deidre is super invested to help all ten books make it to air."

Here's my opening. "A goal we share. Would you mind giving her a ring about joining us, Gilly? Writer to writer."

"If it'll help the show, sure."

Jack circumvents Bobby to lay a hand on Gilly's leg. "Brilliant, love."

I pat his knee as if all this patting is how *The Chieftain's Son* crew rolls. "Careful, Jack. We don't know where the eyes are."

Clearly annoyed, Jack removes his hand.

"The good news is, we've got an entire block of rooms at the hotel and security to keep anyone from poking around."

"Grand," says Jack as he winks at Gilly.

The woman embodies the term "doe-eyed" as she looks at Jack. Not the spirit animal to embrace, love. Let's not forget what happened to Bambi's doe-eyed mum in the meadow.

I slip the tablet out of my bag to start our final briefing before go time. Dash's *"Is it enough?"* clangs loudly in my head, along with visons of the bus and trains wraps we don't have. I'll spend tonight nailing down the list of the additions I can set in motion come dawn.

"I'm leading off with a rather large ask," I say, using nice eyes to draw my actors in. Getting Deidre to Cali Con is my top job, but it's only the first move to knock Dashell Hammond's doubts aside.

"Can I count on the team to be flexible this weekend? I may be asking a bit more of you than we planned."

CHAPTER 5
PREVIEW NIGHT

T he wave of people crashing through the series of double glass doors at the Diego Bay Events Center for today's late Wednesday afternoon preview session is madness. Chip told me they call this first onslaught "The Night Before the Night." I'm told the crowd increases every day, reaching a crescendo on Saturday.

I'm afraid. Not only of the humanity jostling me around, but I'm worried for Jack and Niks. The crush could be dangerous for them. I raise my cell to my lips and add a note.

"Increase security."

After I review the protocol set up for bodyguards, limited access wrist bands, and golf carts to whisk my people to their appearances and secure waiting spaces, I let out a breath. Even so, it would be a lie to say I'm not overwhelmed. My biggest gig to date in Dublin was Lilliputian compared to this Gulliver of an event.

"Beep in on your right," says a magenta-haired girl in the security uniform of the venue.

I lift the badge encased in plastic at the end of my *Star's Shadow* themed lanyard and tap it against an upright post that beeps and flashes a green light. No wonder Dash Everett has a serious man crush on Cian Malley. The P.R. wizard stamped *Star's Shadow* on everything but the paper in the toilets—which I haven't used yet, so it's likely he's managed that too.

I join the stream flowing up the moving staircase to the top level. Most head into a massive space under skylights called The Bright Sky Pavilion. Long tables are set up to hand out convention material and oversized vinyl backpacks. My heart beats a nice rhythm when I start to see *The Chieftain's Son* logo appearing across the backs of attendees. Dash promised True Time had taken care to represent all their shows on their allotted share of the packs but seeing it in the wild is lovely reassurance.

"Is there a *Chieftain's Son* pack there in your pile?" I ask a sandy-haired teen working the table.

"Let me check. They're going fast."

His words are the song I long to hear everywhere in this gathering. It's the song of my success.

"My last one," he says and hands it over.

I want to rub it against my cheek and give it a kiss. It's gorgeous. Jack and Niks look as grand on a vinyl bag as they do on the side of a building, bless them.

My stomach gurgles as I leave the Bright Sky Pavilion and pass a tempting food stand. It's not the moment to sample that chili pie I've got my eye on. I'll wait for dinner at the restaurant Bobby's on and on about with the Jack-Daniels-sauce-covered steak.

Jack Daniels brings a memory of Cian's whiskey tasting. What if we'd met at that bar in the sky without my entire crew wrapped around us? What might have happened after our insides were thoroughly warmed with whiskey? I think of his crumbled business card, the one I took a photo of in case I lost it. If I want to reconnect with his ice blue eyes, a phone call will do it.

I shake off the inkling. "Och, Meg, pull up your socks and get on with your job. Forget the man." There's such a buzz of folks, my talking to the air isn't noticed. In fact, there's a fellow off to the side dressed like a dragon doing his own fine job of soliloquizing while he releases generous puffs of scented smoke into the crowd. Security is on him and his dragon breath in a blazing second.

The Grand Ballroom is just past the food stand. It's the site where

Jack will appear on a panel with other very attractive fellows. The main *Chieftain's Son* event will be held there on Friday. A sign advertising The Grand Ballroom line rises above a row of stanchions.

I pause beneath the sign. In front of the ballroom doors stands a trio of uniformed volunteers. One waves me over. "There's no line. You can go on in."

"Thank you," I say as a woman holds the door for me. I want to get a sense of the place to better prepare my people. I've watched video replays of panels in the room, but they don't give much away about the space.

"Holy socks." I've stepped into an airplane hangar. The room is cavernous with a series of gigantic screens dropping down from the ceiling at intervals, so whichever of the over four thousand seats you end up in it's an inclusive experience. The dais where panelists sit is so far away it's nothing more than a brightly lit blur. To see faces, I've got to rely on the screens.

I move along one of the walls and make my way closer to the front. There are several camera positions recording the festivities to be streamed later, including one trained on the line of fans asking questions. I've looked at floor plans and read seating capacities, but nothing's prepared me for the true scope of where *The Chieftain's Son* will make its first Cali Con splash.

The Grand Ballroom isn't even the biggest of the big. Harborview Hall is the top venue to book. Landing a panel in that massive space announces you've truly arrived. Over six thousand cozy up in there to ogle and swoon over their favorites.

This time next year, I swear I'll be giving Harborview Hall a look to prepare my folks. My future goal is to slap *The Chieftain's Son* images on buildings, trains, buses, backpacks, lanyards, and places I've yet to make a note of.

My breath hitches. If I'm still in the position to be making goals and dreaming dreams. I finger Cian's business card in the pocket of my slacks. Because Dash foisted the man on me as a keeper, my first instinct was never to speak another word to Mr. Malley, but after last night at the bar...

I fidget once again remembering the unexpected intimacy of our whiskey tasting. He so easily stoked feelings from a fire I'd thought I'd successfully banked. And it'll stay banked. I'm not Gilly, and he's not Jack. I suck on my bottom lip. Who is Cian Malley anyway?

I type his name into my phone, and the Internet offers me several pages of answers. Head publicist for *Star's Shadow* is not news, but after a few taps, my jaw dusts the top of my shoes. There are articles mentioning him in major magazines and news outlets. The man's not yet hit thirty-five years and he's won awards I didn't know existed. Cian entered the publicity/marketing scene working for the insanely popular band MetaMeme. Not just working for them...He put the group on the map, rocketing them out of obscurity and onto the charts. MetaMeme has written film scores, broken touring records, and there's even buzz about their own reality show.

Cian Malley's breakout deal was for the band to create music for the RPG game *Star's Shadow*, which the True Time Network turned into the award-winning sci-fi television program *The Chieftain's Son* competes with for top-spot in the ratings. I find an interesting interview where Cian turned down a cushy executive position at True Time to stay directly connected with *Star's Shadow*. Reading between the lines, it seems his choice was not so much loyalty, but rather it gave him the freedom to work the consulting circuit as well. Well then, the man indulges in an extremely lucrative pastime alongside his show responsibilities. I'm sure, at this point in the run of *Star's Shadow*, Cian's underlings do most of the work. He's free to collect consulting money falling from the sky with his butterfly net.

I'm feeling the fool not to at least take a meeting with Mr. Malley to pick his brain about increasing the odds in my current predicament with Dashell Everett. Without, of course, being loose-lipped in regard to my precarious position. I can't look weak. I refuse to look weak.

My phone vibrates in my hand. Bobby's ringing me.

"It's Meg here."

"You want to do a scavenger hunt for fans to find Jack and Niks?"

I try to read his tone. Can't tell if he's surprised or annoyed so I click straight to sales pitch mode. "It'll be brilliant, Bobby. I'll drop hints on social media to where fans might be able to catch a casual peek at our stars. A few autograph signings, T-shirt handouts, and the lovely giveaway couple portraits we made will be promotion gold."

"Security nightmare."

"I've made sure we can be covered nice and tidy."

Someone from an end seat near my side of the room hisses at me to be quiet, and I lower my voice.

"I want to squeeze every bit of traction for the show, Bobby." And keep my job. I'm thinking on my feet for ideas and actions to butter-up my case with Dash. A Jack/Niks scavenger hunt is a bit brilliant, if I do say so myself. It will create additional connection points with our stars. I'll pop out clues each day suggesting a location where Jack and Niks will show up for a small jot of time. It'll give the fans a more personal meet up.

"What do Jack and Niks say?"

"Niks loves it, and you know Jack. He'll do anything for the show."

"And True Time is on board?"

God, I hope Dash won't think I've gone mad with such a last-minute lark. "Like I said, promotion gold." Gone are the days of asking Dash Everett's permission to act. I believe in asking for forgiveness instead, especially now, when proving myself is all important. Cashing in on this weekend is the only way I'll keep from making a bags of my career. I pray my scavenger hunt idea boosts streaming subscriptions and binge watchers to secure my seat as head of P.R. for *The Chieftain's Son*.

"Will you shut up," says a voice from the dark.

"You've got a very wary green light from me then," says Bobby.

I cup a hand around the phone and my mouth. "We're a go," I say and end the call. Not for the first time, I wonder if Bobby has been filled in on the deal I made with Dash. I landed the position as head of P.R. in Ireland for *The Chieftain's Son* because Bobby pushed it through despite my lack of television experience. Should I tell him I'm hanging by a thread? An immediate *no* resounds in my thoughts. Bobby helped get me where I am, but it is up to me not to give him cause for a rescue mission. There's a recipe for loss of respect.

As fast as I can tap and swipe across my screen, I unleash the first clue I stayed up half the night creating and crafting for every social media site.

A trio of hours ere moon takes the sky, there'll be lovers to spy. A bower of fur waits for passions to stir. Time it is true as chance meetings find you.

I've got less than an hour before Jack and Niks make the first clue come true.

I start to call Jack to tell him the scavenger hunt is on but think better of it. Instead, I text Niks and him with directions where to meet up with security and then find me at the True Time booth on the convention floor. Niks's kissy emoji and Jack's thumbs up roll in almost immediately. Damn good sports, the pair of 'em.

"Halle-fucking-lujah," I say loud enough to earn another shush from the nearby seats.

Warm breath against my ear makes me jump.

"Someone needs a lesson on Cali Con etiquette." Cian's close. Our bodies nearly touch. "Lesson one, no loud talking during a panel."

I put distance between us before I turn to face him. "I figured that one out," I say, nodding to my shush-er.

"Surveying the room? Looks bigger on the inside than it does from the outside."

"It's gargantuan."

"Did they show you where to bring in your people?"

I flick a hand to the far side of the dais. "Just there."

He nods. "Bring 'em straight in a few minutes beforehand. Don't get caught up in a crowd before the panel. Fans take it oddly personal if someone they're here to see is late."

We may have had a moment over whiskey, but this man knows nothing about me. I've never been late to anything in my life. No one on my watch will be tardy either.

"Look, Meg. It blows Dash acted like an ass when he suggested I lend you a hand with the Con." He bobs his head to the side. "Allow me to extend the same offer as a kindness, not a condescension. Interested?"

"I might be."

His face relaxes. He was clearly expecting a loud, resounding no. "May I propose a Q & A over dinner?"

The phone in my hand suddenly starts buzzing and doesn't stop. I lift it to see notifications from social media sites flowing in like a storm surge. Fans took my bait. Our *Chieftain's Son* hashtags are blazing with speculations about the scavenger hunt.

A glow from the cell screen lights Cian's questioning look.

I shake my phone. "Saint Brigid is walking with me today. I've got to hop down to the True Time booth."

"Mind if I join you? I haven't seen the spectacle up and running yet."

I'm a bit intimidated by Cian after reading up on him, but that doesn't negate the pleasant feeling his company sparks inside me. "You're very welcome to join me."

We slip out of The Grand Ballroom and to one of the sky-high escalators. I hear the rumble of the crowd from the convention floor before I see it.

It's a mad crush. Lord help us, since this "Night Before the Night" is supposed to be the least crowded of the days. Volunteers waving *end of the line* signs on paddles above their heads appear every couple of meters. Attendees with bags half as big as they are slither through breaks in a writhing wall of humanity.

Cian chuckles as he watches me take in the scene. "Exclusives," he says, jerking a thumb at someone trying to navigate three of the enormous bags without knocking people senseless. "The merch exclusives you can only score tonight."

"I hope their little plastic bobble heads, pins, and T-shirts are worth the risk of being smashed under an over-enthusiastic cosplayer."

He raises an eyebrow. "Those little plastic bobble heads bring in a shit-ton of revenue."

I feel the fool, the green rookie fool Dash and clearly Cian take me for. Settling my face into determination instead of self-recrimination for my inadequacies, I point above the heads of the mob. Suspended from the ceiling, vibrant, lighted, magenta letters spell out TRUE TIME.

"There we are," I say and forge ahead, not looking to see if Cian keeps up.

My first glimpse of the True Time booth tempts me to jump up and down like a kid in primary school who's won a ribbon. A breathtaking, fabricated stone archway frames the perfect replica of Donal Cam's bedchamber. Every detail down to the furs on the bed and deer hide map stretched on its frame give the impression of stepping back in time. Giant black cooking cauldrons flank the entrance, each filled to overflowing with *The Chieftain's Son* giveaways.

T-shirts with our show logo are already a sought-after prize, judging from the length of the line. The folks hired to work my side of the booth are clad in tunics and trappings of the twelfth century.

I make a mental note to have Grady whip up some of his signature pastries back home for our art department as thanks for this beauty.

"It's magnificent," says Cian, who managed his way to my side. "The posing on the bed is quite the provocative move." He gestures at the latest fan, who poses with one of our Donal Cam models atop the furs.

The catcalls and giggles are exactly what I'd hoped for when I came up with the photo op idea for *The Chieftain's Son* half of the True Time booth. Deidre loved it. She's all for indulging fantasies.

I'm surprised to hear Gilly's voice on my other side. "Oh my God, Meg. This is genius. Look, the line circles the booth then along a wall."

My heart catches fire as I look for Jack. It's too early, and God in the garden, if Gilly and Jack came here together—disaster. "Are you alone then?"

She nods. "I wanted to walk the floor before it gets too crazy."

"And this isn't crazy?"

Gilly laughs. "You ain't seen nothing yet."

Cian bobs around me. "Hello, Crystal nominated writer, Gillian Bettencourt. We met last night. Cian Malley."

Her color starts to rise, but she clues into the tease and smiles. "Hi." Gilly looks between Cian and me. "Again."

I don't appreciate the question blooming in her eyes. The woman is a romantic cut from the same cloth as Deidre. She's seen Cian and I together twice now. That's all she needs to get her little heart-covered wheels turning.

I nearly jump when Gilly cups her hand around my ear to whisper. "Jack and Niks are on the way."

"Not alone?"

She shakes her head. "The middle of a security sandwich."

An idea rushes up my middle. "Gilly, I want a photo of you on the bed with the model."

Her face turns as magenta as the overhead sign. "No, it's okay."

"I insist. It'll be lovely fun on socials. Get used to coming out from behind your laptop. You're Crystal Award bound, girl, I feel it."

Cian claps his hands once. "Brilliant." He favors me with a smile that puts the model to shame and shakes a finger at me. "You, woman, think fast on your feet. I'm envious."

The models know me from our briefing before the floor opened. I motion one of them over. "Take this lovely lady to bed for me."

Gilly looks ready to melt into the convention floor carpet. The model earns his pay by sweeping her up into his arms and over to the bed. He poses like a pro, laying her down and hovering above her as if he's descending for a toe-curling kiss. I take shot after shot.

"Got it."

Mortified, Gilly escapes to my side.

"You should at least give her a T-shirt," teases Cian.

The crowd around the booth quadrupled in the bitty time we've been hanging about. My phone alarm chimes. Five o'clock. Three hours before sunset, according to the Internet, and time for the first clue on *The Chieftain's Son* scavenger hunt to become reality.

The roar starts as a distant wave and grows. Right on time, Jack and Niks, with their security, thread through the masses until they reach the stone archway. They stand arm-in-arm, the regal pair they are, posing for pictures. Between smiles and greetings, Jack finds Gilly and winks. His gesture is lost in his interaction with the fans, who press closer and closer.

Jack, ever the showman, holds out a hand to one of our models. "Would you be so kind as to return my crown?" The model bows and offers his headpiece up to Jack, who pops it onto his head and spreads his arms wide. "Ah, now this feels like home."

The fans adore him. A chant of "Kiss, kiss, kiss," rises from the crowd. Jack drops to one knee and kisses Niks's hand. She fakes a swoon and falls into his arms. Their audience goes wild.

I could kiss Jack as he offers himself up to pose on the bed with the women in line for the photo op. His jeans and yet another UCLA T-shirt are far from period, but the fans don't mind. While he plays the seducer, Niks poses near the arch with her share of fan love. Our models hand out *Chieftain's Son* metal water bottles, T-shirts, and oversized cards with directions on how to sign-up for the True Time streaming app and credit *The Chieftain's Son* for their subscription.

I turn to Gilly, but she's disappeared. My heart gives a little hitch. How would I feel to see my husband cuddled up to his costar off-script? I know the fauxmance I've orchestrated between Jack and Niks is a series of gut punches to Gilly, but I won't go soft and back down. We're all in this together for the good of the show.

Cian stands beside me in Gilly's place. "Your fandom knew they'd show up."

I can't help beaming. "I set up a scavenger hunt to let them know. If I don't make the clues a little harder, I'll start a riot."

Cian leans close. "Maybe you should be giving me tips."

A disappointed groan rises around us, and I realized Jack and Niks are saying their good-byes. I break from Cian to blow each a kiss. Not my usual style, but heartfelt. Thirty minutes of my stars' time is worth thirty sacks of gold to me, slightly less of what I'll have to add to their appearance fees for the extra time.

Security whisks the pair away and the models return to the business of seduction. Cian stands at the corner of the True Time booth and gestures for me to join him. I weave my way past the next wave of visitors to Donal Cam's bedchamber.

"My turn to show off a little," he says and nods toward the opposite side of the booth, the world of *Star's Shadow*. He's got the eager face of a kid with a new pup, frightfully adorable.

If my half of the booth takes us back in time, Cian's brings us the future. A multi-colored neon fortress rises from a base of black boulders. Turrets of vibrant orange, lime, raspberry, and indigo taper upward in layers akin to a wedding cake nearly to the exposed metalworks of the convention floor ceiling. A double of Sala Singh, the actress who plays Starry Night, the main character of *Star's Shadow*, is perched at the top of the pulsating sculpture. The replica of her cosmic hideaway is torn right from the screen into reality. She tosses glowing necklaces to the crowd below.

I am transported. The event center fades away, and it's as if my body is slowly rising into the night sky. I wobble as I take in the spectacle, and Cian catches my elbow. The music of MetaMeme swells, and the neon lights of the fortress perform a show to match the song. It's fantasy. It's a rock concert. It's genius.

A cadre of fans surround the booth, wearing the glow necklaces Starry Night sent flying through the air. The lighted circles around each neck pulse in sync with MetaMeme's opening theme of *Star's Shadow*.

This is magic.

The song changes and the necklaces shift to match the new notes. I applaud Cian. "Well done. Grand and beautiful."

Cian bows.

I step away from him. "Enough of that."

"Such a compliment deserves a balanced response." He straightens and squeezes my arm. "Will you wait? I'll be right back."

"Sure." I'm glad to steal a moment to take in the enormity of what Cian orchestrated here. I've convinced myself I think in sweeping scenarios. I'm wrong. My visions are small. Does Dash sense limitations in me? My show is a rare treasure. Time to broaden my visions, shoot for the impossible, and at worst, land in the spectacular.

I watch Cian talking with his crew at the booth, heads together, claps on the shoulders. It's a friendly look, but I see the boss in his eyes. Here is a man that doesn't settle. Here is a man I can learn a thing or two from. I wasn't raised to be fool, but a fool I'll be if I don't accept Cian Malley's offer of sharing advice. I can think of worse things than looking into those eyes over a nice plate of food.

I take the initiative and stroll over to the front of the booth to join Cian. There's pride shining on his face as he looks at his sparkling fortress, well-earned pride.

A bump on his shoulder brings his attention where I want it, on me. "Are you still up for a dinner Q & A?"

I'm gifted with a pleased look from him that sets lower parts of me singing, particularly places I'd worried had forgotten words to the song. This is business now. Pleasant business, but despite the inklings and tingling the man sets off in me, crossing the business line with him isn't something I've time for. Not if I'm to answer Dash's *"Is it enough?"* with a resounding *"So much more than enough, sir."*

His hand brushes mine before he grabs it and starts tugging me through the suffocating tangle of attendees. "First, I'm going to show you how to fly."

CHAPTER 6
TACO WEDNESDAY

The Balboa Sky Bridge could literally scrape the clouds if there were any overhead. The suspended motorway arches over an expanse of glittering blue Pacific. The sea beneath me looks to be napping compared to the wild Atlantic I'm used to back home in Ireland. Today, a cheery sun smiles down on us from a sky straight out of a bright blue tube of acrylic paint.

"Mr. Malley, you might warn a person that when you say flying, you aren't being poetic." My hands brace against the dashboard of Cian's vehicle. The electric jobby is so quiet it's like being trapped in a bubble. No displays on the dash, only a computer screen larger than my laptop running the show. Instead of dinner, he's launching us on a space mission.

Beneath us, the bridge sets my heart crossways. The span feels too thin to sustain the line of cars racing across it. One energetic gust of wind will knock us off for a watery plunge. Heights don't usually bother me, but here in Cian's car, it feels as if I'm sitting in the Gravity Bar at the top of the Guinness Storehouse in Dublin without fine glass windows to prevent a freefall.

Cian laughs. He laughs quite a lot. I hope it's because I'm entertaining and not because he finds me ridiculous.

He clasps a hand to his chest. "The first time I drove over this bridge, a panic attack nearly strangled me. It feels like a one-way trip straight up."

"But here you are, risking fate again."

He turns to me. "Risking it with you."

I stab a finger at the windshield in an *eyes forward* command. "Don't be blaming me for our untimely demise."

"Why not fly high? By staying low, you miss out on the rewards afforded from a lofty perspective."

I lay a hand on his cheek, directing his gaze to the bridge instead of me. "Better alive than lofty."

Cian bends over the wheel like he's on a final push for the finish line. "Point taken. I'm glued to the road."

For a split second, there is no bridge in front of us, only sky. Maybe we're not always destined to feel the earth beneath our feet.

The myth of Oisín and Niamh, the very inspiration for Deidre LaRochelle to write *The Chieftain's Son* series, plays through my mind. Oisín, a mortal bound to his love, Niamh, dwelt with her in Tir na nÓg, realm of eternal youth. When a bout of homesickness hit the fool, he was granted permission to visit the world he left behind with one caveat: no sliding off his enchanted white horse to touch mortal ground. As myths so often go, the eejit disobeyed, turning to dust with his first toe tap on the grass.

If someone asked me right now how I think I'll leave this world, I'd say by way of a speeding car at the hands of Cian Malley. Dizzy relief passes through me as the bridge curves downward with our wheels still touching road.

"I keep my promises," says Cian. "You're alive."

"And grateful for it," I say as we wind through the streets of Coronado Island to approach a classic beauty. The bright white stucco face of Hotel Joya Brillante stretches along a beach dotted with palm trees. Rust-colored tile roofs offer a pleasing contrast to the walls, especially the main inverted cone on the tallest structure. Words such as tropics, veranda, and cabana float on a gentle current through my thoughts.

I click my tongue. "Well now, a hotel on its own island. Not a shabby locale for friendly information sharing."

He pulls into a car park, and we walk along a path lined with plants and flowers toward the beach. A reflection of the hotel wavers on the ocean across an expanse of powdery white sand. Just the sight of the place offers relaxation.

"I can think of worse," says Cian, favoring me with a grin I'll be happy to look at for the rest of the weekend.

"Inside or out?" asks Cian.

"Whatcha mean?"

"Do you want to eat inside or outside?"

I drink in the glorious late afternoon. "It'd be a shame to waste what's left of this beautiful day."

"Correct answer."

I raise an eyebrow at him. "Didn't realize I was taking an exam."

"It's all an exam, a constant test, isn't it, M-Squared? You're testing me. I'm testing you."

"M-Squared?" I hate nicknames as much as I hate pickled beets, but out of Cian's lips, this one isn't so bad. Is he testing me or teasing me? Either way, it is a nice bit of fun. I offer a slight smile to encourage him.

"Meg McGrath. M-Squared."

"Let's keep it at Meg." What's the big draw for people playing with my name? Maureen's always at it, and even Jack O'Leary tried to saddle me with "Megser" a while back.

The waning day gives off too much heat for a suit jacket. I slip out of mine, confident my chocolate-colored silk blouse will do fine.

Cian left his suit coat and tie behind in the car. His deep turquoise dress shirt shifts the color of his eyes—still a glacial sea color, but with added shadings of green swimming through the blue.

"Tell me more of your inspired scavenger hunt." He laughs again as we pass a massive tangle of orange flowers.

"What is it about me you find so hilarious?"

Cian stops short, and his hands hover near the sides of my face but don't touch. "I find you refreshing. I very much enjoy the way you don't hide a thing you're feeling. For example, I knew you were ready to set Dash on fire during our prep meeting. Now, I sense my request for you to elaborate on your scavenger hunt has you drowning in suspicion."

I force my features to relax despite the tingling the proximity of his fingers ignites on my skin. "Direct works well for me. Saves time."

He drops his hands. I imagine a rosy glow on my cheeks from the near contact. "Have no fear, I am not out to steal your ideas. Call me intrigued and leave it there."

We pass manicured lawns where kids turn cartwheels. The surf is background music. The place screams money. I wonder how much it'd put one out to stay here. It's likely the size of the price tag would diminish the pleasure of the experience for me. Then again, a girl's got to splurge once in a while. If I pass through Dash's flaming hoops without burn marks, next year at Cali Con, perhaps I'll treat myself to a few nights in this gem.

Cian's donned a pair of highly reflective sunglasses. I see everything twice, once in real time and a repeat in his lenses. I prefer the color of his eyes to the mirrors.

I push ahead, walking backward to face him. "How far do I have to walk for my supper?"

He slides the sunglasses to the top of his head and squints to a point beyond me. "Fifty feet, give or take."

Up ahead is a lazy-looking food stand under a roof of palm fronds, advertising *TACO TUESDAY* and margaritas. "I'm not overly fond of tequila."

"Oh, no, you don't," says Cian. "I was game for whiskey. You owe me margaritas."

I throw up my hands in surrender. "Your turf, your call. Shame we missed the tacos."

He looks perplexed, so I point to the TACO TUESDAY sign. And he's laughing at me again. "It's not a no-taco thing, it's a cheap-taco thing."

I wear what I hope is a convincing befuddled expression. "Ah, so we're paying top shelf price for Wednesday tacos. We'd best go someplace else. I've got per diem to consider."

"We're fine, Taco Tuesday is a marketing gimmick. You can eat cheap tacos any day, but if you'd rather not do tacos—" he fiddles with his glasses —"There are taco-free options."

Cian's fluster to please me is so sweet, I free my fish from the hook. "I'm slagging, ah, putting you on. If you're ever in Dublin, I know a fine place for Taco Tuesday."

"Well played, M-Squared." The sense of fun behind his smile may be as dangerous as driving off the Balboa Sky Bridge. "I know what's good here. May I order for you?"

This one's a charmer for certain, asking for my taco blessing.

"Taco me, sir."

Cian's laugh coupled with his appreciative eye sweep of my blouse and skirt is as pleasant as the waning day.

While Cian goes to order up Wednesday tacos, I claim one of the high wooden tables nestled in the sand near the walkway and grab the chance to hop onto my cell. Heart rate and breathing rocket in tandem as I snoop through the myriad of *Chieftain's Son* hashtags on Twitter.

My scavenger hunt went viral.

Clicking links to fan sites have message threads swarming with guesses about this afternoon's Jack/Niks sighting, a high percentage correct. A niggle of worry seeps into my euphoria. I'd best be on my guard not to make the clues too easy. The hunt could be in danger of getting out of hand. I shift into a Dash mindset. How big is too big?

Dashell Everett would say there's no such limitation.

Balancing a tray with a quartet of multi-colored, frothy drinks and two bottled waters is just the person who may be able to answer my question if I let him. Such permission requires granting Cian a foot in the door to my business.

I laugh at myself. Hopping in his space car and driving over a skybridge sent a damn clear invitation to my business. So far, Cian's been nothing but kind, a good sport, and willing to help. I'll open the door a crack but keep my foot braced against it in case he tries to push farther than suits me.

Cian rests the tray on the table and lifts the drinks one by one, setting them in a line in front of me as he narrates. "Mango, banana, peach, and melon. I insist you taste in that order."

"I thought you said margaritas. You're tempting me with fruit salad." My eyes rake the road of alcohol. "Don't expect me to make my way through all of these." There's a guaranteed step into bad decisions.

"Keep your two favorites, and I'll be content with the leftovers." He points to the tangerine-colored glass first in line. "Mango. Go."

I raise the bowl-shaped glass, raising the teeny pair of red straws to my lips. "Sláinte."

He snaps his fingers. "There it is: proof you are actually Irish."

"Was there any doubt?"

"You barely have an accent."

"I hear my mother's heart breaking from here."

He licks his lips. "Your doing?"

I nod. "I've worked hard to sound more neutral. Figured it would better suit if I decide to work in your neck of the woods."

"My woods?"

"Hollywood. L.A. In time, it's where I'd like to end up."

A crease appears between his chestnut brows. No laugh. No comment on the life goal I'd plunked on the table. I feel the fool. His silence is comment enough on what he thinks of my dreams. I'd bet Doolin's donkeys back home, chewing on the grassy fields around The Clan, that Mr. Malley doesn't deem me Hollywood material. I'll pour burning coals into Dash's shoes for planting the notion in Cian's head that I need help to do my job.

Cian studies my face. "Don't be too quick to lose the accent altogether. It makes you interesting."

To avoid responding to what reeks of empty flattery, I meet up with the first margarita. The frosty liquid is the perfect amount of sweet. It's like biting into a piece of ripe mango with a kick. Cian's chuckle returns when I wear a fool's grin.

"Obviously, I don't need to tell you mango has me interested."

He folds his arms on the table and rests his chin on them. His eyes are back to frozen blue. "But will it make the top two?"

I raise the next margarita and turn to hide my face as I sip a frozen, ripe banana. Perhaps I will develop an affection for tequila after all.

Cian taps on the table. "You're not playing fair."

I swap banana for the peach margarita and continue to hide my taste test. "You won't know the verdict until I'm ready to share."

When I turn, I catch him sipping the melon margarita. He swallows wrong and chokes.

I point a finger at him. "Serves you right for cheating. If you think I'm going to come 'round and smack you between the shoulder blades, think again, thief."

He slams down half a bottle of water to recover.

I claim the honeydew-colored concoction with both hands, pulling it out of his reach. Instead of turning away, I keep my gaze glued on him while I sip. Holy flight of angels, nothing sweeter'll ever pass my lips in this lifetime or the next. I close my eyes, savoring the icy flow of sweet melon trickling down my throat.

With one hand on the stem of each glass, I pull the mango and melon margaritas to my side of the table, and then slide the banana and peach over to Cian.

"A wise choice, M-Squared." He flicks each of my glasses with a *ping*. "M-Squareds for M-Squared." Laughing at his own joke, he bypasses the mini straws and lifts the banana margarita to his lips for a healthy gulp. When he sets the glass down, he slings an elbow over the back of his chair. "I suppose I owe you business talk. Scavenger hunt...go."

I nod. "If you don't mind."

"I'm all ears."

The man's got charming ears, if such a thing is possible. They're on the small side and rest comfortably against his head. Not the type to stick out and turn red with the sun behind them. I steal a peek at his nose, also just the right amount of smallish and round. I'd not call it dainty, rather nicely compact.

"Do you want to chat about your scavenger hunt, or have you chosen a different topic?" Cian gives me a smile bordering on naughty.

Bless me, I've been caught looking. I tap my phone to avoid staring at Cian. "The hunt came to me on the fly to give fans a little more of their favorite folk. Jack and Niks, good sports that they are, agreed to quick extra fan visits, one for each day of the convention."

I raise my phone so he can watch the swelling stream of likes on #FindJackandNiks.

Cian takes the phone from my hand. "Did I promise not to steal your idea? I'd like to amend that."

I reclaim my cell. "Do you want a push off a very high bridge on our way back?" I dab a bit of margarita froth off my lips with the cocktail napkin. "To tell truth, I'm worried about making the clues too easy. There's a line between a healthy crowd and a mob I'd rather not cross."

"Why don't I try and solve the clues?"

Perfect. If he figures my riddles too easily, I'll know to increase the difficulty.

"Okay—here's what I'm thinking of for tomorrow.

The old, not the new, holds treasures for you. Apart from the throng, Mariachis three fill nighttime with song. As food and drink spread in kind, we invite you to find a moment to bind with the son and his love under stars up above."

"Once more."

I read it to him again, enjoying the way his eyes flick back and forth as he thinks. "Clearly at night, hence the stars. A restaurant, likely a Mexican restaurant if there are Mariachis." He taps a finger against his bottom lip. It's nice and full, perfect for a pout.

I wonder how my own plump lips would fit against his.

"It's on the tough side. Mexican restaurants with music in San Diego aren't exactly scarce. Do you think it's too clever?"

"I did start with 'old not new' which means Old Town San Diego. Under stars is meant to say open air."

He snaps his fingers. "Casa de Fiesta in Old Town."

I reach across the table and squeeze his arm. "You got it. There's also the bit about being away from the throng. The Mariachi trio doesn't start playing before eight. So not too hard?"

"I think you've hit the sweet spot. Not a mob." He shakes his head, smiling. "How did a nice Irish girl like you suss out a subtle local spot?"

"I do my homework, sir, and the food ratings of Casa de Fiesta are through the roof."

The serious look crossing his face dilutes my momentary victory.

"What?" I ask.

"I rescind my last statement. The moment one person figures out the location, it'll be all over social media. There's definite mob potential."

"Bloody hell, you're right. The *Chieftain's Son* lot planned to do dinner there first and end with the hunt. I'll cancel our dinner and make it just a quick appearance."

Cian stretches his legs under the table, making contact he doesn't retract. "Or eat earlier and plan an exit with extra security in place."

"Brilliant. We'll be on the way out when the clue timer buzzes, not trapped in the middle of a meal."

"Don't forget to factor in early arrivals who want first crack at your people."

"Dinner's turning into late lunch." I tip my head to him. "Why don't you join us? You've already met most of *The Chieftain's Son* folks." I nearly choke on a chunk of ice. What in the name of all that is holy am I thinking? Gilly's parents, aka Jack's in-laws, may join us at Casa de Fiesta. No doubt Cian'll sniff out the fauxmance between Jack and Niks if he gets a gander at the happy family breaking tortillas. One melon margarita and I've lost my wits.

"Do you want me to say no, or would you rather rescind the invitation?"

I lay palms to my cheeks. "You can stop reading my face any time."

His lips curve into a gentle smile. "I enjoy reading your face."

For the space of a couple of sips, my eyes meet his. As inconvenient as his clairvoyance is, there's a certain thrill to someone figuring me out.

Cian wipes a hand across his mouth. "Hmm, why would Meg McGrath not want a True Time colleague sharing guacamole with her cast? Could it be I might figure out the public love fest publicized between her stars is bullshit?"

The glass slips from my hand and clanks onto the wooden tabletop. Thanks to the weighted bottom, it doesn't spill. Cian doesn't need finely tuned face-reading chops to know he's hit the mark. "Dash told you?"

Cian shakes his head. "My dear M-Squared, I have eyes. Your Jack fell hard for a certain Crystal-nominated writer, and judging from the way she turned green watching him philander with Niks on the furs, it's mutual."

I stare him down. There will be no reading my face this time.

"You realize the daggers shooting out of those coffee-with-no-cream eyes give you away."

I drop my face with its traitorous eyes into my hands. "How'd you figure it out so fast?"

"I look. I notice. I try not to miss anything." Cian's thumb slides under my chin and he gently lifts. "And I am good at reading people, not only you. Truthfully, you're not easy to read. I just have the knack of it." He reaches for a stray wisp of my hair and then stops himself. "I'm on your side, Meg."

"Jack and Gillian are married. Secret ceremony after we wrapped season one." The moment the confession rides the air, I regret it.

Cian whistles. "They don't make it easy for you, do they?"

"Thank you." Despite my margarita-induced loose lips, it's grand someone appreciates my dilemma for once. "I will gut you if you speak of it to anyone."

He taps a finger on the table. "Jack's fans would roast that poor girl on a spit if they found out. The show could take a ratings hit."

Sharing my deepest, darkest with Cian lifts the pair of rocks I've been balancing on my shoulders over Jack and Gilly. Cian views Mr. and Mrs. O'Leary as nothing more than a business snafu. "And pointing out those very things turned me into a witch on a broom. I've papered my walls with non-disclosures to keep the marriage quiet."

"You're damn lucky Jack and Niks are willing to play your P.R. game."

"Don't I know it. The hell of it is, I've only got until my season two finale. That's all the time I could buy before Gilly admits to the white dress."

Cian's gaze settles on the horizon. I'm beginning to read him as well. His eyes have a think squint. "Timing is key. I'd play up a Cinderella angle with the writer woman. After Jack's tragic breakup with Niks, fans will want their dear boy to smile again. He already wears a prince's crown. You'll be a hero for ending his misery with a deserving princess."

I wrap my fingers around the stem of his remaining margarita and help myself. "I see you're past reading my face and went digging straight into my mind. You pegged the exact scenario I plan to paint."

He softly brushes my fingers aside to reclaim the glass and takes another long drink, appraising me the whole time. "I never doubted you had it under control. You think well on your feet. Dangling Deidre in front of Everett's nose and now an impromptu series of appearances with your scavenger hunt. I am impressed."

"You're not the one I'm trying to impress."

To my surprise, Cian reaches across the table and covers my hand with his. "Well, you have, and for the record, I got cramps when Dash was a complete rude ass to you at the meeting and took credit for your work."

Cian's validation is a welcome boost in the fight for my future. I rest my hand on his, adding to our stack. "Thank you for noticing."

There's a moment between us. Heat surrounds our joined hands. It both unnerves and intrigues me. I slide free to navigate the giant margarita glass while I reset. "Are you up for more questions, Mr. Malley?" The combination of growing intoxication and validation are heady.

His eyes linger on the spot our hands recently occupied. A slight breeze kicks up, raising strands of nut-brown hair from the crown of his head.

"Cian, will you work with me to generate a checklist of things I can add to my equation for a massive *Chieftain's Son* payoff at Cali Con?"

Before he answers, a waiter in a *Taco Tuesday* T-shirt slides a tray onto our table brimming with an assortment of tacos.

I glance around. "Who else are we feeding?"

"I didn't know what you liked, so I ordered some of each. There's carne asada, chicken, carnitas, fish, shrimp, veggie…"

As Cian rattles off our choices, I indulge in the rush of being on the receiving end of an attractive man's attention. I grab for the shrimp taco and nod for him to grab one of the bounties for himself. "How are you at multitasking?"

He works on a monstrous bite of taco. Hiding his chew behind a hand, he manages an answer. "Genius level." Swiping a dribble of hot sauce from the corner of lips that draw more and more of my attention, he starts in. "Deidre LaRochelle is key. She's your vetted draw. You've got legions of fans here who would follow her off the end of a flat earth."

"I'm working on her." I quickly send up a prayer for Gilly's success in coaxing Deidre away from L.A. to land at Cali Con.

"You've got show presence on several panels, good. I always aim for five or more."

I mentally tick off our peoples' appearances, the main *Chieftain's Son* show panel, the one for our podcast, Gilly on *Pages to Screen*, and Jack at *Is it Me or is it Hot in Here?*, which I learned convention-goers dub the *Hot Guy* panel. Four. I'm one slot shy of Cian's minimum. Damn. Did Dash's *"Is it enough?"* stem from the show's thin panel presence? The bastard could have let on five exposures is a magic number.

"Don't take this as criticism, but Dash showed me your line-up for your main show panel."

The tacos form a solid ball in my stomach. "And?"

"You've got your co-stars, showrunner, and a key writer, but it's still a little thin."

A terrible thought seeps into my margarita-fueled brain. Did Dash set me up to fail by not coaching me on these key details?

"Adding Deidre will certainly raise the bar. Are there any other fan favorites you can pad the dais with this late in the game?"

I'd like to smash my fist down next to the fish taco. When I built our panel, I was thinking the fans would want to hear as much as they could from their darlings, Jack and Niks. Small vision. Time to turn the telescope around and look through the right end.

"We get tons of mail for Bowstring, eh, Artie Boyd. He's not much to look at, but he's got a wit about him."

He's nodding. "Grab him if you can. Another flavor to add to the mix. What's your big reveal?"

"I don't get your meaning?"

"Your reveal, an exclusive for Cali Con. Are you screening a segment no one has seen before?"

"We've got a season one montage and a season two preview."

"New footage?"

I shrug. "Up to Bobby. He plays it tight with spoilers."

He looks puzzled. "Tight with you? On a show based on existing books?"

Fans know essential, broad story strokes, but Bobby and the writers settle on which plot threads to weave from Deidre's massive tomes to tell the visual story. Bobby's a master of surprise, leaking miserly bits and pieces of what will eventually make it to screen. He gives fans enough to tantalize but keeps 'em guessing.

Cian hits a sore point. I am top of the need-to-know list since it's my job to blast the show to the world. I'll work on loosening Bobby's reins to include me in secrets so I can craft promos into P.R. fan bait.

The sun dabbles tiny drops of light across the top of the water that in turn blink against the stucco walls of Hotel Joya Brillante. If only I could vanish into the twinkles to be far from my troubles here. As my consciousness dallies with the light show, a stellar reveal jumps into my head, and I smack the table.

"We have a new Chieftain for season two. Everyone knows who the historical figure will be, but we haven't leaked the actor."

Cian clamps his hands on my forearms. "There's your big ticket. A treat for the fans."

I'm boiling over as nervous energy wars with feelings of inadequacy. They manifest in an obsessive need to stack our collection of empty paper taco trays.

Cian stands and walks to my side of the table. "Stop."

A moment later, he's pulled me against his chest to curtail my manic tidying. The clutch shocks me a bit at first. I'm not a hugger, but I don't get the sense this is a gratuitous hug. I am curious, so I allow it. As I suspected, his swimmer's body is built with very tidy muscles. My drunk buzz dampens the instinct to balk at the contact. The man understands my situation better than colleagues who are only privy to thick-skinned Meg or my family, whose answer to the woes of my job is to quit. Cian sees inside me to the human sculpted from a tower of stress knots and offers a moment of comfort. What the hell have I got to lose by taking it? I soften against him.

"It's okay, Meg." He lays a hand on my cheek. "You're doing well your first time out."

"But not on any level in the vicinity of yours. I can't blink without seeing *Star's Shadow* waving at me from every moving vehicle and lanyard."

I'm not sure what does it, tequila, Cian's kindness, or fear I've failed before the Con has barely begun, but a damned tear breaks my defenses and glides toward his fingers. His thumb gently strokes my cheek, blotting away the traitorous drop.

This is madness. I do not cry. I hate the act. It's weak and pathetic. I feel exposed. Where the hell is my armor? I've embraced a life of "me." I control my outcomes. I chart my course. My me-centric life is prepped for bumps and missteps. So why in the name of my entire philosophy am I on the verge of bawling in front this man?

"Let me work with you, Meg."

Another tear follows the first. Tips and advice are a level of support I'm willing to accept. Cian offers more. Giving in is tantamount to an admission of my ineptitude.

"Before you refuse, please hear me out. It's your first gig with a show that rocketed into insane numbers. Knowing Dashell Everett, he's probably been as much help as—" He fishes out a tiny paper umbrella from one of our empty margarita glasses. "This umbrella in a hailstorm."

A laugh I didn't think I could manage finds its way out as he holds the wilted blue toy over his head and looks warily up at the sky.

He settles himself on the stool next to me, keeping an arm draped over my shoulder as we watch waves sneak up on the last holdout of sunbathers on the beach. The perfect blue sky fills with bursts of crimson, a color-coded promise tomorrow will be as warm and friendly as today.

"Why are you so keen on helping me? I know your schedule must be hopping as well."

He draws in a long breath. "My team down here does the heavy lifting."

"Chip?" I don't know I'd trust Chip to butter my bread. "He seems easily distracted."

Cian chuckles. "He's fresh meat, but he's a pleaser. The kid will do well with bottom rung responsibilities." He frowns. "How many assistants did you bring?"

There's no power on earth that'll push me to admit to him I'm a solo act until I hire a new assistant or possibly two. My secretary back at The Clan in Ireland keeps me up to date on the day to day while I'm here.

"Back to your question about why I want to help. I've been where you are. It's scary as hell." As the sun takes its final bow, a spray of burnt orange splashes across the horizon like a spilled margarita. "And if you haven't figured it out yet, I find you intriguing and…"

His gaze locks on mine as he draws closer.

"Inexperienced?"

He slowly shakes his head and brings his mouth barely an inch away from mine, breathing rather than speaking his answer. "Lovely."

The pair of margaritas advise me to go along with the insanity happening here on Taco Wednesday. "You think you're going to kiss me, do you?"

"Oh, I think so. If I may?" He flings a hand to the colors bleeding across the sky. "It's a crime not to kiss someone under this beautiful sunset."

As easily as Cian woke my desire to flirt last night in the bar, he ignites a long dormant wish to be kissed. I tilt my head in invitation. Am I that needy, or is there something special about this man who dropped into my life out of nowhere? "Ah, like being alone at midnight on New Year's Eve."

He brushes his lips across mine. "Exactly." Our kiss is mango and melon and peach and banana. It's sweet and easy. We taste and savor. His lips are soft, full, and live up to the way I imagined them pressed to mine. The tip of his tongue strokes my bottom lip as he gives a contended sigh.

I pull back. "I see you managed to steal another taste of melon margarita after all." The colors of the sunset live in his eyes. My fingers itch to slide into his hair and pull his mouth back down to mine. I'm a careful sort, but the charm of Cian Malley coupled with being thousands of miles from home drive me toward careless. I did let him whisk me on a death-defying ride over a bridge. Our kiss chalks up two for two on my careless tally. I may have underestimated the benefits of careless.

I slip a hand behind his neck. His skin is warm covered with a soft fuzz I'm tempted to stroke. "Don't get the notion kissing is payment for your professional help. I don't barter when it comes to my livelihood."

In one flawless sweep, Cian dips me backward over the side of the stool, the final move of a dance. "M-Squared, we are definitely off the clock."

Careless it is.

CHAPTER 7

SURPRISE GUESTS

Maureen snatches the small cardboard tent bearing the Cali Con logo and her name. "I'm keeping my nametag." She sets it on the long table we're seated behind, positioning it so there's no obstruction of water bottles or microphones between her name and the audience. "They'll have to wrestle me to take it away."

Maureen, Gilly, and I are seated on a stage in the auditorium of the Seaview Library. It's a friendly space with a glass wall behind the audience, overlooking a cozy patio. The side walls are blonde wood, a warm contrast to its glassy backbone. Embedded alcoves in the walls dip in at even intervals, which give the room rich acoustics quite appropriate for a podcasting panel. The room reminds me of a miniature university lecture hall. Each seat is equipped with a small desk that swivels into place. Many of which already support notebooks poised and ready to record memorable pearls our crew imparts.

It's grounding to see the outside world from our dais. Rooms in the events center are carpeted caves without windows. I prefer connecting with sunshine.

We're only a few blocks from the events center, but to my delight, a crowd found our *Chieftain's Son* podcast offering. The three hundred seats spilling out in front of us are full. A gratifying line of people waits outside in hopes someone will leave and give up a seat.

I raise my phone and take a video sweep of the packed house and line. A quick to text to Dash proves I have one overflowing panel on my tally. His minions will double check headcounts on all True Time panels, but a real-time glimpse at how *The Chieftain's Son* presence packs 'em in front and center on his phone can't hurt. The game tips in my favor.

"Meg, we missed you at the bar last night," says Maureen, nudging me. "Bobby sang show tunes on Karaoke. His 'Phantom of the Opera' was terrifying, and not in the way it's meant to be." She side-eyes me with a scolding look. "If you say you were in your room working, I'll have no choice but to take your social life into my own hands."

My face warms as I replay my evening on the beach with Cian in front of the Hotel Joya Brillante. We sobered up with a combination of kisses and minimal shop talk. Our return voyage across the Balboa Sky Bridge was a sweep through the stars. The night sky wasn't all that twinkled. Truth be told, I've never enjoyed my time with a man as much as I did last night with Cian Malley. He's got a brain and a wit about him easy to be drawn to. There's no denying his outside is as appealing as his inside.

"Met a friend for dinner is all."

The disadvantage of our *Chieftain's Son* folks being on the same floor with the *Star's Shadow* crowd is too many folks have the chance to know everyone's business. Any notion Cian and I entertained in our margarita-softened heads for sharing more of the evening was put to rest the moment Bobby grabbed me straight off the lift with personnel updates. If that's not fate intervening to replace twinkling stars in my head with good sense, I'm a donkey at a hurling match.

Lucky for me, Cian is a man who knows how to make an easy exit. I was sorrier to see him go than I should've been. He left Bobby and I quick and casual enough to be nothing but an afterthought. Bobby buzzed like an energy cloud over my confirmation our actor, Artie Boyd, bless his heart, was set to board a plane for San Diego. Adding our resident clown, plus Deidre, to *The Chieftain's Son* show panel better put diamond sparkles in Dash Everett's eyes.

When I moisten my lips, I can almost taste the tropical sweetness I shared with a different pair of lips last night. A very nice pair of lips. A pair of lips I need to put out of my mind. I may need Cian's advice again before the weekend is out. As lovely as kissing the man was, I've checked off indulging in any further California fantasies. All my attentions from here on must be on keeping my position with the show and dazzling Dash.

I cover the mic in front of me with a hand. "Maureen, any word of Bobby dropping in on us?" Even a minor panel like this one for our start-up podcast could benefit from the shine of a showrunner.

"No mention of it last I saw him." She pats her name card. "I hope not. I need a mini break from hashing out future season plot lines. The man never stops working." She flips me an accusing look. "Much like someone else I know."

Gilly leans in, staring at the mic as if it's going to take a bite out of her. "Sorry, Maureen, I almost forgot. I'm supposed to tell you Bobby wants the three of us to meet up for lunch after we're finished to video chat with Danna and the gang back home."

Maureen grumbles. "Meeting before eating."

I tap a nail on the table. "I'll head back with you. I need to speak with him before you go into your writer's cocoon."

Our commander-in-chief is still chewing on the idea I hit him with last night about giving our fans the big reveal Sir Kevin Langston will play Chieftain Brian Boru next season. Bobby's kept the Boru footage on lockdown. There are shadowy shots of Sir Kevin in the reel we're screening, but none of it gives away his identity. The old badger lives in L.A., so he's no more than a heartbeat from us. His people say if I meet his appearance fee, send a fancy car worthy of Sir Kev, and have a luxury suite for him to park his arse, he might be a go. Bobby's cloak of secrecy is my last hurdle on the Langston front.

A tall string bean of a fellow with floppy blond hair and a ring of keys hooked to his belt loop taps each mic and listens. Satisfied, he points a finger at us. "We're good to go as soon as your moderator shows."

I don't want to lose a valuable second singing our show's praises because of a tardy moderator. "I'll start us off, and she can jump in."

The handler from the convention who gave us the whats and whens eyes me. I point to myself and nod at the moderator podium. To remind me who's truly in charge, she flaps her time warning signs and then throws a thumbs up.

As I approach the mic to begin, a curly-headed blond woman clad in a Chieftain's Son T-shirt, an extra-large Celtic knot necklace, bouncy, matching earrings, and a kilt bounds up the three steps to the podium.

"Sorry, I couldn't find the place." She holds out her hand for each of us to shake in turn. "Hi, I'm Bella Baker, president of the San Diego chapter of *The Chieftain's Son* fan club."

I give her hand a perfunctory shake. "Meg McGrath, publicity. You've got the questions I sent?"

She extracts a tablet from a cloth bag with Jack's picture and the phrase, *I'm your Nieve* printed in eye-blinding, Kelly green. "Right here."

"Ms. Baker, I'm counting on you not to stray off topic with fan wonderings in regard to Jack and Niks. Our goal is to pick up steam and new listeners for the podcast."

Bella looks puzzled. "But the more we talk about the show and its stars, the better it is for your podcast."

Here we go. She could be trouble. I'll have to ask Cian how much control he wields over his moderators. True Time foisted Bella on us the same way they stuck me with Cici Storm, the main celebrity interviewer for the *Entertaining for You* program and magazine, to moderate our main show panel. It's been a battle to get Ms. Storm to agree to some decent questions. She's pushing for things like our people telling jokes or singing instead of digging deep into what the show's about. If I hear her say, "Fans will eat it up, Meg," one more time, I may take a bite out of her.

Miss Bella San Diego Fan Club opens by gushing love for *The Chieftain's Son* book series and now it's translated to an even bigger affair of the heart for the show. As we wait for her to finish her verbal Valentine and introduce us, I glance over at Gilly. The girl is as white as the tablecloth.

I lay a hand on her arm. "Gillian?"

She has trouble swallowing and then bows her head to whisper. With a nod to the audience, which includes a fair showing of people cosplaying as Donal Cam, Niks, and Rory O'Conner, season one's chieftain, she leans close. "This is why I'm a writer and not an actor."

"Think of this as a warmup. It's nothing compared to what the main show panel will be."

She squeezes the mic so hard, a scratchy sound leaks from the speakers. "Jack says the lights are so bright in The Grand Ballroom you can't see much of the audience. It helps with nerves. I see every face in here."

Her comment reminds me it's not Jack's first Cali Con. During his days on the sitcom, *Randy in 6B*, his first stint in television, he'd traveled here to the land of sky bridges and margaritas to face the *Randy* fandom.

I'm mustering words of comfort so Gilly doesn't freeze up on me when my stomach takes a massive lurch. Shining on her left hand, are the engagement and wedding rings I asked her to leave off during appearances.

Quickly, I cover her hand with mine and pull her back so we're far from the mics.

She stares at the rings as if they'll shoot flames. "I forgot to take them off."

The anguish on her face stabs right through my chest. I've put it there. The gravity of what I'm asking of her, to keep her marriage on lockdown, presses in on me. I insist Gilly sublimates and hides her happiness. Maureen teases me for my abrupt ways and plow-forward attitude. I never take it to heart, but maybe I should. Perhaps there's a thinly veiled message she's trying to get through. I'm too rigid. Look what I'm doing to Gilly. Diminishing a person's joy is nobody's right.

I cover her ring finger with my hand. "Leave 'em be. Paint this scenario if you're asked: your fella lives in Ireland." I raise my eyes, taking in the black industrial lamps hanging artfully from the ceiling while I think. "He's a local artist you met while doing research for the show." There it is: a lie that's not a lie.

Gilly squeezes my arm. "Thank you, Meg." The dull sheen of her eyes brightens like the rings on her finger.

My insides warm, remembering Cian's compliment about my ability to think on my feet. He's got it right. Ideas do fly fast when a problem heads straight for me.

Ah, Cian. I very much appreciate his suggestions from yesterday, but I am wicked competent at flying on my own. I've got Artie coming in, and my scavenger hunt is attracting fans like bees to the color yellow. I'm determined to coax Bobby into signing off on beloved icon Sir Kevin Langston joining the *Chieftain's Son* panel. He'll stun 'em with the announcement he's stepped out of retirement to be our Brian Boru. Feather after feather in my cap.

I tap a fingernail against the base of the mic. Cian Malley's got to quit popping into my head. I'd forgotten the thrill of gorgeous heat that burns inside when someone wants you. There will come a time when I welcome heat back into my life, but I've got a more urgent agenda this weekend. I'm glad to listen to what Cian has to say about shining up my show's Cali Con presence, but tangling with him beyond that isn't good business.

What would Cian think of me if he knew how precarious my position is with True Time? I picture his compliments and respect unraveling into pity. Am I worthy of his time and advice if I'm on the outs with the network? I give my head a shake as if that'll banish thoughts of Cian.

Maureen's head bobs at us. "Mics, ladies. We're on."

Bella Baker feeds me the right opening question. I'm off and running, describing the inception of the podcast.

When the baton is passed to Gilly, the shy, hesitant girl slips into the persona of a confident and competent artist. She paints a fantastic visual picture of our Post-it-Note-covered topic board and even goes a little fan girl when she talks about actors guesting on the podcast. Exactly the right notes.

"Gillian," says Bella. "You have quite the rags-to-riches story when it comes to the show."

Gilly feigns shock. "Don't let Lawson Graham Premier Sportswear hear you call their Irish Country Lad and Lass collections rags." She looks solemnly out to the audience and raises a hand. "Yes, guilty as charged. I started my writing career with.." Gilly switches to a dreamy tone. "Trekking across a misty landscape alive with myth and mystery, you'll be primed for magic tucked inside the flannel lining of our waterproof teal hiking jacket."

Huge laughs erupt from the audience.

Maureen shakes Gilly. "The woman is selling herself short. Her brilliant novel, *Traipse of Moonlight,* had the whole writing staff, and dare I say, some of the cast, under her spell before she set foot in Ireland."

I shoot Maureen a warning look. The woman likes to tease, but she treads dangerous ground here.

Gilly smiles warmly. "My *Chieftain's Son* journey is a beautiful dream. True fact, when Deidre's first book in the series came out, my mom forced me against my will to read *The Chieftain's Son.*"

It's a deft deflection from our California transplant, but she may have kicked a beehive with the "reading against her will," comment. This loyal *Chieftain's Son* crowd could brand the statement a sacrilege and butter their bread with her.

Bella feigns a dramatic gasp into her mic at Gilly's confession. The audience goes quiet, judging. I'm poised to say something to bail her out, win the fans back to her side, when Gilly continues.

"From the first moment I read Deidre LaRochelle's gorgeous prose, I fell into her world. It's a place I never want to leave." She leans toward the crowd as if she's letting them in on a secret. "I've read the entire series six times, and I'm on my third listen of the audiobooks."

To my relief, the audience goes mad for Gilly. I've underestimated the woman. I will tell her so as soon as we're finished here. I owe her that.

Gilly raises her hands to quiet the cheers. "How many of you out there are writers?"

A smattering of hands rises. "Keep at it. You never know when opportunity is going to jump out at you from behind a tree. A single season writer's assistant job opened a pathway for a new career and a new home for me. Our showrunner, Bobby Provost, took a chance hiring a girl with no television writing experience. I've dedicated my life to live up to his trust."

Her story jars me. Gilly's path is a mirror image of mine. Bobby saw something in both of us that's brought us to this moment in this place. When the surprise passes, the beginning of real affection takes root in me for Gillian Bettencourt O'Leary. Despite the whirlwind her marriage to Jack tossed me into, she's done wonderful things for the show.

Maureen sets the audience laughing over the start-up blunders of our podcast, echo chamber sound nightmares, unfortunate edits, and unintentional spoilers we had to slice out. She stretches her arm to the audience, palm out, as if giving a benediction. "We'll get better at it, we swear."

I ask for a show of hands as to who is already listening to the podcast. Half the room waves at me.

I lean on one elbow and give a conspiratorial wink to the audience. "And after today, who will be listening in?" To my delight, most of the audience jumps to their feet, applauding. When the wave dies down, I gild the lily. "All new and existing subscribers to our True Time app can look forward to even more *Chieftain's Son* bonus material come season two."

Cali Con workers slide down the rows, passing out my freshly minted postcards with Jack and Niks on one side and how to subscribe to True Time and give *The Chieftain's Son* credit on the other. As Bella directs folks to line up at a mic in the aisle to segue way into the Q & A portion, my eyes catch a wave from the end of the first row.

Cian.

Has he been here the whole time?

A flurry of emotions set my heart skittering. The first is an uncensored thrill because he came to see my panel. The second emotion, fraught with unwelcome possibility, follows fast on the heels of the first. Why did he come? Is he checking up on the small-town girl for the big boss? Do his cell phone notes hold a list of all the ways I could have improved our podcast panel? I appreciate his tips and the way he's stretched my peripheral vision, but I'm not keen on unsolicited critique or criticism. I dole out enough of that to myself.

The impossibly long line of people waiting to ask questions pulls my focus. We'll be kicked out before everyone get answers. Inspiration hits. I'll convince Maureen and Gilly to linger outside the auditorium in the lovely patio to answer any remaining fan questions. I'll post pictures. Making sure we've got no disappointed fans will forge an even stronger loyalty to the show. With luck, I'll guide new subscribers to sign up for True Time on their phones as they wait to chat us up.

Before I claim the chance to self-congratulate on my latest instant brainstorm, an imposing figure catches my eye. A silhouette I know well claps one of the doorkeepers on the shoulder and slides into the back of the auditorium.

Holy mutton on a Friday, it's Jack O'Leary.

He wears sunglasses and a baseball cap to hide long golden hair, but jeans and the tight-fitting hoodie advertise an all-too-familiar warrior physique. If a single fan spots him, our closing will be upended in the frenzy.

Jack slinks to the farthest aisle away from the main doors to lean against the wall near one of the niches. I pray his position is shadowy enough to keep him hidden. Next to me, Gilly's phone pings with a message. Her head shoots up after she reads it to search the room. Jack waves, and Gilly's face turns into a blushing rose.

What are the two of them playing at?

Bella points to our timekeeper, who is waving a *last question* sign at the stage. "We've got time for one more question."

A twenty-something woman in a *Chieftain's Son* T-shirt from our booth steps up to the mic. "Can you give us any more scavenger hunt hints about the next Jack and Niks meet up?"

Bella turns to me. "My favorite question so far. What do you say?"

Before I respond and announce our after-panel Q & A on the patio, an ear-splitting squeal rises from the audience.

"Oh my God, it's Jack O'Leary."

Every head in the place whips to where the fan points. Jack gives a friendly wave, which might as well have been the signal for troops to charge.

I'm off the stage in a flash, sprinting to Jack. Cian is there before me. He grabs my hand, and I grab Jack's. With barely a meter to spare before the fandom tsunami swallows us, Cian pushes through a door in the corner of the room I didn't notice.

When we're through, he rolls a rack lined with folding chairs to block the door. "Security should keep anyone from coming through, but we need to make tracks out of here."

"This shitestorm is on me," says Jack, threading an arm through mine. "I'm sorry, Meg."

My first thought is to land a punch in the middle of that broad chest, but I'd only succeed in bruising my fist. Anger is quickly supplanted with the hope someone took pictures to post on social media for Dashell Everett to see. Here's your popularity splash, Mr. E.

Cian leads us out a service entrance at the back of the auditorium to a drive feeding onto a side street. Jack pulls his hat low over his face and glues his gaze at the ground. We wind up and over a couple of blocks. Away from the events center, people go about their daily business. We navigate homeless folks rolled up in blankets sleeping against the front of vacant storefronts despite the heat of the day. Jack reaches over and drops a twenty-dollar bill between a slumbering pair crunched together in a doorway.

"There's a convenience store around the next corner. I'll grab us waters, and we can regroup," says Cian.

"I've got to call Gilly," says Jack, lifting his cell to his ear. "She'll be nuts wondering what happened." His eyes fill with panic. He darts a wary look Cian's way, dropping the hand with the phone to his side. "Bollucks."

I wave, metaphorically erasing the waves of stress pouring off Jack. "It's fine. He knows your situation."

Jack's Adam's apple bobbles as he forces a swallow. "Knows…"

Cian sticks out a hand for Jack to shake. "Congratulations on your wedding, which I vow never to mention until it's old news."

Jack narrows his gaze to size up Cian. "Will you sign one of Meg's fancy NDAs to swear to it? I'm keen on keeping my personal life under wraps."

"Absolutely. I'm a True Time man first and the soul of discretion. You have my word. Nothing to hurt you, Gillian, Meg, or the show will leave these lips."

Jack looks at me for a character reference. I smile and nod, sneaking a peek at Cian's fine lips.

"All right then," says Jack, clasping Cian's waiting hand. He ends the shake quickly and turns away to call Gilly.

I catch Cian's arm before he heads into the store. "Thank you for the assist. If I'da known the fool was going to show up, there'd be triple the security." I shake my head. "No. There'd be no need for security because I'd tie him to a chair in his hotel room."

Cian laughs and jerks his chin at Jack. "They're never as invisible as they think they are."

I blurt without a hint of forethought. "You'd be very welcome to come to dinner with the lot of us in Old Town tonight." My resolve of avoiding the distraction of Cian swirls down the drain. A man riding in on a white horse'll do that to you.

Cian crooks a pinkie finger around mine and swings our joined hands. The familiarity we shared last night returns with a jolt.

"I'd love to hang out with *The Chieftain's Son* bunch to see the next leg of your scavenger hunt firsthand." He leans in. "And maybe after dinner, the lovely head of publicity would continue my private education into the drinking of whiskey."

He's ducked into the store before I draw a mental red slash over any after-dinner connecting. It'll be easy enough to beg out later, even though declining Cian's offer makes me seem ungrateful. He awarded us a blue-ribbon favor, whisking Jack out of a potentially crushing fan encounter.

Yes, dinner with my team will be a grand and appropriate way to say thanks, very businesslike. First and foremost, we are business colleagues despite the generous portion of my personal thoughts devoted to the man. Cian's surely still got a worthwhile nugget or two to toss my way about the Cali Con game. Pinky swinging, kissing, and whiskey tasting belong behind a door I should be careful about opening too far.

I watch him press through the glass doors of the mini market. He's a very nice picture to look at. No harm in appreciating the visual.

Jack takes a few tentative steps in my direction. His sheepish expression is schoolboy caught cheating on exams. "Okay, get to it, Meg. Remind me of the rules, and I'll absorb every last one." He crosses his heart. "I swear I'm finished making your life a misery."

God, he's so serious, I can't help laughing. "I doubt that."

The usual irritation with my Gilly and Jack dilemma doesn't scratch at me. He didn't show up to give me grief. Jack came to support his wife. A woman who's rapidly gaining admiration from me after the way she handled the panel. If I wasn't so damn rigid and paranoid about the two of them, he might have come to me first instead of sneaking in. I've got to be easier on the two of them.

I pat Jack's arm. Lord, the man is made of granite. "Just one rule here," I say, fanning my face to cool down. "And don't you dare fight me on it, you stubborn ox."

He crosses his heart again. "I'll be your obedient beast of burden."

"No legging it back to the hotel, Captain Fitness. We're taking a cab."

CHAPTER 8
CASA DE FIESTA

A large and very fragrant gentleman covered in tunic, leather, and fur scoots his way up the aisle of the train, or trolley, as Cian calls it. To me, trolley brings quaint and horse-drawn to mind, not a group cuddle clanking along metal tracks. We attempt to keep our feet as we stand wedged in the crowd. I slide closer to Cian—professionally closer, not I-kissed-you-on-the-beach-last-night closer.

As challenging as it is to breathe, excitement bubbles in my stomach. The brute in costume is dressed as Donal Cam. This fellow was not one of the Donal Cams at the library earlier. No chance I would have missed someone of his bulk. Even though the wannabe Irish warrior invades my personal trolley space, I'm willing to forgive his squish and stink for the homage he pays to the show. He's added confirmation *The Chieftain's Son* has arrived in force on the Cali Con cosplay scene. For sport, I'll walk the convention floor tomorrow and play *count the Donal Cams and Nieves*. I might even spot a Bowstring or Rory O'Connor in the throng.

I study the trolley stop map above the windows. "You're positive of the place to hop off?"

Cian taps a dot on the trolley brochure in his hand. "Have you forgotten your own clue? Right there, Old Town."

A jerk of the train shifts jumbo-sized Donal Cam into full-body contact with me. I don't want to get a stain on my silk blouse from someone else's sweat, so I press against Cian. He takes it as a signal I don't intend and drapes an arm around my waist to pull me closer. The tang of his spicy chai tea scent is a pleasant diversion to the fragrant clansman canting in my direction.

At the next stop, enough folks slip off the trolley to free up a pair of seats. Cian and I slide in before anyone beats us to it.

"Three rows back. Listen up," says Cian in a low voice. We both lean to eavesdrop on a robust discussion.

"It's going to be Anthony Myhers."

"Anthony Myhers as Brian Boru, a crime against nature!"

Goodness, Lord. They're talking about *The Chieftain's Son* season two.

"We're definitely going to hit the Battle of Clontarf site when we get to Ireland."

"After we check out the Ring of Kerry. I want to sniff out The Clan, where they do the show. I know they'll be filming. We might score seeing Jack or Niks somewhere."

They mention our leads as casually as dinner guests. My protective side inches up but quickly falls. These folks are heading to Ireland because of *The Chieftain's Son*. My days with the travel agency, *Toolin' Around the Isle,* combine with my current job and create a mental spark. A series of *Chieftain's Son* themed tours could be brilliant. Since Deidre's books are based in facts and history, I can bundle actual historic locations and shooting sites. True Time will love the tie-in.

I'm coming for you, Dash.

New voices join the fan pair behind us. "Are you guys following the scavenger hunt?"

"What scavenger hunt?"

My excitement wanes. Maybe my scheme isn't as popular as I reckoned.

The newest member of the fan clique remedies the problem. "Go to hashtag 'find Jack and Niks.'"

My eyes meet Cian's, and we both dive into Twitter. #FindJackandNiks is on fire with speculation on tonight's locale.

I nudge Cian. "You go to hashtag 'Chieftain Son scavenger hunt.' Let's get a sense of how many figured out the riddle."

We simultaneously swipe at our cells.

"Okay," says Cian, scrolling and reading. "The Mariachi three clue is throwing people off." He catches the concern in my eyes. "Good call. Too easy and you'll have more than True Time security can handle."

"There's a debate going on in this thread about what the old or new means. A lot of guesses are Old Town, but there's no consensus."

"Pretty cool, huh?" says Cian, bobbing his head in the direction of the conversation.

"It's got my wheels turning faster."

He widens his eyes in question. "More thinking on your feet?"

I'm protective of the brainstorm brewing in my head. Cian's a help, to be sure, but as Jack pointed out earlier, *Star's Shadow* is also competition. If any of my ideas misfire and help his show, it may get credit for more subscriptions to the True Time streaming app than *The Chieftain's Son*, a death sentence for me.

When I don't answer, Cian turns to stare out the window as building after building pass in a blur. Keeping his eyes out of the equation, he asks softly, "Why is it so hard for you to open up to me?"

If he knew me, he'd realize I've already cracked my comfort zone wide.

Long, slender fingers close on my upper arm. The usual confidence weaving through his voice thins. "What's it going to take for you to see me as a friend on the same team?"

It's a fair question. He's asking why someone in my position wouldn't want to soak in the experience he's willing to give so freely. I'd like to tell him. Explain that the times I've given the *we* model a go, it's blown up in my face. Dominic the fucker, back in secondary school, was the first debacle, followed by group projects at Trinity College where I knew the level of input required to get top marks, but my team preferred bare minimum. When I started adulting and gave Skylar the head-in-the-clouds artist a go, I ended up in the same place. My efforts and investment were sucked out of me until I was left a pathetic afterthought.

Cian clearly wants me to trust him, but that's a commodity I hold close, especially after only two days.

"We're colleagues, Meg."

"Colleagues with competing shows."

I still feel the sting of Dash taking credit for my accomplishments. The bastard gave no effort past an obligatory stamp of approval after I scored the high-profile building wrap and the *Entertaining for You* special Cali Con edition cover.

Cian's graciously let me cipher a few drops off the top of his knowledge pool. If he were going to steal my scavenger hunt idea, it would've already happened. No denying he bailed me out at the podcast panel and hasn't mentioned a peep about it. Isn't it better having Cian take me under his wing instead of one of those jowly, pompous fellows I never even met properly at Tuesday's prep meeting?

Perhaps I should step out of my own way—if I'm honest, something I try to make a habit of. I'm resisting Cian because Dash as much as threw me at him. It's Dash who chafes my confidence, not Cian.

I startle when I see Cian's been watching me think through our scenario.

"Does my question require this much introspection?"

I have an urge to ease away from Cian, to create both physical and interpersonal distance. Since I've breached both boundaries by kissing him and opening the door on my professional life, he's earned an answer to his question. "I do best at trusting myself alone. Relying on others in the past has not gone well for me."

He nods slowly. "Being screwed leaves a mark."

I'm suddenly very interested in marks left behind on Mr. Cian Malley, but I've got no right to dig. "I'm the sort that needs to control a situation."

I expect him to laugh or tease at my admission, but he doesn't. It's his face wearing the mask of introspection now. "It's a need we share, Meg."

"Nothing wrong with it."

He takes a long, slow breath. "Except the isolation tied up with it."

Isolation is the perfect word. That aloneness from wearing all responsibility and consequences is a yoke across my shoulders. Up until now, I've viewed Cian as steering a ship full of crewmates, not the singular type. Not like me. Could it be we're more alike than I've allowed myself to believe?

"Is this where I tell you self-imposed isolation is as much blessing as curse?"

Cian leans his head to the side. "Is it?"

"I trust me to get things done the way I plan them. Less room for cock ups."

"A narrow perspective, M-Squared. What about things you might miss when acting alone?" Cian covers my hand with his. "Ones you don't see coming?" His eyes rest on my lips.

Damn the man, and those eyes, lips, and the kindness he's so eager to throw my way. Is he the *divil* tempting me or a saint riding a sunbeam to shake up the isolation I thought I'd made my peace with?

His fingers find their way between mine and he squeezes. "Let me rephrase my question. 'What can I do to make it easier for you to let me in?' I'm not asking you to change or compromise who you are. Put the impetus on me to forge a way between us."

I may consider throwing a bit more trust Cian's way. If I let him in a little at a time, I'll get a sense of him in small doses. If one step works, I'll take another. My eyes drift to our joined hands, and I nearly laugh. Isn't that what I've already been doing? So far, he's given me no cause to stop opening my door a crack wider. "For starters, let's go over my celebrity escape plan for the Old Town scavenger hunt appearance. You've been to Casa de Fiesta, so you'll know if I've hit the mark."

The right side of his mouth quirks up. "Are you actually asking for my help?"

I shoot him a quick scowl but then plunk my map of Old Town San Diego State Historic Park onto his lap. "I've secured a table here at the restaurant." I tap a spot on the map that lands right on Cian's zipper. A low grunt of surprise and his quiver leave no doubt I've hit a very sensitive target.

To cover embarrassment, I forge on. My voice is higher pitched and faster, which only increases the fire on my cheeks. "We'll be in the far corner away from foot traffic access, but not penned in."

I find a picture of the plaza seating area on my phone to give us both a moment of recovery time. "Here," I say, tipping the screen in his direction. "If I need to get them out in a hurry, we duck between these two potted cacti and through this little shop. Can Chip stand by at the curb just there?"

I position the map at belly height to avoid repeated zipper contact. To my horror, jitters and the pressure of my finger sliding across the designated escape route make me lose my grip. The map and my hand fall right back onto Cian's lap to engage his crotch for a second go.

His face turns as pink as a Christmas ham as his real estate under the map rises in response to my inadvertent poke and clutch. I'm too flustered to apologize or lift my hand as quickly as I should. The sensation of bringing Cian to attention coupled with kiss flashbacks set off my own sensations. Very pleasant ones. Ones that don't belong on a public trolley.

So much for opening my door a crack wider to Cian. I blew it off the hinges.

He lifts my hand from the map and folds up the paper. In a strained voice, he says, "Looks great." A drizzle of sweat parades in front of his ear. "Give me a sec, and I'll call Chip."

By the time we roll up to the Old Town station, the summons to Chip is issued, and Cian regains the ability to spring to his feet and forge a path for us to the door.

As the train/trolley rolls away, Cian leads us across the street toward a large, whitewashed adobe structure with a red tiled roof.

Surely a double crotch pass deserves acknowledgement on my part. "Sorry about the personal poke with the map," I say. "See what happens when you encourage me to open up?"

"I didn't expect your first move would be to get me hot in public transportation."

I sputter, searching for words of denial, but then shrug and play it off. "Your poor little man. All dressed up and nowhere to go."

Cian lets go a snort followed with a belly laugh that breaks the tension from my trolley grope. I join him in a giggle.

His gaze flicks to my lips. "I've stopped guessing what might come out of that gorgeous mouth of yours, Meghan McGrath." Cian takes my hand, and we head down the walkway.

It's another lovely early California evening. I languish in the slow burn of fading light. I let him keep hold of my hand as we stroll alongside Victorian style buildings before turning into an open-air plaza strewn with colored lights and surrounded by multiple species of cacti.

"Don't touch those," says Cian, pointing to one of the succulents with leaves like a million skinny fingers, towering at least a foot over my head. "It's a pencil cactus. My dad calls them 'sticks on fire.' Their oil can literally blind you if it gets in your eyes."

I pull my hand clear of the plant. "Then why in the name of sense do they have so many around here where kids run wild?"

Cian doesn't answer and drops my hand. Looking up, I see he's spotted our group clustered around a bench in front of one of the shops.

"Her folks showed after all," I say aloud, catching sight of a middle-aged couple, the Bettencourts, in close conversation with Gilly, Jack, and Bobby. I met them briefly at Jack and Gilly's private backyard wedding in Sneem. Maureen and Grady sit on a bench nearby, trying to get a wooden ball toy tethered to a stick to land in a cup. Niks is nowhere to be seen. I'm not surprised. The woman loves to make an entrance.

Bobby is first to see me. His eyes shoot to Cian with laser focus, but then he relaxes and waves us over, recognizing my guest from the bar.

"Nice to see you again, Cian," says Bobby as we approach.

Cian shakes Bobby's hand. "Hope you don't mind me crashing the party."

"We're all on True Time's dime," says Bobby.

"Except me," says Grady.

"You can eat off my plate," says Maureen, pulling him in for a quick kiss. "They'll never know."

"Talk business early and often," says the man who must be Gilly's dad. "Voila, you're expensed."

When Gilly gestures at Cian and me, Jack, clad in baseball cap and sunglasses, takes an obvious step away from her, clearly for my benefit. Luckily, no one at Casa de Fiesta seems to take particular notice of him. "Meg, you remember my parents, Amethyst and Rich Bettencourt."

Lord have mercy. Every word of dinner conversation will require my censorship to prevent spillage of details on the O'Leary marriage.

"Mom, Dad, this is our killer head of publicity, Meg McGrath."

Mr. Bettencourt offers me a warm handshake, and to my surprise and discomfort, the Mrs. attacks me with a hug. I can't imagine what stories Gilly's shared about the grief I've given their daughter concerning her relationship with my leading man.

Amethyst whispers in my ear as she nods at Jack. "Do Rich and I sign NDAs concealing the identity of our son-in-law?" Her laughter is as affable as her husband's handshake.

My smile is tight. "Not at the moment." Translation: By God, one will be expressed to your hotel room before midnight.

Rich flips up his Cali Con badge. "Haven't been to The Con in a few years. Lucky we still rate pro badges. I'd hate to miss Gilly's Grand Ballroom debut."

To my surprise, Cian claps Richard Bettencourt on the shoulder. "Nice to have you back at the party, Rich." They embrace and thump backs in the way men hug without hugging.

Cian catches the look on my face before I shift into neutral. "Rich and I worked on a project together a handful of years back."

"That horrible riff on the real life of comedians," Mr. Bettencourt's forehead creases. "What was is called?"

"*Laugh It Off,*" says Cian. "God awful." They share a chuckle at the memory.

Luckily, the table I booked in a strategic zone easily accommodates the addition of two extra Bettencourts and Cian. I arrange the group, making sure Gilly and Jack are separated by Bobby and leave an empty seat for Niks.

I check my phone. No message from our leading lady. "Anyone heard from Niks?"

Jack shakes his head. "She and Marisa are finishing a shopping fling."

Panic rises on his face when he realizes he blabbed a secret in front of Cian.

I scan the table. "Marisa's coming here?" Grand. Now I've got two hush-hush relationships to juggle during dinner.

I grab my phone and text Niks to ask if Marisa, her significant other, is on our guest list. My heart drops from my throat back into place when she answers right away and confirms Marisa's off meeting friends for dinner.

Niks texts again, asking for a car to drive her to Casa de Fiesta. I lean close to Cian. "Has Chip started our way yet, or can he snatch Niks from the hotel lobby and bring her along?"

"I'll make it happen," he says and gets busy on his cell. I've got an inkling whatever Cian wants to happen does. The man does not take a shine to no. It's a trait we share.

"Amethyst and Rich graciously agreed to sit in with me at the production designer interviews tomorrow," says Bobby. "I welcome an impromptu committee."

Jack fills in the blanks for me. "Gilly's folks are TV art directors."

I should know that snippet of background on my Crystal-nominated writer. Another piece of information Cian knew, and I didn't.

"Thanks again for the rescue this afternoon, Cian," says Jack.

Cian waves him off. "Glad to help."

Suspicion I'd tamped down as paranoia bolts to the surface. Cian Malley has been a model of helpful. He's constantly appeared on my flightpath since I arrived in San Diego. Is it a coincidence or something more intentional? Why was he at my panel? I didn't invite him. No denying it was a turn of good luck he did attend, but I'd have managed to secret Jack away on my own. Lord knows I've had plenty of practice at it back home. Tension bursts up my spine to my neck. What's the right question: Why was Cian there or did Dash send him?

I scan the table. Maureen and Grady are in their own world, feeding each other chips and salsa. The Bettencourts, O'Learys, and Bobby chat about renting convertibles for a go up the California coast, giving me a moment with Cian. I lean on an elbow and nearly swallow my question when I meet his shining blue eyes. "Why did you show up today?"

The non-sequitur catches him off guard. I can't figure if his reaction is perplexed or uneasy. "To support you." A muscle in his jaw twitches. "And maybe I wanted to take a shot at clocking more time together."

I want to accept the flattery at face value, I really do. A hitch in my gut fires up a warning as my mouth beats my brain to the punch. "Is clocking time Dash Everett's idea?"

The question hovers in the air like a bad stink. Why in the name of Jaysus H. did I pop off with it? My insecurity is quite the ugly beastie.

I haven't mastered reading Cian. He's either holding in annoyance at the accusation, or I've caught him in a truth. Before he confirms which it is, our server comes to take drink orders.

"Two melon margaritas here," I say flipping a hand between Cian and me, praying the call back to last night works as peace offering if I did offend him. Eyes that read more glacier than gemstone make it clear the offering is rejected. I try to play it off. "Tequila is growing on me."

As soon as everyone orders, Cian circles my wrist with his fingers and jerks his chin toward the little store across the walkway I mapped as our potential escape route. "A word with you, Ms. McGrath."

Maureen catches our interplay and throws me a wink. I wish we were headed for a winkable moment, but the heat of Cian's touch on my pulse is a scorch, not a slow burn.

I glance around the restaurant to check for scavenger hunters. I won't leave Jack alone to be bombarded. It's much earlier than the clue suggested, and all seems fine. We stand, bringing side conversations to a halt. I smile. "We're going to meet Niks and walk her in."

I'm careful not to touch the pencil cacti as I squeeze between two giant clay pots of the stuff. Cian pulls me in front of a candy shop window out of earshot from the others. He gets right in my face. "You don't know me very well yet, so let me clue you in. I'm pissed off."

I lay a hand on his chest to create distance between us, but he presses against it to stay close.

"What's with your crack about Dash?"

I'd be lying if I said his aggression didn't catch me off guard. Mr. Easy Going does have a trigger. I stand my ground. This time, he backs away. My hand falls to my side.

"What are you accusing me of, Meg?"

Before I can backtrack and dilute the impact of bringing Dash's name into the mix, Cian runs a hand across his stubble and glares at me.

"I don't know if your hot and cold routine is an Irish thing or a Meg thing, but it's annoying as hell."

I may have misspoken, but he's an ass going on the attack before I've had a second to clarify. If he's capable of going from zero-to-tosser in under ten seconds, maybe I won't explain and be done with him. "It's a t'ing that's not yer business." So much for keeping my natural accent under wraps.

Cian turns as if he's going to walk away but swivels to face me like lightning to a wet tree. "You're an ice cube to me when we meet and then it's flirty whiskey tasting and kissing on the beach." He drops his head back and slowly rights it. "I thought we'd connected even more today with the panel escape. Then, *blam!*" He smacks a hand to his thigh. "I'm a spy for Dash."

It's not a flattering picture when he lays it out. The apology I'd been considering sours on my lips. I cross my arms and take a breath to tame the Irish trying to push its way out. "But maybe it's a fair one considering Dash was keen to foist you on me since day one." Not to mention the fact Dash has a mind to demote me despite everything I've done for *The Chieftain's Son*. Instead of chiding myself, I decide I have every right to be suspicious of any and all things Dash Everett's hand touches, even Cian.

"I'm not Dashell Everett's lap dog." Cian waves me off. "Sue me for trying to be a decent colleague, and..."

His expression tenses as he battles whether to finish his thought. His sparking gaze locks onto me. "Being attracted, drawn to you." As soon as the confession is out, he heads to the gap between buildings leading to the car park where, hopefully, Chip will soon deposit Niks.

His retreat snaps something in me. *Damn you, Meg.* I'm tilting at windmills because of the position Dash Everett put me in. Dash, not Cian. I don't want Cian running off. It's in no way his problem I'm in a pissing match with Dash over my future. I'm blaming a thoroughly decent man for the shite I've landed in when he's brought nothing but goodwill and sunshine into the scenario.

The situation is a song I've played before. A man gives me an opening for us to go on after a rough patch. My default is to wipe the mess clean by watching him set off without me. It's the safe play, the move to give me the upper hand. I try for a deep breath and come up short. A sharp note clangs over and over in my head as distance grows between Cian and me. For the first time, choosing safe and control over the man walking away gives me no sense of rightness or relief. I can let him go or...

"Cian, wait." I'm after him quick enough to reach a hand to his shoulder. I slide around so I can face him. He tightens his lips into a line, training his eyes past me. There's plain hurt on his face. Here's a sensitive man I took a cheap swing at because of my own fears. Guilt nips my ear with pointed teeth.

"There's a bit of bad blood between Dash and me. It wasn't fair to throw you in the mix."

My initial impression of Cian lumped him, Dash, and the other True Time folks under the same category of slick Hollywood type. I've done him a disservice. There are no visible strings or conditions on the hand he's held out to me. Cian knows his business and, judging from his half of the True Time booth, overflows with uncontested talent. I'm the arrogant ass to play push and pull with him. If someday I want to swim with the big fish in the Hollywood publicity game after *The Chieftain's Son*, Cian is a welcome boon to my education.

And he's a brilliant kisser.

I lay a gentler hand on his arm. "You've been grand with the help. We've gone arseways because of me."

The beginning of a smile plays across his lips. "Arseways?"

Heat rises on my cheeks. "I made a mess of this."

He looks at the finger I'm swinging between his chest and mine. "Is there a this?"

Cian's giving me the opening to shake hands and keep it business between us.

"I'll simplify the question, Meg. Do you want me around or not? And if I haven't made it clear, I'd like to be around."

I'm as low as a toadstool. I've enjoyed his company and kissed the man, but only parceled out trust to him in dribs and drabs.

His patience hourglass with me spilled its sand. It's on me to tip it right again. I meet the gaze of frosty blue eyes. I don't want him to leave. It's brilliant to have a sharp mind to bounce ideas and plans off of. Walking away would be easy, but what do I gain by depriving myself his comradery, know how, and nice set of lips? It's one weekend for feck's sake. No point in putting it in a bigger picture frame. He's shown no sign he's out to compromise my power or control. I lose none of that if I clock the time he's asking for.

"I do want you around, Cian." I set both hands on his shoulders. At first, not an ounce of his tension eases at my touch. "You've been grand to me, and I appreciate every bit of it." I take a step closer, so our bodies nearly touch. Proximity does the trick, and he relaxes slightly. "Every bit of it." I rise on tip toe to plant a kiss on his delicious Hollywood mouth.

His hands drop to my hips, and he gives a little tug, bringing my body against his. Our kiss deepens and makes my head start to swim without the aid of tequila. It's done then, my decision to stick with him through Sunday.

Cian's phone buzzes against my hip. He slowly breaks the kiss, leaving my lips with the urge to go after his.

He holds the phone screen so I can see it. "Chip. Niks is here." His eyes dart toward the parking lot.

I take his chin in my hand and pull his attention to me. "I believe I owe you some quality whiskey time after dinner. I promise to pay up."

"Aye, you do, lassie." He covers my mouth with his. I've never experienced a kiss so brief with the power to knock me off my feet the way Cian's does.

"We don't use lads and lasses as rule. You've been watching too much *Chieftain's Son*."

He grabs my hands and guides me to Chip's waiting car. "What do you say?"

"Let's do this." I imitate his California accent. "And by the way, the hot and cold…" I drop my gaze to the pinkish-purple bougainvillea petals piling up on the walkway. "It's a Meg thing. Don't blame the Irish."

He dots a kiss on my temple. I wait for the panic of a wrong decision to grip my belly. Instead, a pleasant wave of what might be next settles over me. I commit to enjoy the rest of my time at Cali Con with Cian as I obliterate Dash's challenges and keep my job.

We have Niks out of the car and to the table before the second round of drinks are served. I settle her between Jack and Cian. The three gorgeous people in a row are a page from a fashion magazine.

Always playing her part well in the fauxmance with Jack, Niks drapes herself across him. "Here's my sweet." She dabs a kiss to the corner of his lips. Three Bettencourts stiffen in unison.

"Hello, hello," says Niks, addressing the rest of the group in her chirpy Norwegian-accented singsong. "I don't know you or you or you," she says, pointing to Rich, Amethyst, and Cian in turn. She zeroes in on Cian.

I jump in. "Niks Tellefson, meet Cian Malley, head of P.R. for *Star's Shadow*."

"You're okay then," she says and leans over to leave a lingering kiss on his cheek.

I'm more bothered than I have any right to be by Niks's attention to Cian. I remind myself Marisa is the light that sets Niks aglow.

Niks jolts away from Cian like she's been scalded and lightly taps her lips. "Another scratchy face." She molds her body to Jack's side and runs a finger above his upper lip, across his cheek, and down his jaw. "Like this one. Always the stubble." She twists her body to square off with Bobby. "My next show, the men I kiss will be smooooooooth." Niks lets her fingers glide down her own soft cheeks. "Ahhhh."

Gilly smiles at Niks, and they both burst into laughter. Even though they are friends, it's still got to irritate whenever Niks gets too physical around Jack. "Niks, I want you to meet my parents, Rich and Amethyst."

Niks executes the rapid-fire mini claps to signal her delight. "So good to meet you. I love this girl," she says and grabs Gilly's hand across the table.

"Now that we're all together," says Bobby, raising his margarita glass. "To *The Chieftain's Son's* debut at Cali Con."

We clink glasses, baptizing the chips with drips of alcohol.

"And here's to Meg," says Bobby, making me choke mid-sip. "For convincing me to spill the beans at our show panel that Sir Kevin Langston will be our Chieftain, Brian Boru, next season."

"Brian Boru for season two," giggles Niks.

Under the table, Cian squeezes my leg above the knee. The rest of the table applauds. I could sprout wings and fly. I've got my big reveal. Sir Kevin's ass will be in a fancy car headed our way before he zips his fly after his next piss.

Maureen raises her glass. "To Jack, Niks, Bobby, and Gilly for being so damned Crystal Award worthy we all get two trips to California."

Grady breaks into a huge grin. "All, is it? Will you be bringing me along for the award's party as well, Meg?"

I raise my glass to him. "Not a chance." Grady and I clink so hard my glass nearly slips from my hand.

With the group in high spirits, I dare to slap another plan of mine on the table. "Who wants to hear about a little something to sizzle our Con even more?"

Maureen raises her hand like a schoolgirl. "Me. Me. Yes, me."

Niks imitates her. "Me. Me, too."

I crook my foot around Cian's ankle. "Let me paint you the scenario."

"Saint anybody, deliver me from Meg's scenarios," says Bobby, dropping his head onto his hands.

I tap the table in front of Bobby. "No, no. Eyes up. It's pretty wild, but I've seen it done with tidy results." I grab the edge of the table and straighten my arms before leaning in over the table. I wave everyone else to copy me so every head hovers close. I'm eager to let Cian see more of the thinking on my feet he appears to admire. "I plan for it to benefit your charity cause back home, Jack."

The news perks him up. "Go on, you sly one."

I draw an arc with my hands, painting a rainbow. "Win a date with

Jack O'Leary. With the blessing, of course"—I wave a hand toward Niks —"from his lovely lady."

There's loaded silence while everyone looks at Jack.

"Ladies," I amend with a nod at Gilly.

Words rocket out of my mouth before Jack can turn me down. "We can tease it here at the Con. I'll work with the online outfit that sets these things up. You've heard of the organization *Step Up* right? They do tons of celebrity giveaways for charity."

Cian, Heaven bless him, moves in for backup. "We did a similar thing with Sala Singh for our season three premier. Fans love it, and Sala said she had a blast."

"We offer swag incentives for different levels of donation." I shift my focus to Gilly. "I promise you, every minute of the activity is mapped out. Jack will never be alone or put on the spot with the winner. I'm picturing the so-called date as an exclusive tour of The Clan production facility and dinner at the hotel in Waterville. We play up the Waterville/Charlie Chaplin connection. What do we think?"

Cian presses his leg against mine. It's a welcome encouragement.

Jack rubs a hand over his chin, eyes glued on me without blinking. "I've a scenario of my own. We'll barter."

I send up a quick prayer his side of the barter is reasonable or, at worst, doable. "Go on."

Jack rests his arm on the back of Niks's chair, relaxing into his own seat like he's lounging on the beach. "If Gilly and I agree to your mad plan, you'll get me a *Star's Shadow* star trooper costume to wear this weekend." He laughs at what must be a portrait of incredulity on my face. "I want to walk the convention floor, experience The Con without anyone the wiser it's me."

I frown at him. "You're not kidding?"

"I can arrange a suit for you," says Cian.

Mischievous twinkles brighten Jack's eyes. "Say we throw in the Starry Night's metallic bikini get-up for Gilly." He jerks after a well-aimed kick from his wife under the table. "Ouch. Hit the shin, love."

Maureen nearly spits out her drink. "Someone's in a heap of trouble."

I swallow down my own gulp hard at the thought of Jack loose on the convention floor.

"Plan B," says Jack. "How about Starry Night's OG white lacy warrior dress?"

Gilly's look could wither a rose in full bloom. "If we do this, I'll go as Event Horizon in full armor and kick your sexist ass, trooper Jack O'Leary."

Cian bows to her. "Well played, Gillian. I'd be honored to pony up your armor as well."

Niks swats Jack's ample bicep. "Such a troublemaker."

Jack smiles warmly at me. "It can't be called a date if we go for 'adventure.' I'll think on it, Meg."

I experience a warning flash of Jack coaxing an unsuspecting fan into skydiving.

"Now," Jack raises his margarita, licking off grains of salt from his hand. "My turn to toast." His eyes lock on Gilly. "To beautiful second season words from a beautiful woman."

Mrs. Jack O'Leary blushes to the melody of clinking glasses. Jack, the fox, deftly tables discussion of my promo date idea.

Gilly raises her glass. "To Brian Boru, the man I never knew existed before I had to write his moments of glory."

Jack slams both hands on the table and raises his voice. "Blasphemy from the yank. I'll be taking Deidre LaRochelle to wife instead of you." He takes both Gilly's hands in his, and for a hot second, I think he's going to lean across the table and kiss her.

I forget to breathe in the wake of Jack's commotion. My eyes dart around the plaza and down the row of shops, frantic to see if anyone heard them. Next to me, Cian does the same.

Jack drops Gilly's hands, horrified to draw attention to our group.

Cian sits up with a jolt. He hisses quietly to Jack. "Kiss Niks."

Jack looks confused and argues with a sharp shake of his head. I see what Cian spotted. Past the hostess stand on the far side of the patio behind a substantial palm is the long black lens of a paparazzi.

I find Jack's foot under the table and press down on it. "Do it, Jack. Now. Eyes on us."

Jack flashes an apologetic glance at Gilly and then buries his nose in Niks's hair, whispering. She turns to face him. I could be watching a scene from the show. Resting fingertips under her chin, Jack tilts Niks's face up to his and gives her a slow, tender kiss.

Our food arrives as if on cue to end the PDA. Jack and Niks settle into their seats. My appetite's gone. I'm on high alert.

While the others dig in, a trio of Mariachis take the stage in the center of the patio. It's too early. The manager of the restaurant said this act wouldn't take the stage until half-eight. It's barely seven. We're slated to have time for digesting before Jack and Niks fulfill their Thursday night scavenger hunt appearance.

Time to get Gilly and her parents far and away.

I speak in a low voice to Cian. "Would you mind taking a walk around? Scout for fans. Give me a feel for what we might be up against."

He wipes his mouth with the big red cloth napkin. "Back in a flash." Excusing himself, Cian strolls in the direction of the stop where fans who've busted the scavenger hunt clue will leave the trolley to come find their favorites.

When I look across the table to judge how close Gilly and her parents are to finishing their supper so I can relocate them, I find two empty seats where Gilly and her mother were a moment before.

Richard catches me and hikes a finger to the far end of the shop row. "Pit stop."

"Thanks." I should wait for Cian to report in, but this may be my only chance to remove the Bettencourt family from the eyepiece of the paparazzi. I may be overreacting. Gilly would not ring as out of place in our group. The L.A. girl is an integral part of the show. There shouldn't be any lingering danger of anyone here speculating she's the mystery girl who sparked a firestorm of rumors about Jack's love life back in Ireland. I told Dash I had a handle on the Jack/Niks fauxmance. Now I need to assuage the voice screaming "Beware!" in my head.

Still. If Gilly is away, I've got perfect odds of keeping the fauxmance believable.

I clue Bobby in on the camera and excuse myself once again, slipping through succulents to get to the toilets.

Down a short hallway, I find a sign marked *Damas*. I reach for the door next to it when I hear someone crying. Gilly.

"It's alright, Darlin'," Amethyst coos to her daughter. "Frankly, I don't know how you hold up as well as you do with him pulling off a kiss like that right in front of you."

I whip my head around to see if there is anyone close enough to hear them. The passageway is empty all the way to the plaza.

"I'm being stupid. It's his job. Kissing Niks doesn't mean anything."

"It means you're being forced to live a goddamned lie."

I'm hit by a trolley. Part of me has always known how much the Jack and Niks coupling beats Gilly up, but it's a much different experience stepping into her visceral cloud of misery. Long overdue empathy makes my legs shaky.

"They're going to hate me, aren't they, Mom? His fans. They'll think I broke Niks and him up. Theirs is the love story the fandom wants." Her sob echoes in the small room, escaping through the thin opening in the door to dig into me.

"Then tell the truth."

"I can't. Meg says it'll hurt Jack. I won't do that."

"What does Jack say?"

Gilly sniffles, recovering from her cry. Through the slit in the door, I see her putting herself together in the mirror.

"Gillian, it's all a game. You can choose not to play. Jack is your reality. Define that on your terms." I can tell by her tone Mama Bear is ready to rip anyone to shreds who threatens her cub.

"I'm okay, Mom. Meg knows what she's doing. It's not forever."

I'd rather Gilly curse me than defend me. I back far away from the door and lean against the wall near the arch to the patio. I wish I had the luxury of time to slide down to the floor and drop my head to my knees. How many degrees of a horror am I to the people in my life? First, I pissed off a well-meaning Cian tonight and almost broke our connection. Now I stab a wooden stake through Gilly's heart as I offer up her husband to all takers. Add to the list the way I disappointed my sister and belittled her life choice to stay close to home. I've a dark touch.

The door to the toilet squeals open. I pretend I've just started my walk toward it. Gilly and Amethyst greet me with tight smiles. There's nothing 'fore it, but to get to the point.

"I've a favor to ask of you ladies."

Gilly looks hooked and gutted.

"There may be early arrivals for the scavenger hunt. I thought you might like to be off and away from the situation."

Amethyst skewers me with a look that reminds me so much of my own mom I'm about knocked off my feet.

"Sure, Meg," says Gilly. "Whatever you say." They walk past me and cross under the bougainvillea archway to the seating area.

Instead of returning to the table, I hang back. My own tears press, awaiting permission to escape. Permission not granted. I'm well-practiced at holding them in.

After taking a beat to compose myself, I rejoin the group. Gilly and her parents are saying their goodbyes. Jack is wound as tight as an adder ready to strike. The look on his face as he watches Gilly walk away breaks my heart. Niks rubs his arm and whispers words of encouragement.

Cian pulls the chair out for me. "I filled the gang in," he says. "You've got a steady stream of fans congregating outside the entrance arch, but they haven't spotted Jack and Niks yet."

Thankfully, situating my stars with their backs to the entrance embedded in a large group bought us a few minutes. "It's earlier than the time in the hint," I say, taking in the approaching night sky.

Cian bobs his head at the hostess station guarding the main entrance. "Adhering to your timetable is not a priority for the fans." He dips a tortilla chip in salsa. "Early bird catches the worms."

"Flattering." Jack aims a scowl at Cian.

"No offense intended," says Cian. "Sorry."

Jack grabs Gilly's unfinished margarita and downs it.

I lean in, attempting to whisper to Jack and Niks across the table. "Security is heading into position. Once they're in place, you can make yourselves known." I send up a quick prayer no one makes a fuss about the pair before then.

Jack tips his own margarita glass to capture the last drops. I tap out a confirmation text to security and fight to maintain a professional demeanor as nerves and guilt crumble my insides. My latest scenario reduced Gilly to tears, made her mum ready to gut me, and Jack looks like one of his cats was hit by a car. What am I doing to these people?

"Let's sneak in one more round before the hunt commences," says Bobby, as he signals our server.

"Amen to that," hisses Jack while the Mariachis three play on.

CHAPTER 9

CHEESE PLATES AND WHISKEY

I've fallen in love with California nights. They lack the freezing lashes of wind off the ocean we endure back in Kerry. A cooling breeze chases off the sticky heat of the day. Cian and I stroll under the impressive metal arch announcing the entrance to the Gaslamp Quarter of San Diego. My first sight of the arch during the day impressed, but here under a half-moon sky its crown of golden letters on a bed of electric blue lights is magic. Across the street at the events center, late Con panels are closing the place down as the streets of San Diego wake to a nocturnal round of celebrating.

"I love walking through the crowd," says Cian. "The energy is addicting. Adrenaline by proxy."

Lighthearted mayhem encircles us, electrons orbiting a Cian/Meg nucleus. The crowd runs the gambit of couples dolled up at black tie level to Steampunk cosplay with princesses, fairies, and dragons in the mix. Lots of chums laugh together, a mighty craic to be sure.

Delicious smells drift from a nearby food cart. Bacon wrapped sausages sizzle from their bed of onions on a portable grill. "I'm regretting my enchilada combo plate from dinner," says Cian, patting his stomach. "Should have gone ala carte without rice and beans." He veers toward the pops and crackles of the sausages. "Those babies are calling me."

My stomach growls. Being on high alert all through dinner kept me from eating anything but a half-dozen tortilla chips and a sip or two of melon margarita.

Cian bumps my shoulder with his. "You're a woman of few words."

I slip my hand through his elbow. "I'm decompressing." And still wrapping my head around the decision to give this man a go in my life, even if it's just for the weekend.

He squeezes my arm against his body. "Celebrate. It went well. You've got P.R. gold in your stars. Jack radiates good guy, and Niks held the crowd in the palm of her hand."

"Jack is none too pleased with me over detonating the date contest grenade in front of his wife and in-laws." A guilt worm chews on my insides at the strain I'm putting on Jack and Gilly.

"He's a pro. He'll come through for you, Meg. It's a crackin' idea."

"How very Irish of you to say, Mr. Malley. No doubt Jack will work with me. It's the personal toll I've saddled him with, giving me the squirms." Hopefully, the arrival, thanks to Cian, of Jack's Star's Shadow trooper and Gilly's Starry Night costumes at their hotel room will earn me back smile points with the pair of them.

Cian takes a sharp turn and drags me to a line of high tables on a patio outside a restaurant. "Let's grab that seat and people watch." He weaves us through the crowd and pushes aside a low metal gate to snag a table. He pulls the seat out for me and then adjusts his own chair so we're sitting side by side facing the current of humanity flowing down the street.

"Would you think less of me if I kick my shoes off for a bit?" I say, already slipping out of my heels.

"If barefoot is part of your decompression, I'm all for it." He lifts my foot onto his lap and starts kneading the arch. I bite back a protest, worrying after a day walking around, the less than floral fragrance of my feet might send him running. If they do smell like a donkey's arse, he doesn't seem to care.

"Swimming is my way of decompressing at home. My sister, Taryn, owns a Swim and Gym. Gives me 24/7 pool access if I want it." Images of an intimate night swim sans clothes with Cian whirl about in my head. Fatigue makes me saucy.

"Your production facility is in Kerry, right?"

"Just outside Waterville." Where, even in July, it's probably raining and cold.

"Do you live in Waterville?"

"Naw, my place is in Cahersiveen."

"Not far then," Cian says in a knowing tone.

I take a long drink from the heavenly glass of ice water set before me by an angel wearing black slacks, a white blouse, and a skinny red necktie. Cian orders up two whiskey sours with Jameson. The learning between us is not one-sided if I've enlightened him to the virtues of Jameson whiskey.

When the server leaves, I narrow my eyes at him. "You know the distance between Waterville and Cahersiveen? Spend your free time studying maps of Ireland?"

"My grandparents live in Glenbeigh."

I set the water glass down with a bang. 'You're very Irish? And this is the first I'm hearing about it?"

He draws a line down the condensation on the side of my glass with his finger. "Malley didn't give me away?"

"Where's the family from?"

"Dad grew up in Glenbeigh."

I lean on one elbow and stare at him. "A Kerry boy." The world just got a little stranger. Cian Malley's been right in front of me with the tricolor of Ireland superimposed on his forehead, and I missed it entirely.

Oh, Lord, Mommy would insist Cian is a blessing sent. She's big on blessings sent. It's not as if she sees images of Jesus and his ma in a plate of eggs and potatoes. Mommy labels things as "blessings sent" if they move her daughters down certain paths that she sets in her mind we should travel.

My job with *The Chieftain's Son* production team is a blessing sent, one my family and I have trouble seeing eye to eye on. I view it as experience gold and a steppingstone for my future with the Hollywood P.R. machine. Mommy and Taryn define it as experience to launch my own marketing firm in Ireland. One woman's blessing sent is a fear of loss for her mother and sister.

"Technically, I'm an O'Malley. Dad had a falling out with his folks and dropped the O when he came to California to go to med school."

It's a story I've heard over and over. Folks leaving Ireland to make their way somewhere bigger. I'm planning on it being my own story as well.

I nod. "Half of my class at secondary school got itchy feet and headed off mostly to America. The family bites my head off every time I bring up leaving one day."

Cian chuckles. "Same sore spot between my dad and his folks. They'll never forgive him for putting down roots and six grandkids on the shores of the Pacific instead of the Atlantic even though we did spend a couple weeks with them every summer."

"Six of you? That's nearly half a hurling team."

He leans on an elbow. Our faces are close enough to bathe in each other's breath. "All sisters. I'm smack in the middle."

I'm no longer surprised Mr. Cian Malley—correction, O'Malley—is such a gentleman after growing up with seven women in the house. A flood of questions bubbles up in my mind. "How did the only son of a doctor end up in the Hollywood stew?"

He fiddles with a strand of my hair that's come loose from the loop of twisted braid on the back of my head. I'm eager to know more about Cian. He's a surprise to me in a world in which I've tried to eliminate surprises. They lead to uncertainty, opening too many doors. I prefer a predictable road I can shape and regulate. This man breaks my rule in a way I've stopped finding altogether unpleasant.

Cian's face becomes animated in a Christmas morning sort of way when he mentions his sisters. I'm more enamored with every new piece he shares. The man is so open. I look for shields or constructs he may be hiding behind but can't find a one. Maybe he isn't burdened with any.

Is Cian a blessing sent? Even though I go to church at least once a month with my parents, never missing a Christmas midnight mass or sunrise service on Easter, I've long ago split emotionally with religion. I know they're out there, the saints, Blessed Mary, Father, Son, and Holy Spirit, but we haven't had much cause to make dinner plans.

"As a kid, there was lots of filming in my neighborhood. I'd hang around the shoots." His eyes drift upwards. "The atmosphere and all the moving parts of production sucked me in."

"Not stung by the acting bug?" He's certainly got the looks and charisma for it. Cian's like Jack in that way. The two are magnetic without trying while the rest of us are iron filings drawn to their field of attraction.

He shakes his head. "No interest in performing. Getting people excited about a project is what floats my boat. Marketing, publicity, is drawing a treasure map. We create quests for fans to follow and tie themselves to the show or the movie in the process. Take your scavenger hunt. It's such a high when you know you've nabbed your audience." He beams at me. "You know what I mean."

"I do. It's a grand rush to reel them in."

He drapes an elbow over the back of his chair to watch a throng of people marching in step as they sing the theme song to *Randy in 6B*. I make a mental note to tell Jack his former show still gets plenty of love.

Cian chuckles at the group. "I was lucky. Growing up in El Segundo, spitting distance from Hollywood, made marketing internships nicely accessible."

I sit up so fast it rocks the table. "El Segundo! Not the El Segundo with the El Segundo Blue-butterfly preserve."

"The very one."

"Is it close to here? Could we pop over? I'd love to see the place."

The notion amuses Cian to no end. "It's a six-hour round trip if there isn't another car on the road, which between Los Angeles and San Diego is an impossibility."

I scowl at him. "Pardon me for my ignorance. There's no map of California tattooed to my ass."

"May I confirm that?"

I swat his arm. "Not if you keep laughing at me."

His laugh settles into a lovely smirk. "I'm not making fun of you, I promise. It's a matter of perspective. I'll bet you can drive from one side of Ireland to the other and back in the same amount of time."

I purse my lips and give him my best condescending nod as I mock his statement. "Oh, we judge our trips by how many sheep and cows cross the road between Dublin and Kerry."

"Touché," he says and sips from his water glass. "Rewind. How does a girl from Kerry know about the El Segundo Blue?"

I wave him off. The tiny-winged, endangered species, the focus of my secondary school scholarship fail, opens a gateway to bitter memories I'm not eager to share with a veritable stranger, no matter how twinkly his eyes. "It's nothing worth wasting breath on."

Our server delivers a pair of whiskey sours. I commandeer Cian's cherries as well as my own before taking a sip.

Cian trails his fingers gently up my cheeks until he's cupping my face in his hands. "Waste a little breath on me."

I give him more breath than voice. "Why?"

He brushes my nose with his but doesn't kiss me. "Do you know the real reason I can't get enough of you?"

My heart goes from a hard thump to a flutter. "No idea."

"Besides your obvious wit and intelligence, you're one of the most unpredictable creatures I've ever met. Blue butterflies, a constant stream of inspired marketing nuggets...I'm agog anticipating the next surprise to pop out of your..." His finger traces my bottom lip. "Pouty and very nice mouth." He moves in so slowly for a kiss, I'm afraid he might leave himself an opening to change his mind and pull away.

He's not getting that opening on my time. I take matters into my own lips and cover his mouth with mine. At first, it seems we've begun what will end as a short, but worthwhile kiss. Blame it on the Jameson I taste on him that parts my lips, inviting something longer. Sweet shifts to hungry as his tongue finds its way to mine and we linger in a slow dance. His hand on my thigh slides higher. Suddenly a busy street is the last place I want to be with Cian. The evening revelers can keep the moonlight. I'll whisk this gorgeous man into the shadows.

Our private bubble heats up far too rapidly for a public venue and invites a few catcalls. We're both a bit breathless as we break apart.

Cian's kisses are like a bag of wonderfully salty crisps. You want to binge the bag, not just settle for a handful. I tell myself to stop questioning his presence in my life and simply enjoy it.

If he is a blessing sent, then I'll take what I can from it. Cian Malley is not altering the course of my life. He is a weekend, gone come Sunday. An opportunity for me to learn a bit and maybe loosen up the way Taryn and Maureen are always pestering me to do. I can best imagine the pair of them and their smug *"We've been telling you to put it out there, Meg"* faces if I choose to share post-mortem details at home about my time with Cian.

"Another round?" I ask Cian as our server swoops close enough to catch. He nods and orders up, never taking his gaze off me. Holy God, I'm doing the same to him.

I'm usually the worst-case-scenario type. If I see one coming, I avoid stumbling into it. Whatever happens between us in the next thirty-six hours, come hour thirty-seven, we'll return to no more than shared names on a group True Time email. A wicked thought curls my lips into a smile. Maybe we'll be a pair that renews their acquaintance once a year at Cali Con. A weekend ride and nothing more. Shouldn't be too taxing on my part to tangle a bit with a like-minded soul who can shine up my P.R. game and kisses like a house on fire.

Cian slides his chair snug up against mine. He's got one hand on my back and the other on my knee. His lips brush my ear. "So, M-Squared, are you going to waste breath and butterflies on me?"

I try to remember the last time anyone gave a tinker's damn about the details of my life. It's refreshing and deliciously seductive to be asked.

"Butterflies, right. Secondary school competition sponsored by an outfit keen on endangered species. First prize scholarship guaranteed your place as a Trinner."

"A who, what now?"

"Student of Trinity College at the University of Dublin."

Cian tilts his head to the side, a lazy half smile on his face. He makes me feel as if we're alone on this crazy street.

"Did you get the scholarship?"

The honey of the moment abruptly shifts to vinegar as ghosts sketch a vivid memory. I smell the musty auditorium air on the day of the scholarship assembly and relive the double-edged knife of failure and betrayal ripping me open when my boyfriend at the time sabotaged my project. It was the moment the optimist in me turned wary pessimist. "No, but I didn't let it stop me from getting to Trinity."

He sets a wedge of gouda from our cheese platter onto an apple slice and feeds it to me. "I'd wager it's near impossible to stop you from getting what you want."

Cian's compliment distracts from memories I'd prefer to archive forever. Coupled with my expertise at tucking shadows into a tight box, the night finds its calm once more. I bite off half the treat, and he pops the rest into his mouth.

"Oh, it happens. I'm having fits over the damn moderator I'm saddled with for our show panel." I play with Cian's fingers. "Tell me, coach," I twist the silver band etched with a delicate leaf pattern he wears on his righthand ring finger. "How do I get rid of Cici Storm as my moderator?"

Cian looks at me like I've grown antlers. "Cici Storm is a *get* as a moderator."

"She's a vapid fangirl who only got where she got because of her dancing stint on *Stepping Out with the Stars*." I raise a finger. "And marrying the big fellow who does all the action films." His name escapes me, but then I pull it from the catalog in my head. "Christopher St. George."

"My darling, Meg, Cici Storm knew how to cash in on her fifteen minutes of fame to become the face of *Entertaining for You*."

I blow a loud *pfffft* of derision. "She did play the game well."

"Exactly." Cian draws circles over my knuckles. Currents buzz up my arm and then straight to parts near and dear to me. "What's bugging you?"

"Her idea as a great opener was to shout out her initials C.S. for Cici Storm match the show's initials C.S. for *Chieftain's Son*. She swears it was a sign she had to moderate for us."

"I never said she'd win a Pulitzer, but she's got a fan base of her own to help fill the room."

"I'm afraid she's going to turn our panel into a goo-fest over Jack O'Leary. I envisioned someone pithier as a moderator."

"Pithier?" He runs his hand up my spine to the nape of my neck. "This just in, my dear M-Squared. *The Chieftain's Son*, given its romance source material, is a goo-fest, the epic love story of mythical time travelers with benefits."

I swat his hand away. "Let Deidre LaRochelle hear you discounting the historical gravitas of her books into the story fluff of women's magazines, and she'll drown you in the marina."

He holds both hands up in surrender.

"*Star's Shadow* doesn't particularly give old Willie Shakespeare a run for his money."

Cian grabs his heart. "Struck to the quick."

I knock my knee against his under the table. "Don't try to distract me with Bard-speak. Your lead character, Starry Night, hunts down heartbreak, imposing herself into people's lives—"

"And aliens."

"—and aliens' lives to bring them to"—I crimp my fingers in air quotes—"the path of joy as defined in the role-playing video game she sprang from." I tilt my chin down and look at him through my lashes. "And that's not a goo-fest?"

He covers one of my hands with his. "It's hope. Even with her nemesis, Event Horizon, always working against her, Starry Night heals every broken heart she seeks out."

"As does our lovely Chieftain's Son. Love eternal will not be denied no matter the obstacles. It just so happens to be between the same two destined souls."

We face off, and Cian breaks first with his good-humored laugh that I'm growing very fond of, even when it's directed at me.

"We're both in the goo business."

"And a fine business it is," I say, lightly pounding the table.

He captures my fist and kisses each finger one at a time before peeling it open to drop a damp kiss on my palm.

I want him.

Vibrations like the overenthusiastic base rhythm thrumming from the restaurant across the street ripple up my body. I very much doubt I possess enough muscle tone left to stand. Thoughts of dark places and satisfying a need I've denied for too long shut out sounds of the crowd surrounding us. The pulse between my legs answers the beat of music.

I'm finished with playing. It's time for having.

"What do you say we move the evening to one of our rooms?" says Cian. A line of sweat shines on his forehead, proving his internal thermometer hit a level as high as my own. Thank God I'm not alone in my readiness to go over the edge.

"I'd say it's a grand idea."

Cian looks down at our joined fingers. "I'm not going to lie to you, Meg, and pretend taking a gorgeous woman to my room is something I haven't done before." He hesitates a moment before meeting my gaze. There's a seriousness in his eyes ill matched for a prelude to the anything-but-serious fling we're hurtling toward.

"Thanks for the confession, so noted. Now that your soul is cleansed, let's get to it." I lean close and take a nip of his earlobe.

He lays his hands on my shoulders and eases me away. "I don't want to play games with you. Before we take this where we both know it's headed, I need to tell you I see who you are. I respect you, admire you. I want to be with all that is Meg McGrath. You're not just a delightful weekend conquest to me."

If I had any lingering reservation about peeling every stitch of clothes off Cian and taking everything he has to offer, they've run away. I nearly echo his lovely sentiment, but my buttoned-up, cautious side decides to keep it to myself for a bit longer. "Pay the damn bill on your *Star's Shadow* tab before I ride you on top of the cheese platter."

As Cian flicks his wrist at the server, a news alert pings from my cell half-hidden under the plate.

"Holy hell, will you look at this?" I raise the cell so we can both read.

Carnival Studios suspends all production in the light of allegations concerning financial misconduct.

We share identical open-mouthed shock and disbelief. Carnival is a voracious beast that's consumed more than half a dozen smaller studios and independent production companies. They are untouchable. How can this be? All production suspended. A wave of nausea rolls through my middle on their behalf. I can't imagine the ball-busting lost revenue, insurmountable logistics of suspending and remounting God-knows how many current projects.

"Rumors about Carnival's shaky ground have grown fangs lately, but I never thought it would go so far," says Cian. He grabs his phone to dig for more information.

Our cells simultaneously ping with messages. It's a group text from Dash to what looks to be a list of showrunners and P.R. heads for every True Time show.

Harborview Hall opportunity—open Sunday panel slot following Dr. Spacebender secured by True Time. Meeting in my suite in half an hour.

As much as I want to be rubbing my naked body against Cian's, Dash's message means something massive is brewing for us in the wake of Carnival Studios' death knell.

Cian's hand curls around the back of my neck and guides me to one of his short kisses that make my lips brush fire. "Let me be clear, M-Squared, we're pushing pause, not stop on our evening."

I run a hand up his arm. "For the love of cream in your coffee, don't lose that remote."

His laugh takes on a new intimate shade as he holds out a hand to me. After all, lust held at bay holds potential to be more delightful once it's let loose.

CHAPTER 10
HARBORVIEW HALL

C ian and I maneuver our way to the hotel as fast as one can through a barrel of agitated eels. Convention attendees clog every street, sidewalk, and patch of grass. I swear an eejit in an evil clown costume gropes me as we struggle past the line of folks camping overnight under a series of awnings to get a coveted wristband for Friday's Harborview Hall offerings.

Sliding against a bevy of strange bodies is not my activity of choice. Only one body in particular is on my sliding agenda. Dash's call to arms blew that plan off its flight path.

I pull up the Sunday schedule on my cell to see what cancelled to open the coveted slot following *Dr. Spacebender*. I'm met with TO BE ANNOUNCED. Slowing my pace, I dig out the convention *quick guide* from my bag.

"Speed it up, M-Squared. Five minutes until it's time for Dash's summons. We want to be in from the get-go on the True Time feeding frenzy."

I break into a jog to catch up while flipping pages. These heels aren't rated for running. *Found it*. Sunday - Harborview Hall - *Dr. Spacebender*. I trace a finger across the color-coded grid to the next booking. "Cian, hold up. I found the D.O.A. panel. *Bastions of Power* was scheduled in the now *up for grabs* slot."

"Holy shit," says Cian, ushering me through the huge double glass doors of our hotel's main lobby. "*Bastions of Power* was slated to be Carnival's holiday release cash cow."

The main floor bar overflows with a mix of cosplayers and business suits. We sprint into a lift, and Cian hits the twenty-ninth floor where the True Time Network gobbled up a whole wing for the weekend. By some miracle, we're alone as the doors slam shut.

Fast as a whirlwind, Cian traps me against the mirrored wall of the lift, pressing his body into mine. As I suspected, he's as ready to go as I was before our Olympic hurdle run through San Diego. His enthusiasm brings my body into sync with mutual wanting. Cian's lips and tongue are everywhere, on my mouth, behind my ear, the side of my neck. When his hand brushes the side of my breast, he sends me into a state not appropriate for a network meeting.

I'd rather grab his ass and yank his hips tighter against mine, but instead I dive in for one final, rapid-fire deep kiss before gently pushing him off.

He rests his forehead on the glass wall of the lift. I fix my clothes and attempt to catch my breath.

"Business meeting. Business meeting. Business, business, business," he chants, peeking at me under his arm. Panting and grinning, he hisses, "Bussssssssinesssss."

We've got five floors to cool off. Facing the mirror, I wind loose tendrils of hair around my bun before tucking them in. Grabbing lipstick out of my bag, I finish putting myself together. I'm all business on the outside and a roiling vat of burn for Cian on the inside.

As if reading my mind, his hand fiddles with the top button of my blouse. "If I'm not grabbing your bare Irish ass in an hour, I may combust."

"Same," I say, refastening the button while I lean in for a quick peck on his cheek. "Hands off for now."

He tidies his own ensemble and wipes a hand across his face as the lift dings our floor. We head left at a brisk clip to Dash's suite at the end of the hall opposite the block of rooms housing *The Chieftain's Son* people.

Except for Bobby, we're last to arrive. The same collection of True Timers from our Wednesday morning meeting, with the addition of what I'm guessing are a handful of showrunners, populate a pair of couches, a long dining table, and bar stools. The group buzzes like downed electric wires.

I zip a text to Bobby. The reply comes in a flash.

Incoming. Be my eyes and ears.

I'm unexpectedly moved. Bobby's confidence in me hasn't wavered one whit. Am I a fool not to let him in on Dash's plans to rip me out of my position? No, I've got to keep my cliff-hanging status to myself. Bobby would lose his shit and go to bat for me. I'm not convinced that would work in my favor.

Dashell Everett stands in front of a huge picture window overlooking the pool and outdoor bar. He's got a drink in his hand and a mask of victory plastered across his face. He scans the room. "All shows are repped, so to the point then."

Cian pulls out a chair for me at the table and leans against the wall behind me.

Dash throws down the rest of his drink and slams it on the bar. The man certainly has a flair for the dramatic—actor gone executive, no doubt. "Carnival Studios is officially shut down by the federal government, pending investigation. Rumors are flying that Jonah Rossi, their CEO, has been arrested. I've got word their board of directors is locked in an emergency meeting even as we speak."

Speculations erupt around the room, running the gamut from racketeering to a sex scandal.

"Bottom line...They've yanked their presence here at San Diego. Our fleet of foot CEO at True Time knocked aside the other studios and networks to claim the vacant Sunday Harborview Hall slot after *Dr. Spacebender.*"

His eyes sweep the crowd. "Gold, my friends, publicity gold. We're still a fledgling network. This will be True Time's Harborview Hall debut. I need a cataclysmic panel."

We hold a collective breath as we wait to hear which of our shows will be showered with Dash's gold.

He paces and weaves around the room, not directing his words at anyone in particular. "You're my top five shows." He points at each P.R. rep as he names them off. *"Star's Shadow, The Chieftain's Son, Down to the Bone, Best and Boggs,* and *Mage's Wish."*

I squirm in my seat as he goes down the list. I wish *The Chieftain's Son* and not *Star's Shadow* had been first out of his mouth.

"I need solid proposals for Sunday. Who can you guarantee in those panel seats? I want star power, high-profile moderators, I'm talking a hook big enough to lift the events center off its foundation."

My heart refuses to beat in anything resembling a normal rhythm. Who the hell can I pull out of my ass I haven't already? I don't even have a lock on Deidre. After yanking her heart from her chest at dinner by offering Jack up for a fan date, I'm not sure Gilly will be keen on helping me.

"Of course, True Time will cover celebrity appearance fees and expenses. Marketing is already prepping swag bags with merch from every show as giveaways for the Sunday audience." Dash lifts a bottle of champagne from the bar over his head as if he's about to smash it against the wall to christen his suite. "Set the place on fire. Proposals and celebrity guarantees to me in twenty-four hours, midnight tomorrow night, so I can review your ideas after our True Time cruise event. I want to announce the panel to the public by ten o'clock Saturday morning to generate buzz. Give me a spectacle fans will camp overnight for."

He pops the cork on the champagne. "To fucking Harborview Hall!"

The room breaks out in applause and champagne starts flowing. I'm no fool. Networking with this bunch is part of the game, but they are also my competition. I need to retreat to my camp and paint castles in the sky to dazzle Dash and win *The Chieftain's Son* the slot.

Separating from the herd, I make my way to the door of the suite. Cian's right behind me. He pulls the door closed so we're alone in the hall and lifts me off the ground. Spinning in a circle, he crows, "To fucking Harborview Hall!"

"You've lost your mind."

Our shared adrenaline rush surrounds us in a corona of static electricity.

"Haven't you?" He sets me on my feet and grabs my hand. "My room is closer." We practically waltz down the hallway, both whirling in the maelstrom of this new possibility. "We'll pow-wow there."

My thoughts splatter all over the designer wallpaper. Harborview Hall. Scoring the panel will be tantamount to winning The World Cup. If I make it happen, Dashell Everett will have no choice but to leave me be. The bastard has yet to comment on the social media explosion and press coverage I've shared with him about my scavenger hunt. Fool better not be planning ways to renege on our deal now that I'm gaining traction.

Harborview Hall will be my guarantee to keep steering *The Chieftain's Son* and boost my rise in the Hollywood playing field of the publicity game.

Cian chatters behind me, but I don't focus on what he's saying. Apparently, his racket requires an answer because he captures me from behind, trapping me in his arms. A chin digs into my shoulder and hot breath covers my ear as a preamble to his words. "The smart thing to do would be to shut ourselves away in our separate rooms and construct different proposal masterpieces for the boss." His lips draw a sizzling line down the side of my neck.

He's right. That's the responsible and professional action to take.

The tip of his tongue darts into my ear, sending me into a full body shiver.

"The problem is, there's no way in hell I can put together a single coherent thought when I know you're close enough to touch."

I swivel in his arms, so we're face to face. "Now, this is quite the dilemma." I tap a kiss to the underside of his jaw. Niks is right. Scratchy. Oh, so deliciously scratchy. A line of fire runs down my throat, between my breasts, and slides down to the place screaming to feel his scratchy digging deep into my skin.

A ding from the lift startles us apart. Maureen, Grady, Bobby, Gilly, and Jack pour out. Catching sight of me, Bobby launches straight for my position.

"Dammit, did I miss the whole thing?" His eyes dart toward the end of the hall where Dash's suite is surely filled with a firestorm of gossip about Carnival Studios. "We were hanging with Rich and Amethyst over at the Hotel Joya Brillante when I got the text. I got here as fast as I could."

Over his shoulder, I watch the two couples disappear round a bend in the hall. I pray the fools stay away from windows.

I look to the bank of lifts. "Where's Niks?"

Bobby flicks a wrist. "She met up with her manager and Marisa for drinks. Fill me in."

Maureen's voice booms at extra volume from around the corner. "Gilly, where's the key to *our* room. I call first shower. Movie's your pick." Now she's practically shouting, "You boys have a good evening." Raucous laughter fills the hallway. That bit of sass was entirely for my benefit.

Bobby catches the stress pinching my face. "They're playing with you, Meg. Everyone knows to be careful." He includes both Cian and me in the conversation. "Give me the short version before I make an appearance."

"You heard about the feds and Carnival?" asks Cian.

Bobby shakes his cell. "It's all over the news."

"Prime real estate in Harborview Hall opened up on Sunday right after *Dr. Spacebender*. True Time grabbed the slot. Everett wants proposals by tomorrow, Friday, at midnight" I say as Cian nods.

"We got the panel?" asks Bobby, excitement seeping from every pore.

I wince. "Sorry, wasn't clear. He wants proposals of what each of the top five True Time shows can guarantee, hooks and people."

Bobby's light dims. "Hmmm. Makes sense. Did he say what he wants?"

Cian waves an imaginary wand through the air. "Magic."

"Dammit. We've already gone balls-out on the show panel adding Sir Kevin," Bobby rubs his chin. "Should we save him for the new slot? Any confirmation from Deidre? Gilly says she had a conversation with her."

A flush of embarrassment heats my skin. Is Gilly digging at me by telling Bobby she'd spoken to Deidre before cutting me in? I shake it off.

She's not the payback type, and I need to kiss Gilly's ass, not grumble at her.

"What are you thinking, Meg?" asks Bobby with an expression so hopeful he looks like a teen waiting for his first kiss.

I rub a finger across lips, tender from Cian's kisses in the lift. "I've had less than ten minutes to percolate." The deep crease between his brows puts me on the defensive. "I promise I'll pull something brilliant out of my ass."

Bobby's lip crinkles. He's a bullet train thinker. In ten minutes, he'd have a playbook of ideas. "Of course, you will."

I immediately regret being short with him. He's had faith in me from day one. My job is to live up to that. I give him a gentle shove in the direction of Dash's suite. "Go on and get the schmooze over with." I wiggle my phone at him. "I'll text when I've got something."

Bobby nods. "Same. Breakfast strategy session, yes?"

"Nine?"

"I'll meet you in the lobby. G'night, Meg." He nods to Cian before walking so quickly down the hall he could be gliding on a cushion of air. Bobby has two speeds, lightning and intense.

Cian flips his keycard out of a pocket and lays it in my hand.

God, it's tempting, but there's future-busting work to be done. The sexual tension crackling around us is going to make my hair as ratty as a swallow's nest. "I'm wondering if we should keep that button on pause for tonight to write up our panels," I say fingering the keycard.

A rosy wave creeps up Cian's neck. "Or we go with the two-minds-are-better-than-one model."

Our gazes linger on the keycard. "Minds are what's on your mind, eh?"

He moves closer, sliding a hand down my arm to rest on my hip. His focus takes a slow journey down my body. "Everything worthwhile starts with a sharp and willing mind."

As truly grand as Cian's been, Dash's challenge drives us deeper into competition. Parting ways until this is settled is probably smart business. Except the combination of Cian's hand sliding up to my waist and the want setting my insides aflame steal the smarts right out of my head. My sharp and willing mind will have a hell of a time focusing on panel ideas instead of the possibilities Cian's keycard unlocks.

The damn lift dings again, launching me away from Cian. A series of sharp, high-pitched barks follow the chime. Niks slinks out of the lift with her girlfriend, Marisa, who's being dragged by two yipping, white powderpuff mini dogs.

"Shush, babies," Niks coos to the pair of ornamental hounds. She looks up, delighted to find us. "Hello. Hello, again. We had some fun tonight, yes?"

Cian smiles at her. "It's one big party here. Cute pups."

The eejit dogs strike up another chorus of barks. Niks shakes a finger at them. "Not so cute, you naughty girls. We'll put you in a suitcase."

I'd like to put her pooches in a suitcase. The logistics of these yapping hair balls coming from Ireland to San Diego had me plucking out far too many gray hairs.

"Meg, you switched my room to a suite, yes?"

I point toward *The Chieftain's Son* block of rooms. "To the right and all the way to the end."

Niks sets a knuckle against her chin, staring at Cian and me with a knowing look. "I think you are new friends. Yes?" She breaks into a huge smile. "I know these things." One long baby pink fingernail taps a temple.

"Actually," says Cian. "We're on our way to a meeting. Have you heard the Carnival Studios news?"

Marisa nods. "Niks's manager told us."

Niks frowns. "I've worked there. Terrible experience. I'm not surprised." She shushes the barking dogs. "They never shut up. I should get cats."

"Thanks to you both for being such good sports about my scavenger hunt."

"You do know how to keep things hopping, Meg," says Marisa. She's smiling, but there's weariness in her voice. More emotional collateral damage from my best laid plans for the show.

"I am sorry to add to your plate, but there's a very good chance I'll need you for a panel on Sunday, Niks."

One of the dogs lets out a high-pitched whine when Marisa jerks on its leash. The two women exchange an entire conversation with a look. Marisa nods, her chin and bottom lip crinkling.

I'm going to make the woman cry.

Niks takes the leashes out of Marisa's hand and turns to me. "More appearances, your hunt, all good fun for me." She flicks her wrist. "Jack, not so much, but he's a sport."

"Yes, he is." I'm banking on Jack's sportsmanship since I'm cutting his weekend into even smaller slices.

"Goodnight, goodnight," says Niks, kissing both Cian and me on the cheek. "Text me details." She slinks down the hall, her ass swaying side to side. Marisa drifts closer to her despite their annoying fur babies. I'm not the only one who catches it.

Cian gives me a knowing grin. "Another pair of Ireland's secrets."

"You're as yappy as her hounds." I sneak one last glance at his lips and hold the keycard to him.

He stares at it like something a cow left on the path.

"As much as I'm tempted to throw you over my shoulder and carry you into the room"—I shake the keycard at him—"we've both got high-stakes work nipping at our asses."

Cian's eyes are wide. "You hit me with the image of ass nips, being thrown over your shoulder, and dragged into a hotel room, and then walk away?"

I slip the card into his shirt pocket. "I very much appreciate what you said earlier about seeing me for me." I linger on those sparkly, dancing eyes of his.

"I need you to believe I don't see you as a conference hookup." He checks the hall in both directions, the fancy light fixture on the wall next to the lifts, and a dark wood table with a silk flower arrangement before his eyes flit back to mine.

I cock my head to look at him. "What do you see?"

"You're, well, uh, a surprise." He's still for a moment. "Unexpected, but very welcome." A Cian chuckle breaks through. "I'm knocked sideways."

He's certainly done the same to me, sideways and upside down. I don't want to hold out on letting him know any longer. "I'm familiar with the feeling."

Cian lays his hand over the pocket with the keycard, eyes working to read my face. After a moment charged enough to set those silk flowers aflame, he takes a slow, deep breath. "Look, this opportunity is huge. We both want it bad. Even if you are the competition, which"—he holds up a finger—"I won't pretend you're not. We're on a level playing field with a ticking clock to craft a killer panel. Unless you've come up with an idea in the half-second since Bobby flew down the hall, neither of us has a hook in mind. I would really appreciate the chance to bounce ideas off your rapid-fire mind."

I see where he's going, and it makes sense.

"Come to my room for business. We'll break down what we need, what Dash expects, set the groundwork and mine gold." His face is as serious as I've ever seen it.

He catches my chin in his fingers. "Brainstorming, Meg. No other body parts involved. I promise." He holds both hands up, then eases into a sly smile. "For tonight, at least."

I trust him enough to believe he won't pounce like a jungle cat on me the second the door shuts, as nice as that may be. It's distraction I worry about. I pick a stray hair off my skirt to stall. My stakes with Dash are already through the roof. This new wrinkle shoots them past the clouds into star-dotted space. Cian knows Dash better than me. He'll have a more precise handle on what it's going to take to impress the boss enough to win the prized slot. Cian and I are at war with the other three shows, and the decisive battle is only twenty-four hours off.

Damn distraction. The good ally Cian seems to be could make the difference between victory and defeat.

CHAPTER II
GOOD BUSINESS

We follow the hallway branch leading to the ocean-view rooms of the hotel. Cian swipes the keycard and holds the door open, letting me in before throwing the locks behind me. An entire wall of his room is glass. The moon, one click past half, rides low in the sky on a bed of stars.

Cian blows by me and starts pacing the room. "We're both double-dipping already. You've got Jack on *The Chieftain's Son* and *Is it Hot in Here?* panels. I've got Sala on *Star's Shadow* and *Women Taking Charge*. We both need a bang-up triple-dip."

My shoulder blades remain glued to the door.

Cian raps knuckles on the window. "Dash is looking for the unexpected. A mind-blowing fan experience."

Kicking off his shoes, Cian plunks into one of the chairs at the table in front of the window and frees a tablet from the messenger bag on the floor. "I've got my cast on standby." The snap of his fingers is a gunshot as he scrolls furiously across his screen. "Yes! MetaMeme is in L.A. If they'll come down..." He types without looking up at me. "Grab your tablet, Meg. List your resources and every pie-in-the-sky whim you have for the panel. I'll do the same, and then we'll put our heads together and suss this out."

The moment Cian's door closed, my gnarled vines of memory, self-preservation, and previous lapses in judgement rise from the floor, twisting around me until I'm motionless inside their woody prison. Cian is competition, pure and simple. Have I fallen into the same scenario that ripped the guts from my body on the day I lost the Trinity scholarship because I *put my head together* with my then-boyfriend on our competing projects? The bastard abused his inside knowledge and our relationship to belittle and denigrate my presentation and exalt his in front of an auditorium filled with classmates, parents, and judges. My sister Taryn is always at me to get past it, but I lost three things in the space of a breath that day: the scholarship, my first love, and trust in anyone but me to create success.

Cian's stream of consciousness fills the room until he stops cold, catching sight of the statue at his door. "Meg?"

A dozen variations of my own voice hiss warnings in my head. When I kissed Cian on the beach and kept him from walking away from me at Casa de Fiesta, I violated a fundamental truth that's allowed me to move forward in life. Success is the exclusive responsibility of one person, me. Now I've gone and allowed myself to attach to this man. If I felt anything less for him, my feet wouldn't be planted inside the doorway of his room.

But this is Cian. He matters to me. I've already let him in to my life, competition be damned, and I'm not sorry. Staring into the full-length mirror on the wall next to me, I see a fool. Not a fool who is repeating past mistakes, one who believes she's capable of taking a carefree tumble with Cian and writing it off as nothing more than a July weekend. A weekend is not enough.

He approaches slowly, concern on his face. "You're sheet white." His hand finds mine. "Come sit."

Cian's touch is warm. Our contact drives spikes of desire through my bones. His kindness and comradery crack my meticulously constructed barriers and me-centric playbook even more. I do my best to shuck off the unease cementing my feet to the floor. I want to take another step with Cian. I want him. So, I allow him to lead me further into his hotel room. "I'm processing the heft of this new opportunity."

"Don't go cold on me, Meg." Cian captures my other hand. "I know a freak-out brewing when I see one. Talk it through. I'm right here."

Cian must think my reaction is about Dash's challenge, not my splintering reality. The finger-wagger in my head scolds that success is not a team sport. It's insisting I be driven by my own inspirations, aspirations, and ability to spin the world in my direction. I'm trying hard to fight it off, but it keeps at me.

You are Meg McGrath. The Chieftain's Son is your kingdom. You must keep it well and prosperous and not let the enemy behind the gates.

I stare at our joined hands as my stakes with Dash and the Cali Con beast threaten to overwhelm me. Cian's touch is the strength I need to tell the finger-wagger to fuck off. Like upending a Glencairn glass of fine whisky, warmth spreads through me. I don't know how Cian managed, but he found a path to the heart of me. Did I show him the way? Did I plaster a building wrap across my face with directions on how to get close to Meg McGrath?

Cian leads me to a chair at the table. "Stay right there." He grabs the ice bucket sitting on the mini bar and heads out the door. "I'll be right back."

His absence feeds me the last few bites of clarity and courage I need. The urge to flee dissipates. It's done. Cian Malley, O'Malley, has entered my life. I heave the last rubble of mental roadblocks from my past aside. There's no sane reason Cian can't be both business and pleasure. I'm willing. He's willing.

I swallow greedy breaths and pop the tension knots along my neck. After our business of brainstorming new panels is done, we'll see if there are different flavors of business to be explored.

Cian darts back into the room. He fills a glass with ice and then water from the giant bottle sitting on the mini bar. For a moment, I wonder if he's going to hold the cup to my lips and help me drink. I've unsettled the man.

"Thanks." I take the glass from his hand and let a long, slow drink finish resetting my composure.

He sits in the chair opposite me. "You're not used to the heat. It's important to stay hydrated."

I nearly laugh. Cian sounds like Jack, who's always nagging cast and crew on the virtues of hydration and health. After draining the glass, I set in on the table. "That's done it." I reach into my bag, free my tablet, and open a notes screen for our brainstorm.

My quick turnaround might convince Cian I'm not going to keel over, but he doesn't switch into work mode. Instead, he locks me in place with a stare.

"What?"

He cocks his head and tosses me a side-eye squint. "Such a quick recovery." His head bobs toward the door where I froze. "California heat had nothing to do with your stall. You're nervous being in the room with me."

I swallow, or at least try to. My throat goes traitorously dry.

Cian waves his arms. "Is this about me telling you I've brought women to my hotel rooms in the past? It's not a regular thing. I'm not the girl-in-every-port type." He runs a hand through his hair. "I don't even know why I said it. Definitely a TMI verbal vomit. I meant it as an honesty thing."

This semi-unglued version of Cian is damn adorable.

He inhales deeply. "It's important you see who I am the way you've shown me who you are. Am I making any sense at all?"

I reach across the table and cover his hands with mine. "Aren't we a pair? Me with my freezing up and you babbling on like a lunatic."

Cian flips his palms up to grasp my hands. The jolt of desire running through me sparks a shudder. He notices it and smiles. I'm ready to crawl across the table and jump him. When he licks his lips, it's my turn to come unglued.

"Meg, I want you in my room. I don't care if it's for work, or…" His thumbs stroke the insides of my wrists. "Or…" he repeats, sliding from his chair to stand behind me. Strand by strand, he frees my hair from its bun, setting each lock across my shoulders. When he's finished, Cian lifts it all, exposing my neck.

"Or…" Moist lips dot their way across my skin, leaving beads of fire. He spins the chair so I'm facing him. "Or…" He lifts my chin, and those fiery lips ignite my own. The kiss is slow. So slow. So lovely. I moan as heat drifts down my throat, across my breasts, and drops to the place beneath my skirt beating a rhythm that calls to Cian.

He breaks the kiss, keeping true to his measured pace. I grip his shoulders, rising from the chair to mold to his body, hoping to speed things up.

"Or..." His word is ragged around the edges now. Instead of kissing me, hands run down my arms, taking a turn to trace the waist band of my skirt. Reaching inside, he untucks my blouse. Cian's eyes and fingers learn the curve of my hips and then slide around to explore the contours of my backside.

When I try to slip my hands under his shirt, he sets them on his shoulders, shaking his head gently. He isn't finished. The blue of his eyes are the only things lending any coolness to the room. It's all I can do to keep still.

"Or..." The word becomes breath. He repeats it over and over, sending heavenly fog across my collarbone. Fingers undo the buttons of my blouse one at a time. The lusty wind of his breath follows in their wake. He eases fabric from my shoulders, keeping his arms around me to unfasten my bra until it drops to the floor.

My grasp on his shoulders saves me from floating away. He eases me back onto the chair and kneels in front of me. Long fingers draw patterns on my breasts, like he's writing a message he'll read to me later. His touch teases my tight peaks until they rise even more in response, increasing the raw need ripping through me.

Cian leans in, trailing his tongue along the underside of one breast then the other, stopping just shy of the prize. He peeks at me through his lashes. "May I taste?"

I've never had a man ask permission. The words themselves drive me mad. I nod only to drop my head back and moan as the tip of his tongue traces the outline of each nipple.

"Mmm," he says, finding each nub with his teeth. He suckles and flicks his tongue, savoring. I pull him closer, aching for him to take me deeper into his mouth. Relentless waves of desire roar from my breasts straight to my core.

My hand slides down a toned stomach that quivers under my fingers. "Am I tickling you?" I press a bit harder, and his muscles tighten.

"Not saying."

I tuck that bit of fun away for later.

My touch travels lower, past his waistband into his slacks. What I find is glorious. As I explore the length of him, the pulse within my grasp answers my own tempo of need.

I slide down to the carpet and into Cian's arms. My eager mouth attacks those darling lips, my tongue taking his captive. Breathing hard, I back off enough to whisper, "Are you brilliant at everything?"

Grabbing the front of his shirt, I pull us both to standing and walk him backward to the bed. We clutch each other and fall onto the coverlet laughing. The pair of us work as a team to rid ourselves of skirt, pants, and anything else in the way of skin touching skin.

The muscles of Cian's chest are my ideal: defined but not overdone. I lie next to him, one leg thrown over his thigh, gripping his upper arm and running my hands all the way down to his fingers. This body was made for me, lithe steel. I enjoy the soft field of hair across the planes of his chest while his hands trickle down my belly.

A shot of self-consciousness slaps into me as I worry my ample roundness might douse the scorch between us. It's quickly chased off when his hands dance across my thighs and then to the place between.

"So beautifully slippery," he sighs in my ear. Cian's fingers dip and tease until I've forgotten the purpose of breathing. I press into his touch, circling my hips in time with the new patterns he's drawing until I arch against his fingers with a cry.

The sound I make at release raises a growl from Cian. He reaches into the drawer of a bedside table for a box of condoms. Someone came prepared for their weekend. He catches the skeptical look on my face.

"I bought them when I got our waters after our flight from the podcast panel." He holds the packet out as an offering. "A man needs goals."

"Fine answer." I rip it from his hand. "On your back, Malley." I smile and dress him for our dance.

He kisses his way up my body until his mouth takes mine in a fury, teeth scraping my tongue. Hands lift my hips, and I wrap my legs around him. Cian raises above me ever so slightly. Instead of entering, he slides his length against the tenderest part of me until I'm on the doorstep of madness.

"Cian," I breathe. My panting slurs his name. I reach between us to guide his cock where my body cries for it.

He captures my hand and continues to glide up and down against the aching, swollen bits of me until, once again, absolute surrender rises from my lips. When my shudder downgrades to a tremor, I stroke him, reveling in the feel of him harden more in my grasp. Taking the lead, I ease him toward the next target of my yearning.

Damn the man and his dances. Instead of a plunge, he slips well inside, lingers, and then retreats so slowly my ache for him hits a new high. He repeats the move over and over, making a circle with his tip before each new push in. My hands grab his ass to force him deeper, but he controls both pace and depth. And what a brilliant pace it is. Sex is not new ground to me, but this pleasing is.

In Cian, I discover more than a body partnering with mine. I find a lover. To my surprise, within his wondrous touch, I have no problem handing over the control I so violently protect.

His tongue flicks in my ear and hits a trigger in us both. I arch to mirror his maddening cadence. We take a ride together in this glorious California night. My hands dig into his hair, my legs crush him, and finally, his damnable control breaks. I squeeze around each of his thrusts, stealing his sanity the way he's stolen mine.

Together, we truly taste the stars.

CHAPTER 12
IN THE WEE HOURS

I've always believed the still of the night to be a romantic notion, not an absolute state of being. As I stare out the glass wall of Cian's room to the marina, I find stillness. Nothing moves below me. No one strolls the sidewalks near the marina or around the events center. Boats settle atop the water. Cian lies on the bed with a bit of blanket covering only his feet.

I've never experienced the delight of watching a sleeping lover. My first ride, Dominic, from secondary school, was not the situation where you'd share a bed until morning. Back in Dublin after university, I had the misfortune to fall in with Skylar, the artist. To him, sex was fuel for his creative process. Of course, eejit me romanticized I was his muse. Wrong thinking at its finest. He'd never stay with me past a glass of wine and the more athletic portions of our evening. I wanted connection, he wanted convenience. We had a trip to L.A. in the planning stages. All I saw of our trip was the east end of the west bound plane when he left without me.

Now here I am doing a bit of nocturnal sightseeing as I study the contours of my lover's ass. And a brilliant ass it is, firm and flat with well-placed muscles.

I draw the fluffy, white hotel robe tighter. That's what Cian is to me now, my lover. Not in the sense of being in love. Affection, yes, probably too much, given the lack of time we've been acquainted. Respect, absolutely. He's lively and intelligent, a seductive combination. We've offered each other intimacy and accepted. We'll keep that even after Sunday when I leave for home.

Leaving. Such a final word and one I'm loathe to apply to Cian, but what other choice do I have? He's got a life here in California, and mine is five thousand miles away. I run a hand through my hair. I thought I was capable of taking him on a weekend ride and then walking away. That reckoning hadn't considered how glorious this man might turn out to be.

My sleeping lover. If I slide in beside him, trickling fingers down his spine to that bitable ass and wake him, my lover he'll be again. Ours will be the briefest of love stories recounted through a bittersweet lens, a chapter instead of a novel. No geraniums in window boxes on a cottage we call home for us. Such pretty pictures belong to couples like Jack and Gilly. Cian and I have the Balboa Sky Bridge.

He turns onto his back, and the view is just as lovely. To watch the rise and fall of his chest is a calming inspiration. I smile, taking my share of credit for sending him under so deeply. I think we'd still be at it if our day had been less taxing. I envy his ability to sleep. My mind is a series of gears, whirring and grinding against one another, attempting to turn challenges into realities.

I rest my forehead against the cool glass wall. Out a way in the harbor below, a replica of a Viking ship rocks on its mooring. There's a fine piece of off-site marketing. For a tidy fee, fans are clothed as berserkers and ferried out to the ship for photographs.

Settling down into a chair with my back to Cian to lessen the distraction of his physique, I retrieve my tablet and add *harbor presence* to the list of publicity and marketing additions I'll see to at our second Cali Con. My finger pauses over the screen. Will I be with *The Chieftain's Son* looking out over the water from one of True Time's hotel rooms next July?

Cian's tablet rests on the table. I tap the screen, surprised he doesn't have screen lock. His brainstorm file for the Harborview Hall panel pops up. MetaMeme, the now top-shelf band who launched his P.R. career ride the top of his "get" list. *Gamers* is the next bullet point. I nod my head, yes, perfect, pull in the folks who first met *Star's Shadow* on a gaming console. I want to nudge Cian awake and ask him how he sees a panel combining a rock band and video games. What's percolating in his envious brain?

What pairing could I put together for my show? Have I played all my cards with Niks and Jack? I need the Sir Kevin/Brian Boru reveal to kick my main show panel up a notch or two. Who would I wish for on a fairy tree? The air crackles around me with an immediate answer.

Deidre.

The purr in my chest shifts from contented afterglow to a race for its life. Instead of over-saturating the Con with Deidre LaRochelle, beloved story spinner, I'll limit her to exclusive book signings and set her as the crown jewel in the coveted Sunday slot. I tap a fingernail on the table. A simple Q & A with Deidre LaRochelle is too small a scale for the Harborview Hall cathedral.

"Deidre." Why is she so beloved? Her people, her characters. She choreographs hope and the dream of romance. The surety of love and its promises defying any odds or obstacle is the gift she gives readers when Donal Cam and Nieve find each other again in each new book. Deidre's stories stoke our faith in love, in finding the one soul who sizzles yours no matter the cost.

Oh, if I could marry everything Deidre represents with showstoppers like MetaMeme. There's a panel for the ages. Unfortunately, I've no chart-topping band to pull out of my arse.

Or do I?

My gaze floats over to the bed. To Cian, my lately lover. One hand rests on a pillow, long fingers twitching ever so slightly as soft breath steals from his lips.

A mad notion grabs me. What if Cian and I combine our assets? We don't propose two different panels, but one. I dip my head to the tablet as my fingers fly across the screen, giving shape to madness.

I squeak with surprise when hands glide over my shoulders to dangle in front of me. Cian's chin fits to my shoulder.

"Mmm-Squared."

I pop out of the chair and flip my tablet over, knocking Cian in the jaw. "Did you see the Viking ship in the harbor?" I'm not ready for him to see what's on my screen.

He steps back a little and rubs his mouth. "I think you cracked a tooth."

"Sorry." I spin toward him, the tie of my robe coming loose. When his eyes cut a slow path down my body, I snatch the robe closed. It's mad to turn self-conscious after the athletics we've spent the better part of the night engaged in.

"The view's much better in here." He threads his hands inside the robe, pulling it open again for his gazing pleasure. I suppose it's only fair after my surreptitious appreciation of his fine sleeping ass.

He nips my earlobe. "Let's pretend you're a Viking beauty who sailed her ship here to ravage me."

I sweep the robe into place and give a tug on the tie. His strike to rid me of the robe is faster than my efforts to keep it. Cian throws his arms around me and, with a lift and twist, I'm back in bed.

"I forbid this night to end," he says, crawling up over me. His nose presses into the sensitive place behind my ear, drawing tiny circles as targets for his lips.

"Best of luck."

He rises on forearms, looking down at me. "Am I sensing waning enthusiasm here?"

I yank him down and then roll us so I'm on top. To answer his inquiry, I deliver a kiss designed to telegraph the precise level of my enthusiasm. Notes on tablets and plans for panels fly out of my brain as we take one another with savagery to impress any Viking.

Lying on our sides, Cian slings a leg over my thigh to keep me close. I kiss my lover with decadent, slow kisses. Our breaths search for a steady state.

Cian buries his head against my chest and sighs, sending a warm wind between my breasts. "I hate this."

I stop smoothing a lock of hair off his forehead. Those are not the words I choose to hear from a lover's lips.

He gathers me closer. "Not this," he says, running a finger down my spine. "The finite limitations of a weekend."

"Finite but quite nice."

Instead of snuggling down under the covers with me, Cian rises to sitting and leans against the headboard. Long, tan arms bring me along with him. Lips lightly touch my temple. "I didn't expect…"

I nestle into him. "Expect what?"

He pulls the covers over us as the air conditioning blasts through the room. "You to be you." Cian tilts his head back, addressing the ceiling or maybe the stars. "Dash painted you as a very green, skittish, barely competent woman who'd lucked into her position."

Anger pounds in my chest. Dashell Everett can burn in the blue fire of hell. He's got no grounds to define me as such or scatter his toxic slander to my True Time colleagues.

Cian watches me with a half-cocked grin. "There's a look Dash would be ill-advised to turn his back on." His expression softens, and he lifts my chin. "Instead of a bumbling newbie, a savvy, driven beauty with wit and a brain that doesn't quit blows into our first meeting like a tempest."

It's the second time he's called me a beauty. A hairline fracture runs across the surface of my heart, knowing I won't be hearing that word or any others from him for much longer.

Cian laughs. "You handled Dash's rudeness like a champ. When you lied to his face about Deidre LaRochelle, I wanted to kiss you right there." He looks out the window to the harbor lights. "I felt an urge to connect with you. Talk to you. You intrigued me. I wanted more of you."

"And I was quite the ice queen." Resentment and bile kept me from bothering to connect with Cian at the meeting. I laser focused on changing Dash's opinion of me.

Cian's thumb strokes my jaw. "When you turned down my offer to help you…Ouch, freezer burn."

"Turning you down was about me, not you." I drag a finger through those soft brown hairs on his chest. "I never figured a self-assured Hollywood hot-shot would be bothered by rejection."

Cian closes his eyes. Ever so slowly, the corners of his lips curl up. "I went to drink alone to convince myself it was idiocy to give a single shit over you blowing me off." He opens his eyes to look at me. "And who should walk in?"

It's my turn to laugh. I raise my hand. He captures it and presses it to his lips.

"It wasn't enough for you to interrupt my pity party, you flirted with me."

"Not flirted. Tried to be a friendlier sort than I was at first go by educating you on the finer points of Irish whiskey."

He takes my face in his hands and kisses me slowly as if to thaw any remnants of the ice queen lurking below my surface. "Not only did the bruises on my ego fade, but the urge to spend more time with you kicked into overdrive."

The way Cian watched me that night before he left the bar comes into sharp focus. "I'd be a lying fool to say it wasn't the same for me."

"You're unsettling."

I trickle a hand to the small of his back and tug at the patch of hair nestled in its curve.

He drops a line of kisses down the side of my neck. "And then there you were in The Grand Ballroom Thursday morning."

I tap a finger to his lips. "Talking too loud."

"Breaching etiquette and going a mile a minute. I saw it again, your dedication, unstoppable forward motion." His head rests in the hollow of my shoulder, eyes closer to a royal blue in the dim light. "You're addictive."

I lean my head against his. "And here I was thinking the same about you."

Cian tenses for a moment and then strokes my hair. "We'd be a formidable team. If we were ever given the chance."

It's my body's turn to shift from the languid state of intimacy into wariness. I touch Cian's side but pull my knees up and wrap my arms around them. "Team has never been a pretty word for me in life or career. I'm at my best when I'm on my own." Cian stares at me so long I start to squirm.

"There's no rule that you have to do it all on your own. It took me some time, but I've learned to let others shoulder some of the responsibility, and I do pretty well." He pries my arms free, pressing down on my knees until I'm stretched out beside him.

I stiffen for a second, worried he's privy to Dash's ultimatum. In the next second, I wonder if confiding in him might be worth the risk. By the third second, I've locked my dilemma inside the box marked *Meg's Eyes Only*. "Relying on yourself is not a bad thing."

"I didn't say it was, but neither is including others to energize your momentum." His arms circle my waist to draw me closer.

I want to roll away from him before I detect even a whiff of judgement in his eyes. His hold is iron, as if he knows my mind.

"I know it's a struggle for you to let me in, Meg. I'm grateful you did." He plays with a strand of my hair. "Why did you push me away that first morning?"

"I didn't know you." I let my hand drift down to his hip. "All I saw was a soldier of True Time."

"An enemy soldier?"

"What else could you be to me?"

"Oh, I can think of a few more things." He sucks my earlobe and chuckles. I relax a bit, then a bit more. A sensation begins slowly at first, but then gains traction. I want to trust Cian. I do want to tell him what I'm up against with Dash. Why wouldn't he help me the way he's been doing since I've allowed it? Suddenly, I'm bursting to throw wide my gates to this man.

I lay my hand flat on his chest. His heart thumps like a horse taking a hurdle. If there's a time for talking, it'll be now, before my body decides on a different type of communication with him. "I'm in a bit of a bad situation with True Time."

Cian's heart stutters beneath my fingers. His brows tilt down and lips press together. I don't know him well enough to read these signs. Are they concern for me, or am I mad for bringing True Time into bed with us? I'm about to put him on the spot with knowledge probably best caged between Dash and me.

"Never mind." I turn and hug a pillow for comfort. "There's no need to blather on." Cian's laugh sends me rolling back in his direction. "Funny, am I?"

He presses his forehead to mine. "You never blather." Cian kisses the corners of my eyes one at a time. "I hope I've convinced you I'm on your team, Meg, whether you want to be on a team or not." He pinches my ass. "Evidence points to some willingness not to do everything on your own." Cian rubs his nose against my cheek. "Tell me."

I gather both his hands in mine, holding them between us, and speak to our joined fingers. "Dash wants to boot me from *The Chieftain's Son.*" I'm gratified when his body gives a shake of surprise.

"You're kidding!"

"Well, not boot me, exactly. He wants to send in one of you Hollywood fools to take the helm and keep me on as the number two." I rest my head on our hands. There. My shame is out in the cold world.

"That is a legit sucker punch."

I nod. "A big one." I raise my eyes to his. "I won't hand off my bone-breaking work and sit back for scraps."

He circles my wrists with his fingers. "You'd quit?"

Instead of answering, I slide out of bed and retrieve the robe. For a long moment, I stare at the sky as the first iris purple streaks rest atop the horizon.

Cian, now clad in his boxers, wraps his arms around me from behind. He's set to comfort and support, not seduce. I appreciate him all the more for it.

I lay my hands over his. "I made a deal with Dashell Everett." My derisive grunt fogs up the window. "Which explains his less-than-flattering attitude to me at the meeting."

I watch his reflection in the window chew its lips. "Thus, the lie about snagging Deidre LaRochelle."

"It was my shot across Dash's bow."

Cian twirls me to face him. "Tell me, Meg. Tell me everything. If it's a battle, I'm on your side."

"Even if it makes you a traitor to the crown?"

"Not a traitor. We're on the same side." Cian frames my predicament in a pretty way. We are still rivals at the end of the day. Rivals for King

Dash the Abhorrent's affection and rewards. I must push rivalry aside if it buys me a chance at the Sunday slot.

I guide Cian into a chair and take the seat across from him at the table. The light of tablets illuminates our faces. "I'm sorry, but I looked at your tablet."

He waves me off. "I was going to show it to you anyway." Cian leans on an elbow to stare me down. "You've got an idea."

"I have." I slide my tablet until it's next to his and tap both screens. "Look at these assets: your stars, my stars, Deidre LaRochelle, MetaMeme." He rolls his fingers in the universal signal for *keep going*. "I say we combine them. Share the panel."

Cian's face goes through the steps of a dance. The first move is dismissal, but a tap of finger to lips shifts his eyes into processing mode. His eyes brighten. "Go on."

"We'll call it *The Ship of Dreams*."

Cian cocks his head to the side. "Like the Titanic?"

"Stop now." I give his arm a playful slap. "Ship as in shipping couples, you know, putting people together in a romance."

"I'm aware of the practice."

"Our star couples compete for the audience's favor. Donal Cam and Nieve against Starry Night and Event Horizon. Here's the first kicker. Deidre LaRochelle not only moderates but delves into both onscreen romances and what makes them tick. She'll blur the line between actors and their characters. A merry chase such as this will be fair bait to lure her here. The woman loves love, and the opportunity to give her lovers the chance to shine against another popular pair is the sort of challenge she feeds on."

Cian's eyes wobble the way Bobby's do when he's streaming content through his brain. "And the second kicker?"

I stab a finger at the bullet point for MetaMeme on Cian's tablet. "We end with a concert. Do you think your fellers could play some of *The Chieftain's Son* music as well as the *Star's Shadow* songs? We include audience participation with voting along the way. A *who answered it best* live poll. I watched a hundred hours of Cali Con panels online and seen it done. Marketing will churn out paddles with pictures of the competing couples on either side."

Cian chews on a fingernail while I hold my breath to see if his wind will blow my way. His gaze remains glued to our side-by-side tablets.

After what should be long enough for any fool to make a comment or at least ask questions, I reach across the table and lay a hand on his arm. "Cian, say it now if you think the proposal is me dreaming. Do you believe it has a chance?"

He raises his head, stare boring into mine. "Holy shit, Meg. This could be huge."

I smack a hand to the table. "Massive."

"None of the other shows can touch this." Cian smashes out of his chair. He grabs the front of my robe to yank me in and crush his mouth to mine. I swear we fly across the room onto the bed, leaving robes and boxers on the carpet.

As Cian lights me up brighter than the hot streaks of sunlight breaking over the watery horizon, my mind hums with visions of victory. We have a crackin' proposal.

CHAPTER 13
GOOD MORNING TO YOU

A quiet purr pulls me through the bleary tunnel between sleep and usefulness. The electronic rooster is my cell vibrating against the glass top of the bedside table.

Cian traps me under a dual limb configuration. He drapes an arm across my shoulder and a leg is slung over mine. This is new territory for me, sharing a morning bed after a night of uncharted pleasures. In the dark, Cian encouraged boldness I'd never dared to let loose before.

Now, it's full morning, a time where flaws can't be hidden in shadows. Considering the numerous expeditions we undertook across each other's terrain last night, I should have no reason to be self-conscious about the size of my belly or bum, but I do and draw the sheet over me.

I've no idea what etiquette is for our situation. Do I slither out and dress first or wake him with a kiss? Either choice has its merits.

The cell chimes with a new voice mail. I stretch my arm to the phone so as not to wake Cian. I smile as the back of my hand brushes his limp fingers. Damn the proper thing to do, I'll check the message and then go with the morning kiss option. As I slide the cell across the sheet, Cian's snores skitter and skip as he turns away from me, taking his arm and leg with him. I nearly giggle when his unconscious ass fits against mine like we've practiced the position dozens of times.

The number of unread texts start my heart clanging with anxiety. It's barely past six. What in heaven and hell could be brewing this early? As I read, excitement sets my insides tingling.

I let out a squeak of surprise when a hand snakes down my arm to grab my phone. Cian steals it from my hand and turns it screen side down on the bed.

"I claim bed squatters right to be the only one allowed to bring that sound out of you, Meg McGrath." Cian's sleepy voice slips over my skin. A lovely part of him is pressing against my ass.

I reach behind me to assess the rising situation. "Christ sakes, man. How'd you go from zero to primed before your eyes open?"

"Who said my eyes are open?" Cian's hand covers mine, suggesting a certain rhythm to prime him to another level. "It's the great gift of morning."

"Every morning?"

He chuckles, sending a tiny gust of warmth down my spine. "Do I have the honor of being your first foray into the discovery of such a gift?"

"I'm not saying."

His other hand lifts my hair so moist lips can worship my neck. The feel of him both high and low on my body sets off my own morning gifts. I want to take him in fast and without mercy. He darts his tongue into my ear, and I reward him with a version of the squeak he's so proud to ring out of me.

"I'm honored, M-Squared."

He tenses, stopping the sly morning seduction. I bite my lip to keep from pushing him onto his back and jumping on. "Meg, is this okay?"

Damn the man. Still the considerate gentleman after the night we had and asking my permission to play on. Cian Malley spoils me, setting my emotions and desire far past boiling, a place they've no right to tread considering, at best, we've got two more nights together. Last night he said he hated our limitations. Well, by God, I'm with him there.

I flip so we are face-to-face, thread my fingers in his hair to bring him to me, and kiss him with the ferocity of a last wish. "I'm never one to refuse a gift."

We unwrap the morning gift as a preamble to getting on with the day. Once we finish and manage a duet of regular breathing, I reach for my phone. I can't find it in the sheets, so I peer off the side of the bed and see it laying on the floor in the vicinity of the now half-empty box of condoms.

Cian gives my bottom a playful slap. "What are you doing?"

I raise the box first and pop it in the bedside drawer. "Sparing housekeeping a bit of embarrassment."

"Thoughtful and beautiful," Cian says, dropping a kiss on my shoulder as I retrieve the phone.

"Who dares to message their way into our bed?"

Our bed. I like the notion of that too much. Our bed is nothing more than a few nights of lust and desire. Two very fine states of being, but I live in reality. A long dormant corner of my brain reminds me solid relationships in my own family flamed from those initial sparks of lust and desire. My sister, Taryn, was smitten with her husband, Roy, early on and it stuck. God knows my parents were bound for the altar far sooner than their folks thought wise.

My romp here with Cian lacks the gift of time to kindle. A tiny gold thread of hope dares to wrap around my heart. The Hollywood game is my dream. Once I've traded Ireland for L.A., could there be a maybe for us? I tamp down my postcoital wisps of insanity.

A look of unease crosses Cian's mushy morning face. "Dash?"

I tug the sheet to cover me up to the neck, not feeling my news is best served naked. "No, thank God." I pull in a long, slow breath to purge Dash from my thoughts. "The day Dash Everett doesn't insist on granting his sainted permission for every move I make, songbirds will fly from my ass."

Cian laughs. "That would be quite something to see. I'd better be around for it."

I wonder at Cian's freedom with the network. "How long is your leash with Dash?"

His quiet stretches enough to make me regret the question. I shouldn't have told him about my problems with Dash at all. Does it put him in a difficult position? Of anyone, Cian understands the intricacies I deal with every day on the job. I don't regret letting him in on my dilemma.

"The color of your eyes makes me crave the dark chocolate syrup I drizzle over mint chocolate chip ice cream."

The one and only time my prolonged Dublin fling took the color of my eyes into consideration at all, he'd called them bittersweet chocolate, emphasis on the bittersweet. I prefer Cian's drizzle.

Is Cian deflecting my question with the ice cream comparison? Could it be that Cian survived his own trial-by-fire from Dash and has no desire to dredge up the memory? I don't press the point. If Cian wants to elaborate on his relationship with True Time and Dash, he will. More likely, he doesn't want my position to seem any more precarious by flaunting his own security in my face. That is the gentlemanly thing to do, and he's proven himself worthy of the title.

I allow the deflection. "I'd take you for a more exotic ice cream kind of guy." I study his face. "Espresso mocha chip with a bourbon swirl."

"Mmmm," he says, nuzzling my neck. "With dark chocolate syrup."

"It's Bobby Provost blowing up my phone. He's dancing naked in the forest over our joint panel idea."

Cian's eyebrows pull together. "When did you talk to him?"

There's a teeny nudge of guilt in my belly for working while Cian slept in the aftermath of our lovemaking. "I'm not a good sleeper, and I promised Bobby I'd let him know if I came up with anything."

He sits up and scratches at his overnight growth of beard. "I take it Bobby isn't a good sleeper either."

There's an odd tone to his voice. I suppose if I'd discovered that Cian snuck out of bed to do business while I slept, I'd be a bit put off too. Best not to go down that road and ruin the glossy shine of our night together.

"It's a bit of good news for me and the both of us."

Cian puffs up his pillows and settles to hear me out. "Sir Kevin is on his way here, so True Time and Bobby greenlit previewing the premier episode of season two for *The Chieftain's Son* panel audience. The slot after us was another Carnival Studios show, so there's leeway to extend our time." I plant a hit-and-run kiss on Cian's lips. He doesn't respond the way he's been doing for the past few hours.

Cian dons a poker face. "You never mentioned you were gunning for a full episode reveal."

"I've you to thank for it."

"Me?" He frowns.

"You've got me thinking bigger than I'd ever dared. I put the bee in Bobby and Dash's bonnets yesterday afternoon about the preview being an exclusive to complement Sir Kevin's arrival."

Cian chews his lip. "The dominoes fell in your direction." He stretches and slings his legs over the side of the bed, showing me his back.

Disappointment nibbles at me. I thought he'd be more excited on my behalf. I chalk it up to morning grumps about leaving our bed to start the workday. If it wasn't for the good news, I'd be grumping along with him.

He shivers in the air conditioning and grabs the hotel robe from the floor at the end of the bed. "How does your good news include me?"

I'm a bit knocked off. He's asking a *me* and not an *us* question. "Good news for us, our shared panel."

Something in my expression must speak to him because he drops onto the bed and takes my hand. "Sorry. I've got a bad habit of detaching so I can run the day through my head when I wake up. What's our good news?" He leans on one elbow.

Relief raises the corners of my mouth. "And here I thought I was the only one with a scroll constantly blazing through my brain."

He slides a hand under my chin to guide my lips to his. We say a second good morning with a lazy kiss.

"Bobby's hell bent on convincing Deidre to moderate our shipping panel." I reorder stray locks of Cian's Nutella drizzle hair. "Those two are a mutual admiration society. Between both Bobby and Gilly making their cases, I believe we'll get her. Deidre's pushing for a commitment from True Time to bring her whole *Chieftain's Son* series to screen, not just the first five books. Bobby'll work that angle, convincing her an appearance could well tip the scales of the network decision in her favor."

In a swift attack, Cian plucks me from the sheet to dip me into the final pose of a ballroom dance. "You, my dear, are definitely a force to be reckoned with."

After a luscious kiss, he playfully pushes me away. "Time to work. Let's bang out the rest of the details, then I'll get on the horn to convince MetaMeme to join us."

"Not without a shower and a change of clothes." I steal the sheet to cover up since Cian commandeered the robe. "Meet for breakfast downstairs." I check the time, it's nearly seven. I meet Bobby at nine. "Forty-five minutes?"

"Thirty-five."

"You're bargaining with me?"

Cian crosses the room to take me in his arms. "I'll bargain for as many minutes as I can with you." Our kiss is anything but bittersweet. "While we're bargaining, may I request the honor of another night, Ms. McGrath?"

I tap a finger to his chin. "I think that can be arranged, Mr. Malley."

He kisses my forehead and leaves me standing wrapped in a sheet in front of the great glass window as he heads into shower. I slip my sore but happy body into clothes, toss shoes and tablet into my bag, and with wistful regret, leave Cian's room.

As I zip past the shallow lift bay, I smack dead into Jack. He's in running gear and dripping head to toe in sweat. He clutches my upper arms to keep me from rebounding off him and landing on my bottom.

"Whoa there, Meg. Sorry. Are you okay?"

"Please tell me you've come from the hotel gym?"

He looks guilty. "I took a fine run along the water."

"Without security?" I shake my head. I've warned both Jack and Niks not to venture out without security. Sometimes I wonder if sound comes out of my lips when I speak to them. I tone down my usual song of annoyance. I'm still in the process of repairing things with Jack after my less than supportive behavior to his marriage. I don't want to lose any ground by scolding him. "What am I going to do with you, Jack

O'Leary?" I grasp his blue-ribbon bicep and turn him toward our bank of rooms.

"I reckoned early was safe as long as I didn't collide with one of your scavenger clues."

It's my turn to take a bite of guilt sandwich for piling more obligations on Jack. "I hope you know how much I appreciate the way you put up with me. Gilly too."

Jack brushes a hand across my back. "We know your heart for the show is what drives you."

We. I look up at this kind soul. He and Gilly make *we* a place to long for. As short-lived as the *we* Cian and me will make, I'm glad for it.

My hotel room comes up first. I open the door with the keycard. "I'll see you and Gilly at noon at the restaurant with Bobby's new Jack Daniel's steak obsession." I consider spilling the Sunday slot details but decide to wait until I can paint a clearer scenario about the benefits of yet another obligation piled on to Jack's weekend. My laser focus today must be the main show panel and the avalanche of app subscriptions I'm praying it sets off. "We have a lot to review before this afternoon gets going."

"We'll be there." Spots of heat rise on my cheeks when I catch Jack glancing past me at the far too-perfectly made bed for the early hour. His eyes switch back to me and take inventory of my uncharacteristically loose hair and rumpled clothing. The easy smile on his face doesn't tease or judge. It's warm with a nod of congratulations as if I've just won top honors. Jack, bless him, leaves it at that and heads to his own bed.

I shut the door and lean against it, an idiotic smile on my face with thoughts of Cian. Sharing *our* bed for another night will be grand, but I'm also jiggly with the joy of talking with him over breakfast. I crave his company and comradery as well as his other talents. "Top honors, to be sure."

I've an urge to call my sister, Taryn. Who else can I gush and giggle with about hooking up with a man who'd be exactly what I'd custom order from a menu? I'm sure Maureen will corner me for Cian details soon, but I'm not keen on talking with anyone from the show. God knows Dash can't get wind of how far his suggestion of Cian *showing me the ropes* has gone, not when the Bossman's opinion of my competence already teeters on disastrous.

I feel in my bones I'm close to turning him around with *The Chieftain's Son* strong showing at Cali Con.

CHAPTER 14
THE HOT GUY PANEL

The crowd on the convention floor exploded since Cian and I checked out the True Time booth on Wednesday. Taryn begged me for a *Star's Shadow* robot dress she'd seen someone wearing online. It'd been a helluva hunt, but I tracked one down.

This festival of nerd-dom isn't exclusively Dungeons and Dragons gamers with tape on their glasses or legions of pop culture cosplayers. Sure, those fans are represented, but everyone from families, couples in matching outfits, and solo guests craning their necks to take in statues of giant robots, to folks who look as if they've strolled in from a beach picnic are in the mix.

I'm told it's abject madness to secure passes to Cali Con. These people glued themselves to computer screens and prayed personal longing would be enough to gain them admittance. I'm a bit awed by the perseverance it takes to walk these aisles or park your carcass into a seat hours before a favorite panel to insure your place in the room.

After getting my foot run over twice by buggies with small wailing children, I give up on civility and use my shoulder to carve a path between a T-shirt booth towering up to the ceiling and a trio of superheroes built entirely of LEGO® blocks to make my way to the True Time booth.

The line for *The Chieftain's Son* fur-covered bed photo-op snakes out of sight. I grab my tall, sandy-haired booth lead and hand off the box of postcards with the details of my *Win an Adventure with Jack O'Leary* promotion. God bless the True Time marketing department for their lightning speed, and the O'Learys' willingness to run with my intrusive idea.

"Hide 'em good until after the end of *The Chieftain's Son* panel. I don't want any leaks before our reveal." I chew on my lip. "Bust them out at half-six." When the tunic-clad clansman looks confused, I translate. "Six thirty."

"Will do," he says, stowing the box under a curtained table.

"My man Chip will bring you more boxes for Saturday and Sunday. How are you on giveaway merch?"

"Lookin' good, Ms. McGrath." He shoots me a thumbs up.

"I'll leave you to it then," I say and nod at the bed. "Thanks for holding down the furs."

The route through the lobby of the events center and up the moving stairs requires a shoving strategy as well. I meet up with Jack, Gilly, and Maureen in a secure ready room. They mingle with the rest of the panel participants waiting to be escorted to The Grand Ballroom. Security forms a loose perimeter around the throng, protecting but not interfering. My folks wear green wristbands of the chosen few who will mount daises throughout the day to bestow their presence on adoring fans.

"Ready, Jack?" I ask.

He shrugs his shoulders. "Is any fool ever really ready for these things?"

I point a finger at him. "If any fool is, it'll be you. Do you want us to wait and walk over with you?"

His smile is for Gilly alone. "Go on. I'll see you after." He touches two fingers to his lips.

We three women head toward the Grand Ballroom doors with our magic green wristbands. I lay a hand on Gilly's arm before we pop in. "Maureen, do you mind seeing to our seats? We'll be right along."

She tosses me a look of, *"You'll be explaining later."* "Sure."

As soon as we're alone, I lay what I hope feels like a sisterly hand on Gilly's shoulder. I can tell she's wary. A rush of sympathy for her warms my chest. "I feel I owe you a private apology for hitting you with both the scavenger hunt and the adventure day with Jack without discussing it first."

Her shrug telegraphs her distaste of both my brainchildren. Instead of making eye contact, her gaze locks on the blue California sky outside the wall of glass.

"I regret that thinking on my feet hasn't been kind to either you or Jack. Please understand I only intend the plans to boost the show."

Her smile is sad and full of resignation. "I get it."

I breath in courage. "I've been insensitive to ignore the personal impact on you." I've categorized Jack and Gilly as an impediment instead of being awed two people who deserve it have found one another. Cian is to blame or to thank for such an epiphany. The bead of cynicism I've kept so close over the concept of finding your perfect match, or dare I say, soulmate like Gilly and Jack begins to shatter. Before these last couple of days, I never believed in quick and powerful connections like the one I've made with Cian. Even if it can't last, it's been a gift to know it's possible.

"The ideas and decisions I've thrown at you and Jack are about an ideal image, not reality." Gilly stares at me as if she can't believe she's hearing these words come out of my mouth. "I am truly sorry I've been less than supportive of your relationship and marriage. It won't be the case anymore."

Gilly's eyes glisten. Oh Lord, I've gone and turned on her tears again.

"And for the record, the two of you are grand together."

I stumble backward from the force of Gilly's hug. "You don't know how much those words mean to me, Meg. It's been so hard."

I return the hug with the silent sisterhood of those who've found a light in someone else to make their own shine brighter. "I'll do my part to change up a bit." I break off. "Let's go watch your man dazzle the room."

Maureen waves us to a block of empty chairs in the first row and we sit. The sound of more than four thousand voices gives The Grand Ballroom the feel of a living entity. I peer at the back of the room.

"Maureen, can you tell how full it is?"

"Looks bursting to me," she says, holding a hand over her eyes to block out the glare from a giant screen.

Fantastic. I'm confident a lordly share of the crowd has come to see Jack.

Maureen tugs at my sleeve to whisper. "Your dinner guest is playing at something up there." She nods in the direction of the dais.

I spot Cian right away. He's chatting up one of the Con personnel. "Playing at what?"

"He's swapped positions of the nametags."

A nasty chill runs down my spine. "What do you mean?"

"Jack was in the spot next to the moderator, but now he's bumped to second spot."

Gilly stands. "That's not fair."

My chill ignites into anger. "It's more than not fair. I negotiated positions." Leaving the two ladies behind, I stalk up to Cian. "Well, here's a tip you never shared with me, last-minute name swapping."

He's rattled, as he should be, at being caught in the act. "It's not what it looks like?"

"So, it's not you switching your boy into Jack's position?"

Surprise shifts to tight lips. "It was True Time's call, not mine."

I shake my cell at him. "A call I didn't get from them or you."

Tight lips bloom into an angry scowl to match mine. "I don't have a crystal ball to know when Dash is keeping you in the dark."

Fingernails press into my palm. "After what I told you about my situation, I think it's clear I'm purposefully in the dark when it comes to the boss man."

Before we continue, one of the Con folks asks us to take our seats. I'm fuming as I drop down next to Maureen.

Cian tails me. "Would you ladies mind scooting down so I can sit next to Meg?"

"Our pleasure," says Maureen, shifting seats before the reserved section fills with publicists and guests of the panelists.

"Look, Meg," Cian tries to take my hand, but I pull free. The look of hurt in his eyes makes me as low as a bottom-feeding river fish. "The reason they moved Malakai Bono from my show into Jack's spot is because *Star's Shadow* needs the boost."

Curiosity tempers my anger. "Boost?"

The strain on his lovely face intensifies. "*The Chieftain's Son* is kicking our ass in bringing in new app subscriptions."

I jab my screen to check emails. Sure enough, there's one waiting for me with the latest tally of which True Time show is credited with the rise in subscribers. We're in first place with a decent gap before *Star's Shadow's* second place. It's working. My mad scavenger hunt, the photo op in the booth, the building wrap, and everything else I've set in place for my show are paying off.

"I assume new subscriptions are part of the blood sacrifice Dash demands from you to keep your job." There's a bite to Cian's tone. His eyes fix on the dais.

I deserve his agitation after being quite the dark witch to Cian just now. After everything he's done for me, and with me, I accused him of sabotage without giving the man a breath to explain. For the love of Mommy's boxty pancakes, we're good faith partners on a rock-solid proposal for a panel sure to be chosen for Harborview Hall honors. My lips still bear the imprint of his goodbye kiss from breakfast, yet I went raging at him. What's wrong with me? Cian's got cause for bitterness after my madwoman charge.

"Dashell shoulda cut me in on the change." Wrong choice. Too defensive. I should come in softer. I am pathetic at personal. My old habits don't die hard, they take a bite out of folks.

Cian whips his head to face me. "Well, now you know." He turns away, arms crossed.

I've definitely stepped in it. Damn my full-steam-ahead default. "Cian." My voice is drowned out by the introduction of the moderator, Hooper Katt, the handsome with a Jimmy Smits vibe, fifty-something male lead of *Truth, Justice, and the American Dream*. Maureen leans over Gilly to loud whisper. "If he's a promise of things to come, I see why they call this the hot guy panel."

Hooper holds his arms wide to the room, acknowledging their reception. "Thank you, Cali Con!" More applause fills the space. "Welcome to *Is it Hot in Here or is it Just Me?*" He fans his face to another swell of approval.

When I turn back to Cian with an apology tingling on my lips, his rigid posture nearly makes me lose my nerve. I lay a hand on his arm. "I'm sorry. I was an ass for jumping all over you."

There's no heat from this hot guy.

The room explodes when Malakai Bono and Jack O'Leary enter the scene.

I risk sliding my hand to Cian's and try to twine my fingers with his. He neither resists nor welcomes the contact. It's like petting a slab of rock. "Can I buy you an apology whiskey later? Or two?"

From the row behind us, someone calls Cian's name. I recognize Chip and other faces from the *Star's Shadow* team who beckon him to an empty seat in their midst.

"Business," is all he says before slipping off.

CHAPTER 15
TIME TO SHINE

A human wall of security surrounds the members of *The Chieftain's Son* panel as we exit golf carts that whisked us to a discreet events center entrance. Fans holler, hoping to get a slice of attention from Jack, Niks, Cici Storm, and even Bobby as we make our way inside. Sir Kevin might as well be wearing a shroud he's so bundled up in hood, hat, and sunglasses so he isn't recognized before the reveal.

Cici threads her arm through Jack's as we make our way inside. "You were hilarious on *Hot Guy*. Any more jokes up your sleeve for ours?"

The way Cici fawns over Jack makes me grateful Gilly doesn't keep a knife tucked in her belt the way Nieve does on the show. We're led into the same small room behind a row of black drapes designated as a green room, where panelists and their handlers wait. It's a short walk from here to the side door of The Grand Ballroom. Everyone is prepped and primed.

I take a head count and come up one short. "Where's Artie?" Arthur Boyd, our Bowstring and comic relief, isn't with the pack.

"Here," he calls from the doorway, chewing on a soft pretzel.

"You nipped out for food?" I bite my tongue to keep from a full scolding.

"Where's mine?" says Jack, using the request as an excuse to peel himself off Cici.

Artie tears off a hunk of his salty treat and hands it to him. "What's mine is yours, my chieftain," says Artie with a bow.

While they continue to mess about, I check my phone for the hundredth time since Bobby told me to expect a call from Deidre. Nothing yet. The name I most want to see doesn't grace my screen either. Cian promised he'd join me in the audience for *The Chieftain's Son* panel as moral support. I know he's out there now for the *Star's Shadow* panel.

Business.

My mind comes up with dozens of interpretations of what Cian meant by *business*. I hope it referred to his obligations to his show and people. I'm gutted to think it meant everything between us from now on must be strictly business after I jumped down the man's throat over nametags.

Didn't I make my heart a promise to keep it shallow and fun with Cian? In true Meg McGrath form, I barreled forward with the man and created damage to tidy up in the wake of my impulses. I spent years teaching myself to assess before I leap. With the stakes of Cali Con so high for my future, I got sloppy. I can't afford another slip.

Bobby nudges my elbow. Discreetly, he nods to where Henry Troost, our season one chieftain, Rory O'Connor, is flashing a sour milk face in the direction of Sir Kevin Langston, our season two chieftain, Brian Boru. Sir Kevin retains a proper entourage of clothes fluffers and hair straighteners. He's quite the peacock.

"Ladies and gentlemen, welcome to the chieftain smack down," Bobby whispers to me. When I don't laugh, he lays a hand on my shoulder. "It's all good, Meg. You've done a perfect job upping the ante on our show panel."

A smile breaks through my nerves and I pat his hand. "The lot of you will be grand out there."

"Grand or brilliant?"

Before I can answer, he nods to the doorway. I follow his gaze and nearly drop dead when Deidre LaRochelle marches into the room.

Our group breaks into applause as herself drops into a curtsey.

My eyes dart to my phone as if I've missed the message announcing our grand dame's entrance. "How, when..." I stammer.

Bobby throws an arm around my shoulder. "Very last minute. Obviously. You know Deidre. I didn't want to say anything until we saw the whites of her eyes."

In a panic, I check Deidre's wrist for the band that grants her celebrity entry privileges. It's there. She's here.

"True Time fast-tracked the logistics with Dash's blessing," says Bobby as Deidre performs a round of cheek kissing. "Surprise." Our showrunner is as pleased with himself as he's ever been.

My heart turns to stone and sinks to the bottom of my stomach. I know Bobby's thinking he's given me a massive Christmas morning gift, but he's shot an arrow straight through me. Dash will find out coaxing Deidre is Bobby's doing, not mine. He aimed a fecking spotlight at the lie I told Dash about securing Deidre LaRochelle.

"Is she in for Sunday as well?"

My question is clearly shy of the grateful reaction Bobby expected. His thinking eye wobble takes off at a gallop.

I hop in before he settles on something unpleasant and wave my hands as if I'm erasing the question. "Well done, Bobby. Well done."

He side-eyes me. The man is too intuitive not to realize I'm hiding something. Thankfully, Deidre's rounds catch up with us.

"You're very welcome to Cali Con, Deidre," I say.

"Thank our girl there." She throws a kiss to Gilly. "Seeing this insanity through fresh eyes kicked the ass of my jaded perspective. I'm all yours, Meg."

I click straight into P.R. mode. "I've got two exclusive signings on hold for tomorrow if you're game. We'll have a ticket drawing at the booth for folks to attend. My big ask is for you to lead a panel on Sunday."

"I knew you'd keep me hopping, Meg." Deidre pats my shoulder. "Corner me later, and I'll sign in blood."

I do corner Cici Storm and force her to quickly add Deidre details and questions for our first lady in her moderator script. Thinking on my feet fills me with a rush of confidence as I reshape the panel. I can finally answer Dash's question.

Is it enough?

Yes, Dashell Everett, it fucking is.

And then it's time. I leave my folks to double check name tags and answer any last-minute questions from The Grand Ballroom crew. Everything is in place. All that's left for me is to sit and pray.

I make my way to the first row of seats. There are two left. The rest are filled with the man himself, Dashell Everett, and a handful of other True Time suits. Dash nods at me, and I stroll over to him, trying to come off sure, but not cocky.

"Meg." He sticks out a hand for me to shake. "Your scavenger hunt is causing quite a stir."

"And we're only half done," I say.

End of conversation. He turns to his cronies. Not a word over the streaming app subscriptions, Deidre, or questions about my proposal for Sunday. Is he miffed I didn't consult him for approval on my impromptu hunt first? I'm sure he plans to take credit himself for anything I pull off. Does he regret our deal? His brevity doesn't give me a whit of confidence.

Claiming one of the empty reserved seats, I scan the area for Cian. In a last ditch hope he'll keep his word, I set my bag on the chair next to me. Assistants, guests of the panel, and the ever-present Chip fill the row behind me. The face I long to see doesn't appear from the shadows of The Grand Ballroom.

Taryn once confessed her wedding day was a blur. She had dribs and drabs of specific memories, but it mostly runs together like water on a still wet painting. That's how the panel goes for me.

Cici spews banality as she fangirls over Jack at the introductions. As I hastily scripted, Deidre appears unannounced and brings the crowd to glorious madness. The reveal of Sir Kevin Langston as Brian Boru nearly rips the roof off the ballroom. Henry Troost, Sir Kevin, and Jack improvise a passing-of-the-baton interchange from chieftain to chieftain that turns out to be truly moving. Bobby shares the story of our production setting off a location fire in Northern Ireland during season one. His expert charm skills were required to allow the show to use the place again.

The Q & A portion strings me as tight as Artie Boyd's bowstring. Deidre deftly fields a question on the topic of her not being Irish.

"Darling, once you've stepped foot in Ireland, you'd sell your soul to be Irish. Writing *The Chieftain's Son* stories is my soul price."

Of course, there's the inevitable question about Jack and Niks being engaged. Maureen stands up, raising her arms to the sky.

"Step aside, Ms. Tellefson, I'm Jack O'Leary's fiancée."

What in the bejaysus is the woman doing? I grip the seat on my chair and nearly snap my fingernails.

Cici Storm is next to chime in. "Take a seat, Maureen, I'm Jack O'Leary's fiancée."

On the heels of her proclamation, Artie Boyd stands. "How dare you both? I am Jack O'Leary's fiancée."

The audience bellows with laughter as Jack's face flames red. Thank the Lord, he and Gilly avoid eye contact.

To my horror, Deidre commands the crowd's attention. "We've only one blushing bride on this panel, our darling Gillian Bettencourt."

Oh, holy hell. Gilly looks terrified. Jack, thank Christ, saves the day. He pounds a fist on the table. "Damn the lucky bastard who beat the rest of us to you."

Niks playfully slaps him, and equilibrium is reestablished. I'd bet Mommy's prize-winning cottage pie the video of this panel will be watched a thousand times for hints the day news of Jack and Gilly's wedding becomes public.

A question flies to Gilly and Maureen from a woman in a white wig dressed in an impressive copy of Nieve's green gown and fur-lined collar from our building wrap. "How close are the writers to the cast?"

Unable to contain themselves, the two fools, Gilly and Maureen burst out in laughter. Maureen grabs the mic they share. "Close enough to touch."

The last question is to Deidre concerning her ability to sustain interest in Donal Cam and Nieve over so many books. She gazes out over the audience as if she's sitting down to a cozy meal with them instead of a woman addressing nearly five thousand hearts.

"Imagine passion as a sky so blue no name or label will do its color justice, or the miracle of waves endlessly singing their song to the shore. Do we ever tire of such things? No. So it is with love."

I understand why applause can be called thunderous. The term does not rise from hyperbole. The reaction to Deidre's statement sets the walls and floor to rumbling, as a roar fills my ears. Vibrations rise up chair legs and end in the roots of my teeth. All we need is lightning and we'd be in a proper storm. I stare at my bag, taking up the seat beside me. I ache to have Cian next to me, hearing Deidre's words and wondering if somewhere inside them we might find a chance to exist.

But he is not here. He did not hear her words. That's my doing.

Cici Storm's reveal of the *Win an Adventure Day with Jack O'Leary* contest and Bobby's announcement the folks gathered in The Grand Ballroom will be treated to the premier episode of season two brings forth wave after wave of monstrous approval.

As soon as the room goes dark and the first shot of Jack in his golden-haired glory awakening by the River Boyne fills the screens, I watch my pre-scheduled flurry of tweets, posts, and new pictures from the panel blaze across the Internet. Scores of hashtags old and new for the contest, the premier Cali Con exclusive, Sir Kevin Langston as Brian Boru, Deidre's quote on love, and the promise of a new scavenger hunt clue coming soon explode online. My "invitation" to subscribe to the True Time streaming app with a nudge to credit *The Chieftain's Son* for signing up is my posting finale. As soon as I brief Deidre on her schedule, I'll cloister in my room and flood the rest of social media with more *Chieftain's Son* news. I feel the void of not having an assistant or two.

The dais is empty. My people are gone. The two rows of reserved seats are vacant except for me, and the ghost of the man who never showed up.

My proposal needs polish. Will it be *Ship of Dreams* with Cian's show or is Meg McGrath a solo act once again? An empty chair is a very loud answer.

CHAPTER 16

TRACTION

Gillian Bettencourt is a better human being than I will ever be. I torture the woman by parading her husband around like a prize rooster, yet here she sits with Maureen across from me at the table in my hotel room to help me write the next scavenger hunt clue.

When Gilly checks her watch, Maureen knocks knees with her. "Is it time to wake the hubs up from his power nap?"

Gilly shakes her head. "I've got a few minutes. He wants to eat before we hit the True Time party boat."

"Party boat," shouts Maureen as she pops out of her chair to execute a very hip-thrusty dance move. I love the woman dearly, but subtle is not in her wheelhouse.

I slide a pen behind my ear. "It's no party. Believe me. We kiss asses, make nice with the execs, and dodge inappropriate questions from the likes of Cici Storm."

Gilly looks pained. Maureen throws an arm around her shoulders. "Think of me as your date instead of that blond brute you cavort with. I'll show you a grand time."

I twirl my hand over the table, eager to put the next leg of the hunt behind me. "Let's finish. Time's a-wasting. Read me tonight's clue once more before I unleash it."

Maureen lifts the pad she's scribbled on. "To rendezvous with our couple fair, seek moon shine at True three-quarter Time, lighting their golden hair. A fleeting glimpse may come your way where boats in line do gently sway behind the place you've spent your day."

Gilly taps a pen on the table. "Except for the time, it's super on the nose."

I tap the table. "Point taken. The bitty sidewalk behind the events center could clog up fast."

"On the other hand, the clue is going live with not a whole lot of time to crack it. There is a bit of buffer since they want us on the boat earlier," says Gilly. "Technically, we'll be pulling out of the slip by nine."

Maureen chews on a pen. "True three-quarter Time could be interpreted as eight forty-five instead of nine. That'll kill the buffer." She starts muttering rhymes. "Nine, sublime, dime, slime…"

I swipe at my cell. *The Chieftain's Son* is blowing up on social media thanks to our brilliant panel. Details are leaking like mad online even though our screening of the premier episode isn't even finished yet over in The Grand Ballroom.

Maureen plops her elbows on the table and leans on them. "You'll have a right fam jam mess on your hands, Megsie, if you make the clue too easy peasy."

I frown at Maureen for the "Megsie."

Gilly jabs a pencil at Maureen's pad. "What if you cut out the last part and don't capitalize the True and the Time?"

I nod. "Then we don't advertise the True Time party boat outright." I rework the clue on my tablet.

To rendezvous with our couple fair, clock's three-quarter time will light their golden hair. A fleeting glimpse may come your way where watercraft do gently sway.

I chew on my lower lip as I slide my screen so Gilly and Maureen can see my revision. "It still feels like a bloody signpost pointing straight to the marina." If I hadn't mucked it up with Cian, he would be here now, chiming in.

Gilly looks out the window. "Okay, we lost *the place you've spent your day,* and since the marina stretches almost all the way to the airport, our clue is murkier."

Maureen slams a hand on the table. "Another fix. Don't give 'em as much time as you've been doing. Release the clue at eight or even a quarter past. They'll scatter up and not figure out the exact spot until the True Time party boat is spotted. No time to form a mob."

I nod. "And if Jack and Niks are on board by half-eight, they won't jam up the works signing autographs on their way to the boat. It'll just be a smile-and-wave encounter. I'll have our folks from the booth hand out swag to fans." I blow out a long breath. "It's done then. Thank you both. I'll be tapping you for the Saturday clue as well."

Gilly looks a bit green. "Once they figure it out, won't the fans wait for the boat to come back?"

"No worries there," I say. "The party cruise isn't ending in the same spot we started to avoid True Time's stars being overwhelmed. The network lined up ample security for the back end." I shove her foot with my chair. "Now go wake your man and get food down his gullet."

Maureen plops bare feet on the table. "What does one wear to a party boat?"

I need to shoo them. Cian's disappearing act makes it clear I've got to write a new panel proposal for my show alone in less than two hours before the bloody party boat nightmare begins. Now that Deidre is a go, there are more *Chieftain's Son* exclusive resources to work with. Judging from the reactions to our posts across social media, Cali Con can't get enough of our show.

I stand. "I'll see you all at eight in Bobby's suite. We'll go down together from there."

Maureen jumps to her feet and salutes me. "Aye, aye captain."

As soon as the door closes, I schedule my scavenger hunt tweet, and stare at a new blank page. "All right then, Meghan, what's your Harborview Hall Plan B?"

In those wee hours while I watched Cian sleep, my first grain of an idea was a rags-to-riches panel. Jack was a small-town Irish boy who worked his way up the ladder from stage to supporting actor in a sitcom to a fecking god. Gilly went from writing about fancy clothes to a Crystal Award nomination in a year. Deidre was a high school history teacher who had a hankering to see Ireland. It's the Everyman angle. Totally relatable.

My fingers fly across the keys, painting a scenario, until I hit a wall. I'm not feeling the sizzle I did when I envisioned the *Ship of Dreams* panel. Gazing out the window, I speak to the clouds. "What bit is missing?" No revelation rains from the sky to answer me.

I've got three different paths in my plan but no connection. Just the fact they've all landed on the same show isn't enough. I pace while tapping a pen to my lips, then it comes to me.

"Bobby Provost," I inform the clouds.

Our showrunner is my glue. Every dream needs a believer, and Bobby is that person for every one of us. Our panel will be a celebration of potential. Personal journeys. Inspiration. It'll give our fans hope someday they might find a golden path to their dreams.

Is it enough?

Dash's challenge is a fear that never leaves me. As the sun rose over Cali Con, my *Ship of Dreams* idea grew legs and danced as Cian and I fleshed it out. Our proposal was truly *enough* on the Dash scale of excellence. How fast a dream can die.

I've glazed the top of my new offering with a shiny coat of sugar when there's a knock at my door. Actually, it's a bang—most likely from housekeeping in a final offer to freshen my towels before they head home for the night.

"Thanks all the same, but I'm fine," I call out and glance at the time. I've barely burned fifteen minutes redesigning our shot at Harborside Hall. Mommy always says when something is right, it flows like water from the faucet. I email a draft of the proposal to Bobby. I'm hoping we can steal time on the boat to add a bit more luster. I'd grab him sooner, but he and Gilly's folks are squeezing in one more production designer interview over dinner before the True Time promo cruise.

Clunk. A fist connects with the door.

I flash an annoyed glance. "Who is it?"

Clunk. Clunk.

Someone's playing games with me, and I'm in no mood for it. If it's Maureen asking about her boat attire, we're going to have words. I stomp barefoot to the door and throw it open to find a bottle of Jameson Gold Reserve whiskey and two Glencairn whiskey glasses hovering before my eyes. Cian halts his attempt to thump his elbow on the door.

"I believe I'm the one who owes you whiskey," says Cian.

I'm a steel and glass tower with a foundation of surprise and a cap of confusion. Cian foots the door to keep it from closing.

"May I come in?"

I step aside without a word and let him pass. Once again, I'm leaning on the inside of a hotel room door while Cian Malley graces the middle of the room.

He cracks open the bottle and pours us both a glass.

"Ice?"

Crossing the room, I take the glass from his hand and throw back dark amber liquid. "No thanks."

"I've heard apology goes down smoother with a whiskey chaser."

"You've nothing to apologize for." Except for stomping off like a child and standing me up at the panel where he promised to support me. Mercy, I sound like a neglected wife. This man owes me nothing. Cian's got his own show and business to attend to, not to mention I was a rare tosser to him first.

He stares at the whiskey in his glass, giving it a swirl before he drinks. "There's something I haven't told you, Meg." He stares me down. "I can be a real ass."

Ass or not, a part of me that should be locked up tight so it doesn't get me in any deeper with him than I already am is very glad he's here.

I pour more whiskey into my glass, and slowly inhale its healing aroma. "Ah, there's another bit we have in common."

Cian's eyes stretch into two perfect circles under raised eyebrows.

I swallow more whiskey. "I led with a bite over the name tag switching before giving you a chance to explain, then went cold on you —something I promised I'd stop doing. There's the apology I'll be washing down with more of this fine stuff."

We stand like two eejits in a staring contest.

Cian breaks the standoff and collapses into the chair lately vacated by Gilly and drops his head into his hands. "It was a slap in the face you thought I was trying to pull something on you. My reaction was completely over-sensitive." He scratches at his hair before looking at me. "That's not me. Shit usually rolls off my back. I don't allow anyone to make me feel the way you did, especially over a less than nothing issue." Cian shakes his head. "It blew my mind you could so easily throw me off my game."

I drop into the chair across from him. He's speaking a language I understand, one I can translate. "We're sharing a problem here, Cian. I've already told you I'm much better as a *'me'* than a *'we.'* I sense the same tendency still lingering in you even if you've come farther from it than I have. We're nearsighted fools." I laugh, focusing in on a truth. "Here we've cozied into a bit of a *'we'* situation."

His shoulders droop. "Nearsighted fools? Were we lonely and pathetic before?"

"Neither. *Me* is how I raised up *The Chieftain's Son*. I learned not to depend on anyone but myself, and I'm blazing dependable." I shift my gaze to the window. "It's too easy for others to let you down." I meet his eyes. "Or take you down."

He adds another splash of whiskey to our glasses. "To clarify, we're paranoid instead of pathetic?"

"Let's leave it at...we prefer to set the pace instead of following it." I raise my glass and Cian clinks his against it.

"What do you Irish say?"

"Sláinte."

"Sláinte," he says, savoring the toast as much as the whiskey. "And how do you say 'I'm sorry'?"

"Oh, that'll do fine."

I hadn't realized how heavily the spill of bad blood between us had weighed me down. Relief lifts the rock from my chest.

"You didn't need to come here with your fine spirit and spirits, but I'm glad you did." I turn the glass in a circle on the table. "We're game pieces an ocean apart, serving the same master. Let's drink to our moments together here at Cali Con."

"What if we had the chance for more moments?"

I give him a sad smile. "During the weekend?"

Cian lays his hand on mine. "I came to *The Chieftain's Son* panel."

My body gives a little shake of surprise. "Why?"

"I promised." He twines his fingers through mine and squeezes. "Even an ass can keep his promise."

"What are you on about? Asking after chances to be more and keeping promises?"

He leans forward until his forehead touches the tabletop. "I have no idea." Cian slowly lifts his darling face to look me in the eye. "It may sound idiotic, but you need to know you mean something to me, M-Squared."

His blue beauties continue to peer up at me. "I'm not the type who genuinely clicks with people right away even though I'm excellent at giving that impression. It's part of the game, but it's not true in most cases." He slides a hand up my thigh. "This thing between you and me... You can't deny it's an honest-to-God click."

"Click, huh? Is that the California term for falling into bed?"

He squeezes, sending a jolt from his fingers straight under my skirt. "I'm not kidding, Meg. I make a conscious effort to avoid clicking, and I think you do too. Yet here we are."

I've been feeling the fool but sitting right here is a man who's fallen down the hole alongside me. We're not playing a game with each other. Given the choice, I'm certain neither of us would sign up for this. "Dare I say the term you might be looking for, Mr. Malley, is kindred spirits."

He rolls the idea around. "While I like the sound of that as I sit here, thinking how much I want the opportunity to talk with you every day, spar with you, pick your brain and..." A smile sneaks onto his lips. "Slip into bed with you, it also unnerves the shit out of me."

Unnerving is the perfect word for the skitters inside me. "Like you're breaking your own rules?"

Cian lets go of me and raises his glass. "Sláinte to that."

I clink my glass to his, and we drink.

Cian relaxes into his chair. "Does the appearance of Deidre LaRochelle bode well for our *Ship of Dreams* panel?"

We're back to *our*. I shouldn't be as happy as I am. Cian and I have a big red expiration date stamped across our asses. Working together is a one-and-done. "She's in. What about your folks?"

He's up and pacing the room. "Malakai Bono is in, but I'm waiting for a green light from Sala Singh's people."

"When'll you know?"

He rolls his shoulders and then shrugs. "Waiting for the call makes me crazy. Unfinished business is my kryptonite."

I grin like a fool. "I believe we are cut from the same cloth, sir."

He stands and lifts me to my feet. "That's what makes us a winning team." His hands slide down my sides to my hips. With a swift jerk, he pulls me flush against him.

As his lips brush mine, I whisper. "General wisdom warns matching personalities may rip each other to shreds. It's the knowing of each other's weaknesses that's the danger."

"Permission to rip you to shreds?" he asks before diving into the type of kiss I thought I'd forfeited after the way I'd treated him at the name tag incident.

I run my hands across his shoulders and into his hair as the kindling of our apologies burst into flames. His touch is everywhere, under my skirt, down my blouse. We fall onto the bed and roll with each kiss, trading the top spot. I'm so ready for him, the next switch may be our last.

Suddenly, Cian pushes up away from me. "Shit."

I don't bother to catch my breath before asking, "What?"

His face pinks up. "The necessary equipment for our current activity is in my room."

My fingers trail down the alluring bulge filling the front of his slacks. "Not all of it." The darling moan from his slightly puffy lips drives me closer to losing my own power of speech.

"I'll grab them and come back."

I roll him again so I'm top dog. "What do you say to a houseguest?"

He sits up so I'm in his lap. "I say, bust out the welcome mat."

We jump off the bed, and he takes my hand. I grab my bag with the other and we make tracks to his room. Once the door slams, we leave a fine trail of clothing to his bed. Our bed.

I've never experienced a man being so gentle yet tantalizingly rough at the same time. I'm no demure, little flower as I match his grind and take him full in. Our lovely bout is quick but efficient.

Lying on our backs with legs tangled, Cian collects my hand and brings it to his lips. "You'll spend tonight with me, Meg?" He leans his head on my shoulder. "I want another chance to see the way the morning light catches those lovely streaks of auburn hiding in your hair."

I rest my head against his. "It might be very late when I come to you. I'll be at Bobby Provost's mercy on the cruise and after tonight."

He kisses my temple. "I don't care."

Cian is like the first bite of food you take after you swear up and down you're not hungry. As soon as flavor hits your tongue, you're suddenly ravenous for the rest of what's on the plate in front of you. I'm starving to give Cian more value than a brilliant weekend ride. "What's your favorite book?"

He pulls back to look me in the eye. I see the question strikes him as odd, but then he laughs in his special way that says he's enjoying me. "I never know what's going to come out of these lips." Cian presses his mouth to mine, initiating an *I've got all the time in the world* kiss. Somewhere in the middle, he says, "*How to Think Like Leonardo DaVinci.* Have you read it?"

I shake my head. "But I will."

He drizzles kisses across my jaw to my ear. "Yours?"

"*The Importance of Being Earnest.*"

My answer brings him up short. "A play? Huh, I never expected you to favor the story of people pretending to be someone they are not."

I tilt my head. "And why is that?"

"You're so straightforward and honest. My no-nonsense M-Squared."

My alarm sounds. "Holy mother." I've got less than half an hour to rinse off and change before I meet my people for the damnable True Time party boat. I'm up out of bed, diving for clothes.

Cian, sharing a similar timetable, tosses me pieces of my outfit from the floor as he rushes toward the bathroom. "I'm going to hop in the shower. See you on the high seas." He plants a kiss on my lips, earning gold medals for both brevity and intensity before he closes the door.

Once I've covered the necessary bits, I reach for my bag next to Cian's cell on the table. A text message buzzes in for him. I check it out of reflex before my brain registers the text is none of my business.

It's from Sala Singh, *Starry Night*, to fans of *Star's Shadow*.

Are we still on for the Sunday panel? Must chat re: script changes.

I stare at the screen. *Still* on for Sunday? That makes no sense. Cian said he was waiting for confirmation from Sala's people. Why is the woman herself hailing him? Script changes? What script? Cian and I finished a rough outline for the panelists at breakfast. There's no script.

A dark and twisty storm rises in my gut. Is Sala Singh, Cian's leading lady, talking about *Ship of Dreams* or another scenario not shared with me?

I surge to the bathroom door with a plan to fling it open and demand clarification. As soon as I touch the knob, a gust of doubt blows Hurricane Meg back offshore. Here I go again, ready to jump down the man's throat. I take three deep breaths. One for me, one for Cian, and one for good sense. It does the trick to help me see the logical and quite simple explanation here. Cian's done the same as me after our rocky afternoon by rustling up a solo panel idea in case my people don't come through for our joint *Ship of Dreams*. His Plan B. What else could Ms. Singh's text possibly refer to?

I step back from the door and swallow the last drabs of suspicion burning my throat. "Cut from the same cloth indeed."

CHAPTER 17

PARTY BOAT

My *Chieftain's Son* clan and I stare out the window of Bobby's room at the gaudy replica of a Hawaiian luau venue docked in the marina.

Maureen barks out a laugh. "There's the tackiest thing I've ever seen."

"Will it stay afloat?" asks Grady.

The top deck of the ship is spotted with fake palm trees scattered next to Tiki huts with sun-faded palm frond roofs. The taco bar Cian took me to at the Hotel Joya Brillante is a five-star establishment next to this farce of tropical paradise. Mounted high on one end of the ship is a giant screen. Flashing against the dimming sky are montages from True Time's most popular shows as well as teasers for next season's new offerings.

"Aloha," says Jack, emphasizing the "ha."

Niks claps her hands. "We'll do the hula dance up there, yes?"

I'd heard snippets of Dash bragging about his party boat at the meeting in his suite. Did he bother to preview this cheesy spectacle? If size matters, he got what he paid for. The tropical nightmare is massive.

Near the floating monstrosity where prop palm trees go to die, my scavenger hunters at #FindJack&Niks will have no trouble zeroing in on their favorite couple's whereabouts. Spying a mob of spectators pressing against the circle of security, I brush the air with my hands to sweep our group out of the room. "Let's get down there fast, before the crowd gets any bigger."

From the lobby, we speed out a side door to where True Time rolled out a red carpet leading to the marina. We're hustled through a trio of press tents where voices call out to our stars, as well as Bobby, Gilly, and Maureen, for quick photos or sound bites. Once we break cover onto the open-air portion of the carpet, cries of "I love you, Jack," and "Marry me, Niks," rise from the throng of fans.

Jack shouts in my ear so I can hear him over the commotion. "Are we to stop and sign autographs?"

"God, no. You'll never make it on board the Isle of Dash if we do that," I say and herd everyone down the red carpet, running along the marina to the party boat. "Once we're on the ship, you two'll pop to the top deck for a nice wave and smile."

To my relief, both Cali Con and True Time's security are out in force. We're hustled through a tunnel of muscle adorned with True Time wristbands and past two checkpoints before reaching the bobbing venue.

We enter onto an enclosed lower deck every bit as tropicalized as the upper deck. A rack of splashy Hawaiian shirts in as many colors as flowers in a Kauai rainforest sits between us and the stairs leading up top. Each shirt has a hibiscus decal where the breast pocket would be emblazoned with the True Time Network logo. We're instructed to choose our favorite and "Go tropical."

Past wardrobe, lovely lasses toss leis of silk flowers around our necks, kiss our cheeks, and wish us, "Aloha." Our progress stalls when each girl takes her turn dabbing a kiss on Jack. He walks away with five leis to everyone else's one.

Once past the lei gauntlet, Jack pulls the extras off his neck, adding one each to Gilly, Niks, and Maureen. "These itch my neck something fierce."

Gilly starts to reach a hand to rub Jack's neck but catches herself in time. Her instinct is as natural as if the two of them have been together for longer than a single year. Oddly, the sign of their intimacy validates the speed at which I've fallen for Cian. My life script always warned fast is not real despite the people in my life who've proved me wrong. In my experience, instant attraction is a buzz that only lasts until you've finished the glass in your hand. Jack and Gilly feed my experience into a shredder.

Our last stop before the stairs is a long bar draped in a green grass skirt with a brightly painted, miniaturized version of an outrigger canoe mounted on the wall behind. Pre-poured, on-theme drinks line up behind tiny tent signs advertising: Mai Tai, Piña Colada, Rum Runner, Bahama Mama, and a cocktail called a Killer Bee.

The bartender spreads his arms wide "Help yourselves. Two-fisted drinking encouraged." He claps his hands and flicks his wrists, a Blackjack dealer leaving the table. "There's an open bar on the top deck if you don't find something here to your liking."

I give the Killer Bee a go and am pleased with the mix of fruit, honey, and what I guess is rum.

"Jack!" None other than Cici Storm comes flying down the steps from the upper deck. She's got her arm through his in a millisecond. "Come dance with me."

Niks deftly captures Cici's other arm to avoid being left out of the equation. "Dancing, pretty drinks, boats with palm trees...I love San Diego." In a move worthy of a prima ballerina, Niks executes a twirl and shift to sandwich Jack between Cici and her. The shift effectively creates a tug-of-war with Jack as the rope.

I fall a little bit in love with Niks as she quenches Cici's predatory attempt to separate Jack from his herd.

A nonplussed Cici quickly recovers. "I'd love a quick chat with the both of you for our *Entertaining for You* Cali Con live stream." She runs a hand up Jack's arm. "We've got a darling setup on deck, complete with luscious flowers and twinkle lights." Ms. Storm rises on tiptoe to mock whisper in Jack's ear. "There's even a parrot."

Good soldiers that they are, Jack and Niks look to me for permission.

I smile. "Sounds grand, Cici."

Jack and Niks have dozens of duo interviews under their belts. I trust 'em. Every bit of coverage, even from gossipy queen, Cici Storm, has potential to translate into more True Time streaming subscriptions on our show's tally to gild my future.

I slip my own arm through Gilly's and hold her back for a quick whisper. "I'm sorry to be selling him off again."

She adjusts her pair of leis and trails a look after the retreating trio. "I'll always hate it, but thank God, I'm getting used to it."

The trust in her eyes for Jack makes my own heart thump a mushy beat. Bless me, I do envy the O'Learys. I've always considered the notion of soulmates a brew of bosh and bother, but watching Gilly look after her man spikes a bit of doubt on my long-held belief.

What if the rapid-fire attraction I harbor for Cian is elixir from the same well that gave rise to the love story of Jack and Gilly? I admire the man. He's sharp with layers I've only caught glimpses of. I could never settle for a simple man. Cian's galloping intellect is a siren's song. The kindness at his core draws me as powerfully as the physical and cerebral attraction. Cian Malley is a sounding board I'm eager to keep playing.

My head drops back, inciting a muscle crack in my neck. I've gone mad. Why did Cian ever bring up the "more" question? It's got my own galloping mind heading straight for a cliff.

Bobby steps up behind us. He lays a hand on Gilly's shoulder. "Have your parents headed home yet?"

"When I left them, they were debating between tonight and tomorrow morning."

He curses. "Tell me what it will take to keep your folks here through the weekend to help with the production designer interviews. I should have insisted Jeffrey Palmer come with us to muddle through portfolios and meet ups with me before he steps away. I need artists' eyes."

A fistful of nerves mixes with the Killer Bee in my stomach. "I set Jeff up to do video chats at your interviews."

Bobby frowns. "Given the time difference and him running around like a madman with crews to be ready for the our insane shooting schedule as soon as we hit the ground back in Ireland, he hasn't logged in."

Gilly pulls out her cell and taps a contact. "Crank up your Bobby

Provost signature sweet talk. You'll hook my folks." She plops the phone in Bobby's palm. "Or you could steal their car."

While Gilly and Bobby stay behind, I head up the steps to somewhat dusty, decorated paradise. The glare from the vanishing sun momentarily blinds me, but my ears have no such impediment.

"Where's your 'Top of the Mawrnin' Clan, Cian?"

The slur gives me reason to pause before stepping out into the light. It's the same dig I heard the first day outside the prep meeting, but not from the same voice. The "your" is what makes my hackles rise. Is *The Chieftain's Son* now presumed to be Cian's business, too, since I took him up on Dash's suggestion to give me pointers?

I relax fists and shake out my hands. I'm too sensitive. Cali Con is going brilliantly for us. My show is outshining the rest of True Time's roster, so the lot of them can go straight to hell.

The eejit whose voice I can't place chimes in again. "Gotten in pretty thick with them, eh, Malley?"

Instead of Cian, Dash's deep baritone answers. "You should all take a page from Cian's playbook on wooing the competition."

My hackles harden into steel spikes. Is Dash referring to my show as the competition, or is his flapping gob aimed at me personally? Cian and I have been friendly to one another in public. God willing, our time spent together is not enough for Dash to make assumptions.

My gut drops to my knees. Unless Cian is telling tales out of school about us. Either way, it's time to bust up the True Time ole boys' confab. I step through the hatch into the sunlight. Two long strides bring me to the center of puffed-up egos. As expected, my presence kills the current thread of conversation. I take a swift inventory as if the owner of the "*Top of the Mawrnin'*" crack has a detectable glow.

"Dash," I say raising my glass, "this is quite the craic you've got going here."

"Brilliant celebration," says Cian as if translating me for Dash.

An ear-splitting crash from the screen above shakes the deck as Jack in Donal Cam glory shatters a boulder with a mighty Gallowglass sword, igniting a conflagration of golden light. From the center of the blaze, a shadow form moves forward until Nieve is revealed. The lovers reunite in a kiss sure to set hearts and loins pounding as the image snaps to black, and our updated and much bigger budget *The Chieftain's Son* season two logo crackles overhead.

Everyone on deck explodes with applause, whistles, and even a few cat calls. Ah, our show may be the prettiest girl at the party.

I look to Dash for some sign of acknowledgement, but he's flung a paternal arm around Cian's shoulder. As the two trade private words, I slip away. Dash has proven himself to be a man of many faces this weekend, not a one looking kindly in my direction. His buddy-up with Cian irks me. Even a bloody smile in my direction would do after *The Chieftain's Son* made its splash across the screen.

The party ship sets off, surging past the events center and out to the bay. I make my way to the open bar to trade my empty Killer Bee glass for something with more sting. Grinding in my gut cries out for a straight shot of whiskey or two to take the edge off a full-blown case of anger. I can't let Dash and his passel of True Time ballbags throw me off my game. It's hard to tell what rankles me more, the truth Dashell Everett has a death grip on my future, the politics required to kiss my boss's ever-loving California ass, or the game of pretending his caustic repartee flows over me like a designer scarf.

I settle for a blended Hurricane instead of the shots. I'll stick to watered-down, candied-up rum drinks or what Mommy calls fancy boy sodas tonight. I've got to keep alert and keep careful eyes trained on my people and the likes of Cici Storm.

I tap on my cell screen with the True Time subscription numbers. *The Chieftain's Son* surge continues. We've got a splendid lead. I'm meeting Dash's challenges with full panels, numbers, and then some. I start to toast myself with the Hurricane when it's plucked from my hand.

"Clandestinely texting your other Cali Con conquests behind my back?" Cian takes a long sip and smacks lips that never fail to catch my attention. I sneak a glance at the True Time cabal to see if they notice his proprietary move.

I slip my cell into a pocket. Cian avoids comment on the subscription count he couldn't miss on my phone.

"You've caught me, Mr. Malley." I let loose a loud sigh. "Juggling my men is quite the challenge." I'm tempted to bring up his clandestine text from Sala Singh about script changes, but I bite my tongue. Not the time nor the place to pick at that wondering.

Cian takes a long, slow sip of my Hurricane, keeping his eyes trained on me over the top of the glass. "Umm, this gives mango margaritas a run for their money."

He offers the drink back to me, but I wave it off. "Consider it a bribe to tell me what your True Time pals over there are saying about my show. I'll order another."

"I'd like to request a different bribe." His lips stretch into a sly smile. "Perhaps a dance involving nothing but a grass skirt and a coconut bra. I'm sure there's a wardrobe closet somewhere on board."

I dart a quick look around our vicinity to make sure no one's listening. "And what'll you bring to our party?"

Cian adds teeth to his grin. "I've got plans for my own coconuts."

I shake a finger at him. "You're a very naughty sort."

Cian nods at the bow framed by the distant Balboa Sky Bridge. "Grab a drink and meet me up there, M-Squared. We'll toast to the memory of our first date."

Up ahead, the bridge sketches a lovely dark curve against the mango margarita sky. Cian dips in for an icy-lipped peck that's over in an eye blink. He saunters to a circular, rattan bench wedged into the bow lit by the glow of a giant Tiki torch.

First date, eh? Am I counting our night of margaritas and kisses as such? If so, isn't it brilliantly economical our first date and first kiss are wrapped up in the same evening. Simplifies the retelling of us. I brush off a stray hair tickling my cheek. Wouldn't a simple date tonight be lovely? I'd let my hair fly loose in the rising evening breeze while I snuggle with Cian under the citronella scented haze of a Tiki torch.

What I should do is pour the icy Hurricane over my head to shock my business brain into its proper position. Across the deck, Dash looks every bit the arrogant son of a bitch as he lords over Jack and Niks's interview with Cici Storm and *Entertaining for You*. His voice booms above the crowd buzz, taking the lion's share of credit for the success of the show. I search for Bobby, prepared to launch him at Dash's arrogance. Bobby Provost is the beating heart of *The Chieftain's Son*, not Dash Everett. You could throw a million Euros at a sheep, and that doesn't make it a prince. It's Bobby's creative genius, not Dash's coin, making our show royal.

A commotion near the hatch by the steps to the lower deck interrupts the current of conversation swirling around me. Under her floral arch, Cici swivels toward the noise, targeting fresh prey.

Making a grand entrance in matching Hawaiian shirts are Sala Singh and Malakai Bono, the *it* couple from *Star's Shadow*. Cian darts through the crowd at vampiric speed to their side before Cici gets to them. I shake off a spike of unease. Did I misstep not sticking with Jack and Niks until they were free of Ms. Storm. Did Dash notice? Is that why he insinuated himself in their interview? My stock might lose crucial points in the boss man's reckoning.

I abandon my Hurricane without a sip and thread through a troop of tipsy True Time folks to get to Jack and Niks.

"How'd you go with Cici?"

Niks leans close to whisper. "The She Storm pats Jack's biceps the way I do to my pups."

Jack flushes. "At least mine don't yap and bark."

I shake my head. "I should have stuck with the pair of you. Sorry."

Jack looks guilty. "It's fine, Meg. You shouldn't have to hold our hand every time a reporter jams a mic up our asses." He gives me one of his Jack O'Leary smiles that incites a rush of well-being warmer than a sunny day.

Niks's scolding expression burning a hole through Jack's forehead brings me up short. I study one and then the other. "You're keeping something from me."

Jack tosses Niks a look of pure helplessness.

She crosses her arms, tapping one finger against her upper arm. "It's your story to tell, *lover*."

I've never heard her sound so cross with Jack. His hands find Niks lower back as well as mine as he guides us to the rattan bench at the bow that should be occupied by Cian and me. My nerves ratchet higher with every step.

Jack takes a breath, puffing his chest to twice its size. "If you want to go off on me, I'll take it."

I force words through clenched teeth. "I'm going to start screaming anyway if you don't explain."

He rubs a hand over the stubble on his chin. "I might've let slip the word engaged."

"No might about it, Sweet One," says Niks.

"Fine," says Jack. "At least I didn't say married. Cici riled me. She tried to cause a dust up between Niks and me—"

I hold hands up to stop him. "Your solution was to admit to Cici Storm you may be engaged to someone who isn't Niks Tellefson?"

Jack looks as if he swallowed a fully lit Tiki torch.

A thousand nightmares cloud my thoughts. Cici will telegraph the news to millions. Jack and Niks will be painted as liars. Och, I hear it now. Hollywood fakery. Disrespect and game playing. Fan love will turn into coal black disgust.

"No, no," says Niks. "Jack zipped his lip. No messy details."

Jack studies his very expensive runners. "Niks cleaned up my mess."

"Cleaned it how?" I say very slowly.

"I think you will be buying me a very big ring," Niks says, eyes narrowed at Jack. "You buy one for Marisa too."

I gape at the pair of them. "Wait. Cici Storm thinks the two of *you* are engaged?"

Niks leans against Jack. "We played your game, Meg."

I curse myself for not being there to redirect Cici Storm. Cian would never let such a slip happen.

Jack and Niks stare at me wide-eyed, waiting. Waiting for what? An apology I did my job by shipping them to the world? Their pairing has been the catalyst for a fan frenzy that's only helped the show. I won't apologize for the payoff from my strategy.

I rock my head to speed up my ability to put a lucid sentence together. Did I not just apologize to Gilly for throwing Jack into Niks's arms once again? And what of Marisa, the true love of Niks's life? Gilly and Marisa are now both collateral damage in this war for fame and ratings. A mess indeed. I've been so hellbent on the publicity boon of the Jack/Niks fabrication, it's warped my moral compass. The mess to clean is of my making. It's time to grab a mop and bucket.

The swell of panic at Jack's blunder flattens. I close my eyes for a clarifying think, then slowly open them. "Thank you both. You've played this game brilliantly. I owe you my absolute appreciation." Confusion replaces anticipation in my stars. "It's time we stop playing."

Hopefulness sparkles in Jack's eyes.

I chew on my lip. "We've got to spin it just right to keep you two shining in the fan's estimation. After the Cali Con rush calms down, we'll write a new story. An engagement tease between the two of you is not farfetched." I spin a finger in the air. "You portray a high-octane love story on screen. It makes perfect sense it might spill over into real life. We'll paint a mutual parting, not an ugly break-up." I take my turn at patting Jack's bicep. "Your close friendship is no lie. Everyone will understand that won't dissolve even as your 'passion' does."

"Oh, thank God." Niks claps her hands but then shoots a quick glance at Jack. "I do love you, but it's weary being Jack O'Leary's woman all the time."

Jack takes Niks's hands in his and kisses her forehead. "Truer words were never spoke. Ask my Gilly."

Did I sell my cash cow at market for a handful of magic beans by short sheeting Niks's and Jack's fauxmance? Surprisingly, relief, not dread settles over me. These are good people. Folks who gave me their trust and allowed loyalty to the show to impact their personal lives. I have been a bit of a bully, but I'll justify my actions to my last breath as dedication to the success of *The Chieftain's Son*. There's no disaster brewing from their interview. Jack's slip simply hastens the next chapter of my original scenario. We'll build a buzz toward a different exit of the roundabout.

Jack's eyes roam the deck. "Do you know where Gilly's gone off to?"

I bob my head toward the stern. "Bobby grabbed her and Maureen and slipped just there."

Jack's a runner poised for the starting gun to go off. I lay a hand on his over-patted bicep. "Remember, lots of nosey eyes on you here."

Niks links arms with Jack. "I stay with him, yes. Eyes see Jack and me together. Everyone is happy." She winks at me. "Go find your pretty man."

Well, doesn't her description wrap Cian up in a neat package. A lovely warmth simmers behind my breastbone. That pretty man taught me so much. He blunts the sharp edges of business with humanity. Sala Singh's text to him I peeped at earlier changes hues to comradery instead of suspicion. Cian and his folks are a team. I want to be a tight weave in the fabric of *The Chieftain's Son* in the same way. Maybe being a *"we"* is growing on me.

The space between bodies here on deck shrinks to a minimum. The inhabitants of the lower deck pour topside as we cross under the Balboa Sky Bridge. Off to the west, fireworks scatter across the newborn night sky, adding another festive layer to the party. Amid this bubbling True Time pool of dealmakers, a lazy sense of summer brushes over me.

I weave my way to Cian's last known location, eager to find out if he's possibly locked in his stars for our *Ship of Dreams* panel. I'm certain Dash will love our mash-up of the two shows, and God willing, it will finally put *The Chieftain's Son* on equal footing with *Star's Shadow* in the big man's estimation.

I spot the back of Cian's head in the joined-at-the-hip group of True Time execs. His tall, lanky frame contrasts his thick-middled colleagues. After a brief stop at the open bar for a pair of fresh Hurricanes, I wander through the crowd, anticipation building. I've at least two more potential "date" nights with Cian Malley. I plan to make the most of them.

As I slip through the final layer of humanity blocking me from Cian, a pair of voices stop me as effectively as a blow to the head. There's no mistaking who they belong to, Dash and Cian.

"It's past time Cian here claims the helm and whips our Irish country bumpkin of a publicity department head into shape."

"Come on, Dash. It's not exactly a backwater team. Meghan McGrath's got fantastic potential. With her under me, I'll crank up the solid momentum on *The Chieftain's Son* and do True Time proud," says Cian, thumping Dash on the back.

"I'd love to have her under me," another fool chimes in, and I finally identify the fucker who's been taking shots at me all night. The entire bevy of bastards laugh. Their wave of toxic misogynistic masculinity smacks into me. With his back to me, I can't read Cian's reaction. Urges to run, punch, or heave my pair of Hurricane's in their overfed faces battle inside me. Turmoil glues my pair of maroon pumps to the sand-sprinkled wooden deck.

Dash catches sight of me first. The *Oh shit!* composition of his features results in the collective turn of half a dozen heads.

My eyes find Cian's, praying beyond hope what I'm hearing can't be real. This isn't about *my* show, and *my* future. It's a bloody royal cock-up I've somehow misinterpreted. In the single moment when Cian's look meets mine, my life bursts into flames.

He reaches out in time to catch the two Hurricane glasses before they slip out of my grasp. Dash is at my side, fingers clamped on my elbow to guide me away.

"I'm sorry, Meghan. This is certainly not the way I wanted you to find out. You knew it was more probability than possibility your position was in jeopardy. I warned you."

He maneuvers us into a small space between the hatch to the lower deck and the side rail of the ship.

I rip my arm from his grasp. "You promised me a chance." I flash my cell at him. The screen shows the latest tally of True Time subscriptions. "My show is wiping the floor with your other prize ponies."

Annoyance mixed with a dropper full of anger crosses Dash's face. "As I said before, your talents are valued. There's no question you should stay with *The Chieftain's Son*." He guides my phone away from his face. "A show that's exploded in popularity like yours demands a more experienced hand at the wheel. It's business, Meghan. There's marketing potential you lack the experience to tap into. We agreed to take you on because you're Bobby's golden girl. Putting you in the top spot alone was never fair."

"Then be a better mentor to me, Dash." I tamp down the urgency to list the ways he hasn't lived up to the scenario he painted for me when I was hired. Our weekly calls were supposed to be more than a sign-off.

He was supposed to be guiding me, sharpening my potential, inspiring and educating me.

A wave of Dash's hand dismisses me. I've caught him in his empty promise to me, and he's hot over it. Dashell Everett never expected *The Chieftain's Son* to become what it is. He sees Meghan McGrath as steady, but Cian Malley is stellar. Dash never intended to honor our deal for me to keep my position.

"I stepped into the *Entertaining for You* interview..." says Dash, jerking his chin at Cici Storm's palm arch. "Once your Jack and Niks farce threatened to go off the rails. It was a ridiculous rookie gamble from the start. Obviously, more than you could handle. Fans are far more daunting foes than you ever imagined, Meghan. You've given Cian a hotbed of shit to shovel up."

When I open my mouth to breathe fire, Dash flashes me a warning look. "I strongly suggest you don't say another word. This is not the place." He lays a hand on my shoulder. "Stay with the show. Accept the number two slot. Cian is the mentor to take you to the next level. After working with him for a few years, you'll be ready to handle a top show on your own."

I want to smash Dash's fingers with a rock.

As if sensing the danger to his digits, he withdraws his hand. "We'll meet Sunday night before you leave and resolve your future with True Time." He gives me a dismissive nod and walks off.

My new reality rips through my body. Fury burns away tears. I grip the rail tight enough to snap a fingernail. Behind me, in low tones, a different voice breathes my name.

CHAPTER 18

ROCKY SEAS

I don't turn. I don't speak. I don't do anything but stare out over the water. Pulsing light from the jumbo screen bounces off the half wall surrounding the deck, giving a strobe effect to the darkness.

"Meg." There are layers stacked upon layers in Cian's single word: guilt, resolve, fear, arrogance, questioning. There's nothing he can ask that I have the inclination to answer.

He's closer. Heat from his body pierces the cool night breeze. I move down the rail until the welcome chill returns.

Still, he follows. His hand rests on the rail near mine while he stands in silence next to me.

"I've nothing to say to you, Cian."

It takes every drop of energy not to drive my fist into his solar plexus and leave him gasping on the deck.

His hand slides closer as if to make contact. I rip mine off the rail. The thought of his touch sends my mind into spasms of rage. If we physically connect, I'll lose the final thread of control left to me. Crying is out of the question, although tears prick my eyes. Screaming at him will only bring attention I can't handle.

"I'm asking you to walk away."

"I'm asking you to listen to me, Meg."

How dare he? Red, busting anger wipes away my meager thread of control. I whip around to face him before I can do a thing to stop myself. "What in bloody hell could you say to make a fucking difference?"

Cian opens his mouth to speak, but I cut him off. "How many lies are going to bolt out of that mouth of yours?" I ball my hands into fists. "Or should I say, how many *more* lies?" I smash one fist against the side of the ship. "You're a bastard, Cian Malley, a thieving monster."

All I see is the top of Cian's head as he stares at the uneven boards of the deck. "You're absolutely right, Meg." He raises his face slowly as if giving me the opportunity not to meet his eyes. "This is destroying me."

"Ha!" My voice is so loud it cuts through buzz of the party. I back away from the open deck until Cian and I are out of everyone's eyeline. We're wedged between the rail and a hut. "Destroying you? I think we both know who's been destroyed."

He claims my hands. I try to pull away, but he's got me trapped. "I need to apologize and explain."

I go as still as a pond on a windless day. "Did you know you were set to replace me before you came to San Diego?"

Cian presses his lips together so tightly they glow white in the dark. "Yes."

"There's all the explanation I need." I struggle to get loose. "Let me go or I'll loudly fight my way free of you."

Cian's breathing becomes rapid, and his body heat raises the temperature in our little cranny. "Kick or scream or whatever you need to do, but you're going to hear me out. I can't let you walk away. You're too important to me."

Unbelievable. This raving ass is going to hold me captive to cleanse his traitor's soul. "Important to your new job, you mean. Was your ultimatum from Dash to keep me on as your number two?"

With a swift jerk, Cian's brought my body against his. "I wasn't supposed to fucking like you. All I needed to do was tolerate you. Dash warned me you were a handful, so I was prepared to win you over and talk you into staying with the show."

I attempt to swivel out of his grasp. The feel of him breaks me. All the while I was falling for this man, I was his project. I should have read the room better that first day. Dash as much as admitted Cian was in charge of me. Eejit me believed I had a shot at keeping my job.

"Please let me go."

"I don't want to let you go, Meg. Yes, I was supposed to bring you to heel, but there you were, a whip-smart, sharp-edged, goddamned beautiful genius who could match me blow to blow at my own game. Dash is clueless to the perfection he has in you."

For half a heartbeat, I think he's going to kiss me. Instead, he lets go and turns to the water. I'm momentarily hypnotized by strands of his hair dancing in the breeze. Strands I still yearn to touch.

"What was I supposed to do with that, Meg?"

I try to smash the pull lingering between us. "Be a decent human being, for starters. Not paint the scenario of being my benevolent mentor with no strings. Not team up with me on the panel idea. Not lie. Not sleep with me."

Cian's shoulders slump. He pivots to face me. "Is there ever anyone in your scenarios, Meg, beside yourself?" It's his turn to pound the rail. "You're so damned determined to be a solo act you won't give an inch. It's much easier to villainize me because I handled this badly instead of admitting the show has become too big for your current skillset."

I press fists against my temples. "You are the villain here, not my learning curve. I went against my instincts and look where it's gotten me. I never worry about betrayal when I'm a 'solo act'."

"Please, Meg. Work with me to get past this. Give me a chance."

I hate the part of me wanting to give in. I've gone mad. No one's ever stirred my guts the way Cian's done. "Where's my chance to keep my position? You ploughed right over me to get my job. Is it the challenge of raising up a fledgling project? Oh, wait. I've already rocketed my show to a top spot. You're just sniffing around to capitalize on my success and turn me into an afterthought. I'm a non-person to you, Cian, the next paving stone in your tidy, little garden path to a bigger and better future."

A growl surrounds Cian's words. "Your job was already lost."

My solar plexus takes this punch.

"I'm Dash's logical choice because I have family in Ireland and am willing to relocate for the length of the series." He runs a hand through his hair. "And I'm fucking great at my job. I made *Star's Shadow* a phenomenon."

"As I did with *The Chieftain's Son.*"

"Yes, you did, but with how many potential P.R. disasters and NDA leaks ready to blow up in your face? Jack and Niks. Jack and Gilly. Unhappy guest cast."

"What?" My stomach contracts into a knot of fear.

Cian grasps my shoulders. "This is the point I'm trying to make. A pair of your actors gave negative interviews under your nose. You don't have a multilayered grasp on how many balls you juggle with a hit show. Your P.R. world is micro-focused. Hollywood has a far and dangerous reach. I can show you how to handle it all."

"Control me."

"Teach you."

"Disgrace me." The damn tears sting again.

"We'll spin the new situation to prevent that."

I take one step backward and then another. "Who's not going to know I've been squashed? Not Dash. Not True Time. Not Bobby. No one. You've ruined me, Cian."

I want him to tell me I'm wrong. The space between us increases as I wait for him to explain his magical spin. The man of so many words has none for me now. I give Cian Malley one final nod and show him my back.

Curse my urge to shake Cian until an idea to save me spills from him. I crave any solution to prevent my downfall, to save my pride, my job, and Lord help me, my connection to Cian.

Survival screams for me to run fast and far, but I'm on a goddamn boat trussed up as a luau. I seek faces I can trust to keep me from jumping overboard and swimming for it. I ache to swim. How many laps would it take to grant me the ability to sort this out?

I take a turn around the top deck, looking for my people while avoiding Dash and Cian. The party crowd is growing more raucous as Killer Bees and Hurricanes flood the crowd. Searching for a respite, I take the steps to the lower deck. More music and a group lesson on Polynesian dancing greet me. I push through the lines of swinging hips until I spot an arch at the far end leading outside.

Glory be, I find my tribe. Five glum expressions stare up at me from a round wooden table. A collection of margarita glasses in various levels between full and empty glow from the multi-colored string of pineapple-shaped lights looped over the table. At least I don't need to put on a happy face with this lot.

I locate an unused glass near the middle of the table and fill from a pitcher of what I hope is full strength margarita. Raising my glass, I mumble, "Sláinte."

"Sláinte, my balls," grumbles Maureen.

After gulping half a glass of warm margarita, I study the group. It's oddly comforting to be part of a group as miserable as I am. "Out with it then."

"Fuck San Diego," says Maureen. "Grady is asking me to postpone the wedding so he can fly his ass back here for two months and study with a dessert chef he met at Bobby's Jack Daniels steak restaurant."

I reach across the table to grasp her hand. "Can't he do it after the wedding? You'll go with him."

She shakes our joined hands. "I can't. We'll be deep into writing the next season."

Bobby looks pathetically guilty.

Maureen waves a hand at him. "Keep your hang-dog look to yourself, Bobby. It's not you stirring the pot."

Gilly slides her hand over Maureen's shoulder and pulls her in for a hug.

Niks starts waving her phone over her head. "Damn, damn, damn. I can't keep a signal." She presses her lips to the end of her phone and yells. "Marisa, can you hear me."

"That won't help," says Jack in a voice laced with impatience. "Walk around until you get more bars."

Niks smacks the phone onto the table and glares at Jack. "Marisa is doing the freaking out. Cici woman is blah, blah, blah-ing about the engagement everywhere. How do you say bad thing? A 'cocks-up.'"

Niks's attempt at slang bursts the tension bubble encapsulating the table. Jack laughs so hard tears stream down his face. Maureen bangs on the table over and over to catch her breath. Bobby raises his glass. "Cocks up, everyone."

We all drink.

"Full disclosure," Gilly says, pointing a shaky finger at me. I don't know if I've ever seen her so tipsy. "When I said I'm getting used to the bullshit of Jack's fame and fabricated life...I lied."

Jack raises his glass. "Fuck fabrication."

I tip the pitcher and refill everyone's glasses before lifting my own. "Fuck fabrication."

The pissed lot of us shout the phrase to the sky, drawing surprised faces over the rail of the top deck to look down on the lunatics.

Maureen grabs Niks's phone and leads her away in search of more bars. Gilly slides closer to Jack and the two whisper. Their legs bump into mine under the table as they secretly twine around each other's ankles out of public view. I've half a mind to tell them to shout the news of their marriage to the sky and damn the fallout. It's Cian's problem now.

Naw, that would launch the pair straight into a tidal wave of fan backlash. Neither they nor the show deserve such treatment. Despite the shitestorm falling on my head, I care deeply for *The Chieftain's Son*.

Bobby stares at a crack in the wooden table. I nudge him with my shoulder. "How did you earn your ticket to our pity party?"

He digs an elbow into the table and rests his head on his hand. "The interviews for a new production designer are a bust. No one I've seen is up for the scope, challenge, and insane pace of our show."

My eye twitches. That's exactly what Dash is saying about me.

I pat his shoulder. "You've just started the process."

"Thank God, Amethyst and Rich agreed to help me find someone new. I'm going to stay a week in L.A. before heading home to see if I can nail down at least a short list of candidates There's an Elodie Pettipas who's worked with a pal of mine. She comes highly recommended." He narrows his eyes when the corner of my lip hitches up. "What?"

"You said home."

He looks surprised.

"I've never heard you call Ireland home before." A nice warmth replaces the wall of ice Cian planted in my chest.

Bobby shrugs. "They say home is where your family is. *The Chieftain's Son* is my family."

I glance over to Maureen and Niks, who's given up on the phone. They giggle and hug. Across from me, Jack and Gilly are deep in conversation. The way they're drawn to one another sweetens the saltiness of the sea breeze.

No one is alone tonight. Every one of these fine people relies on someone in their lives. Does that paint them as weak and incapable? It does not. On the contrary, I'm surrounded by proof of strength, comradery, and trust. As painful as my experience with Cian is, I got a taste of what everyone here already knew. There is joy and support and success in plurality instead of singularity. Even though Cian, that bastard, had ulterior motives, our short time together did inspire me. It made me better. Maybe a life of *"we"* isn't the devil's doin' I've convinced myself it is.

Finally, I meet Bobby's eyes. He studies me with a look, cutting artifice down to the truth.

Bobby inclines his head toward Jack. "Don't kick yourself over the engagement leak, Meg. You'll work your magic on the wrinkle."

I've been a fool not to include Bobby in my situation with Dash. Bobby believed in me before I trusted myself with the enormity of our show. This man brought me onto his team with every confidence I would do him proud. I will honor his trust until the day I'm forced out the door. Withholding troubles from Bobby hurt rather than helped. I may be a casualty of war, but *The Chieftain's Son* still has potential momentum to gain here at Cali Con. I won't let my accomplishments with the show go up in a wildfire to burn my career for good. I admit, this is one scenario where the wisdom not to go it alone makes perfect sense.

I lay a hand on Bobby's and speak words that come hardest to me.

"I need your help."

CHAPTER 19

FRIENDS

Bobby and I walk alone behind the Diego Bay Events Center. Jack and Niks did their usual brilliant job signing autographs and posing for selfies. I winced at every shout of congratulations on their engagement.

With the moon still high in the July sky, our friends retired to hotel rooms to make up or make love. The only folks left on the party boat are a clean-up crew and fellows dismantling the giant screen.

There's an hour and some change before the outline of my plan B panel proposal is due to Dash. At least, with Deidre in the mix, I've got a strong contender with albeit ragged edges. Air stutters and catches in my throat. Plan B doesn't touch the brilliance of the *Ship of Dreams* Cian and I crafted. I may have Deidre, but he's got MetaMeme.

Bobby and I walk in silence along the sidewalk next to the marina. He doesn't pry or poke. It's very strange being so close to a silent sea. I'm used to the wild Atlantic with its symphony of crashes and fizzes as it battles for dominance over the shore.

Each time I'm ready to share with Bobby, the shock of my reality batters me. A crack against my soul followed by an eerie silence until the next crack. Bobby doesn't push.

We reach a collection of shops and restaurants called Seaside Village.

It's mostly deserted save a restaurant or two with a Cali Con late-night crowd. I hear the strains of an acoustic guitar and a voice singing, *"I'll follow you into darkness."*

I'm headed straight into darkness. The man I let myself believe a handful of hours ago might brighten my life ended up being ole Hades himself.

I can't tell if it's the soulful acoustic melody, the words, or the look of concern on Bobby's face that finally breaks me, but broken I am. My heel catches an uneven piece of the walkway and I trip. The final insult to my shredded control. Bobby catches me on the way down. In his arms, I crumble.

Sobs work their way up from my chest. Bobby guides me to a wooden bench facing the water and holds me as my spectacular ugly cry drowns out the music. I wail for the loss of my dream job. I wail for disappointing Bobby. I wail for letting down everyone who depended on me. I wail for the way I've bruised and battered people's personal lives.

I wail for the embarrassment of telling my family what's happened.

I'm the first of my family to go to college and make a splash on a bigger stage than Cahersiveen, County Kerry, Ireland. Sure, Taryn's giving her Swim and Gym a grand go, and my parents are content running their "Shades of Light" gallery, but I aimed higher. Losing my job is proof to Mommy and Daddy it's time for me to abandon my lofty goals and hang out my publicist shingle in the hometown, cater to local artists, and accept the small and tidy life they adore.

"I'm going to get you napkins," says Bobby, spying my soggy wad of tissues.

I nod. He gently releases me to head for the nearest food window.

Once alone, a mighty sob shakes me to the core. It's for Cian. For gain and loss. For trust and betrayal. For the fleeting dream of wanting him to be more than a weekend. I was seduced by a taste of *"we"* and set aside the *"me"* that's always served. Damn it all, the *"we"* felt right. It opened my eyes to the *"we"* I'm a part of with my Chieftain's Son folks. I believed Cian to be genuine, and our connection to be mutual and glorious. How many have said the same as the tip of a knife sinks between their shoulder blades?

God bless Bobby Provost. He's back, allowing me to unravel, asking for nothing. His embrace isn't sensual, it's steady and true. Like Bobby. Like Jack. Like Maureen. Like Taryn. Like the decent people in my life.

I blow my nose and regain the power of speech. "I'd ask you to turn away, but I think you've seen the worst of it."

"How long have I known you, Meg? Four, five years? In all that time, under inhuman pressure and insane circumstances, I've never seen you cry."

"It's not something I choose to do..." I sniff. "For an audience."

"It's kind of beautiful."

I find the last dry corner of the napkin wad and dab my eyes. "If you look directly at this right now"—I draw a circle around my puffy face—"You may well turn into a pillar of stone."

"Definitely beautiful. Another layer of a deeply complicated person."

He's kindness and compliments, but I need his pillar of stone. "Dash fired me."

Bobby stares as if attempting to translate my words into a language he understands. His eyes begin to wobble with the look he gets when he thinks at a speed imperceptible to most humans.

"He can't."

"He did."

He runs a hand through his hair. "What am I missing here, Meg?"

I swallow hard to keep from dissolving. "Before we left home, Dash told me True Time doesn't think I'm handling the show as well as it needs to be." I pat the last puddles on my face. "They're sending someone with more experience over to The Clan to take over. I'll be demoted to Cian Malley's assistant."

It's Bobby's turn to shake. The man is livid. "What a pair of pompous, two-faced bastards. It's my damn show. Cian knew all this time he was replacing you?"

"Appears so." The arm around my shoulders squeezes so forcefully I let out a little squeak.

Bobby pulls his arm away. "Sorry, Meg." He shoots to his feet and starts pacing in front of the bench. "How dare he go behind my back to you. Fucking network." He stops. "Why didn't you tell me?"

I grip the seat. This is embarrassing. I should have told Bobby, but I've been so determined to do everything on my own. Meghan McGrath, queen of "*Me.*" "Fool that I am, I made a deal with Dash I believed he meant to honor. Long story short, he promised if I handled Cali Con up to his standards, and *The Chieftain's Son* increased True Time's streaming subscription enough to beat out their other shows this weekend, my position would hold steady."

"Handled Cali Con? You've done an amazing job. What nebulous standards are we talking about? *The Chieftain's Son* couldn't be making a bigger splash."

I pray there's enough air in my lungs to continue the conversation. "I thought I'd figured out what his standards were, but I didn't shoot high enough. Didja see *Star's Shadow* on every bus and train car? True Time wants the visibility Cian Malley pulled off for his show." I forcefully relax my body before something snaps. "Dash threw me at Cian from day one to illustrate my inadequacy."

Cian's name knocks the breath from me. I'm nearly panting. "Please understand, Bobby. I can't be the number two at a job where I've been number one. It's humiliating."

Bobby sits next to me and grabs his cell. "Dashell Everett has a lot to answer for."

I lay my hand on his phone. "No, please."

Bobby raises his eyebrows.

I guide the phone to his side. "It's not Dash I need your help with." My face tenses, ready to unleash a fresh flurry of tears, but I manage to keep control. "I'd lost my battle with him before I ever got on a plane."

"Please tell me what I can do, Meg." A muscle in his jaw ticks. "I need a distraction to keep from kicking down Dashell Everett's door, forcibly removing his head from where it currently resides up his ass, and punching him."

I gather what's left of my wits. "The proposal Cian and I worked up for the open Sunday Harborview Hall spot with *Star's Shadow* and *The Chieftain's Son* main couples vying for popularity is off the table." I can't imagine working with the lying bastard on anything. That text on Cian's cell from

Sala Singh about changes to the "script" flashes in my mind. Was that about our panel or a different one he was hiding in his back pocket? My stomach knots. Was his teamwork angle a ploy to show me how well we could work together once he nabbed my job? One thing is certain. I will not be his number two, and our Ship of Dreams just sank to the bottom of the bay.

Damn if I'm not on the verge of another crying jag. I wave my hand as if to knock down my unstable emotions. I need to hold it together. Time I can't get back flashes by.

"What? Why?" Bobby windmills his hands. He likes a direct line from point A to point B, and I'm not giving him one.

"We're not working together anymore. Cian Malley is your new head of publicity and marketing." I stamp my feet on the ground and growl to get control.

Bobby stares me down. "Do you know why I insisted True Time hire you?"

Insisted.

Bobby's question alone is proof enough that Dash Everett doubted me from the beginning.

"You pulled off a miracle in Dublin with your brainchild of the native Irish artist's festival. International press, the establishment and backing for awards, scholarships, grants. You finagled me and other more impressive names to come to Dublin and judge the indie film competition. The event rivaled the Rose of Tralee festival or Bloom's Day. You snapped your fingers at the global artistic community and said, 'Eyes to Ireland.'"

I nod. "It was quite wonderful. I'm glad it's taken off as an annual event."

He sits and grabs my shoulders. "It's your wonderful, your legacy. You can handle *The Chieftain's Son* no matter how big it gets. Don't let Dashell Everett make you feel small."

"He's already taken it from me. It'll be worse if there's any fallout for you or the show because I put up a fuss."

A battle rages across Bobby's features. He can scratch and scream at Dash, but in the end, True Time holds the power. Network money is what builds or breaks our world. Resignation is not a look Bobby wears well.

"Meg, tell me what you need from me. I'll make it happen," says Bobby the showrunner, the problem solver, a true chieftain.

Here is my crossroads. The place I shed my skin and admit I can't score the panel win for *The Chieftain's Son* with willpower or my plough-ahead-damn-the-consequences style alone. I need help. In a stroke of grand irony, I realize it's the steps I took to let Cian in that allow me to reach out to Bobby now.

I check my watch. Forty-five minutes left to polish my plan B so brightly it will blind anyone who looks directly at it. What was it my granddad always said, *"If I'm going down, I'm going down in a ball of piss and fire."* Yanking the tablet out of my bag, I click on my proposal and hand it to Bobby. "Help me make this proposal unbeatable so True Time must give *The Chieftain's Son* the Sunday spot in Harborview Hall."

His eyes skim the outline at lightning speed. He's got his phone against his ear even faster, yammering at someone. "Show emergency. Meet me in my room. Five minutes."

Bobby's on his feet and dragging me along with him as we jog toward the hotel. "Your outline is a fantastic start, Meg. Solid. Fun. Imaginative. Let's see how much farther we can take it."

"Mind telling me who we're meeting in your room?" Every heartbeat is painful. More people will be privy to my failure. I must shake off the resentment, fear, and mortification threatening to drive me under bed covers for the rest of the weekend. This is about our show grabbing the choice spot, not me.

I've already lost.

Bobby breaks into something closer to a skip than a run. "Our secret weapon. The Queen of Hearts, Deidre LaRochelle."

The breakfast crowd at San Diego's stab at an Irish Pub is small. The real mob streams along the sidewalk in front of the events center half a block away, waiting for the doors to open. It's Saturday, and from what I hear, the craziest, body-slam day of a day at the Con.

Deidre reaches across the table and tips an airplane-sized Jameson bottle into my coffee.

"It's caffeine I need, not something to put me under the table," I say, pushing her hand away.

She empties the rest into her own coffee and produces another tiny bottle. "It's five o'clock in Kerry, darlin'."

Her man, Doolin, shakes her purse and listens for a rattle. "How many are in there?"

Deidre leans an elbow on the table and stares me down with a look to peel skin back to see what's inside. "Not enough."

Bobby and I watch our phones perched side by side. We know damn well Dash made his decision on the Sunday panel. The press release is due out at 10:00am when the convention floor opens, and it's half-nine already. Thousands of flyers are printed, waiting to be stuffed into every information rack and stacked in the True Time booth to announce the replacement.

I check the Cali Con app again to see if the schedule has been updated to stir up even more hype.

Deidre reaches across the table and clasps my hand. "Your proposal is a beautiful love letter to the show and fans. Bobby and I simply added lacy lingerie and chocolate. True Time won't pass up such class."

The panel Bobby, Deidre, and I banged out in less than an hour last night is a gift to the fans who've sent the show soaring. It's for the sweet folk who cosplay as Donal Cam and Nieve, the patient collective waiting in endless lines for a smile from Jack or a wink from Niks, and the bubbling throng of enthusiasm tracking down my scavenger hunt clues for a glimpse of their favorites.

Bobby added more gold by agreeing to show the gag reel from the season one Blu-ray about to release, a personal, insider offering of charm and good fun. Deidre devised a wooing contest mid-panel where every male actor from Sir Kevin to Artie Boyd will read tongue-in-cheek poetry to Niks in an attempt to win a kiss. Of course, Jack will triumph and kiss Niks right there in front of God and everyone. The audience will go mad for the real-life smooch, especially given the rumors of the pair's engagement.

Maureen and Gilly are in a writing frenzy at the hotel to script the panel. The gorgeous marzipan flower on top of our sweetie is Deidre herself reading an excerpt from the next tightly guarded *Chieftain's Son* novel not due out until next year.

We'll send the fans on their way with a challenge. As my last act, a final farewell, I'll open two Instagram accounts, "Love Letters to Donal Cam," and "Love Letters to Nieve." The loveliest pairing of picture and prose posted on each will win trips to The Clan and an outing with Jack and Niks. The contest is on Bobby's dime. He's footing the bill for airfare and will put the luckies up at our Clan housing in Waterville. True Time can't bitch over the expense.

Our proposal gives and gives and gives to the fans. Nearly two hundred fans waited in line during our Grand Ballroom show panel and never got in. The Sunday bonus offers another chance for the fan base to be in the presence of the characters they love. We're going to provide an experience they'll be tweeting about until their fingertips bruise.

If I think too hard about Bobby and Deidre's generosity, I will dissolve like the sugar in my whiskey-enhanced coffee.

I swear Deidre possesses emotional radar. She reaches across the table and squeezes my hand. "How you holding up, Meg?"

Like an unwanted surprise visitor at your front door when you're in pajamas, her question pops Cian into my head. How sparkly is his Plan B? I can't imagine it's any more dazzling than what we've cooked up. My bones ache with a sense of loss when I think of the *Ship of Dreams* that will never be. I would love to watch Donal Cam and Nieve wipe the floor with Starry Night and Event Horizon in a couple smackdown. At least Cian loses our panel as well. There's one small victory.

I take a long swig of coffee. Deidre's right, whiskey helps. "No news is bad news."

Bobby scoops up his phone, sliding his finger across the screen. "No messages from Dash. Nothing on social media. What's he waiting for?"

My phone rings. "It's Grady." Our man inside the events center. "Grady, you're on speaker with Bobby, Doolin, and Deidre."

"Maureen said to ring you straight away. I'm inside the lobby and there are no inserts or flyers I can see about the Sunday spot."

The table shares a look of confusion.

"Thanks, Grady. Keep an eye out, will you?"

"Sure," he says, and before I say goodbye, Bobby's phone trills with an incoming call.

He and I stare at his screen and then each other.

Dash.

Bobby gestures at the speaker icon, but I shake my head. I'd rather hear the news from a person I trust. That man isn't Dashell Everett.

It's unnerving feeling fragile. I'm not used to it and don't wear it well.

Bobby scowls as he listens to Dash, but then suddenly his face brightens. "If Meg told you our people are on board, they're on board." He positions the phone between us so Dash can hear my voice.

An excited buzz resonates in my chest. "All of Team *Chieftain's Son* are game for another go."

Deidre raises her coffee and whiskey to toast me as Bobby rests the phone against his ear. Doolin waves a dismissive hand at us ready to be finished with this business.

I lift my own cup and clink with Deidre. Before the rim touches my lips, the look on Bobby's face and his growl send my cup crashing onto its saucer.

"Absolutely not the right call, Dash." His eyes go cold as a winter wind off the Atlantic. He slams his phone onto the table.

My phone buzzes with an alert. It's the press release.

The True Time Network is delighted to announce a new addition to our line-up at San Diego Cali Con. Join us for the Ship of Dreams panel at Cali Con this Sunday at 1:00pm in Harborview Hall where fans will decide which romantic pairing will triumph as the ultimate "ship" between our two blockbuster programs, "The Chieftain's Son" and "Star's Shadow."

A chorus of shrieks rise from a group of twenty-somethings stuffed into a corner booth. At our table, I can't judge whose string of curses is more colorful, Bobby's or Deidre's.

She points a blood red fingernail at Bobby's phone. "You call that son-of-a-bitch and tell him to kiss my ass. I'm won't do any panel except the one we wrote with Meg."

Doolin scoots his chair back, escaping the line of fire.

I'm gutted. How could Cian do this to me? It's beyond betrayal. He submitted our *Ship of Dreams* to Dash as his own.

My head fills with white noise. I'm deaf to the heated words flying across the table, but I see faces seething with fury. In counterpoint to their anger, I'm filled with unexpected calm. Bobby and Deidre prepare to arm themselves for battle on my behalf. I can't let them fight for an irrevocably lost cause. Before the moment erupts into complete chaos, I grip each of their arms.

"Don't take a bite out of Dash. It won't change what's already in place." I release my hold and collapse against the chair. "Let the panel go forward. It's a brilliant idea and will be grand for the show. Do it for me."

I'm not one who appreciates the spotlight. It's on me full blast as Bobby, Deidre, and Doolin focus on me.

"That's a generous perspective, Meg," says Bobby.

After his front-row seat to my teary breakdown last night, he seems surprised at my acquiescence, and why not. I've only shown my confrontational side since I first stepped into my office at The Clan. I never backed down in the face of a challenge even though my full-steam-ahead style of decision making didn't make me popular. I invented a strong-armor Meg who buried compassion inside the shell I believed would strengthen my position as a rookie, as a woman competing against True Time's men's club.

I let that one aspect overrule the rest and look where it's gotten me.

Deidre's up and around behind me. She folds me in her arms. "The road to success rarely looks the way you picture it." There's conviction in her voice one uses when sharing life's great wisdoms. She should know. It took her the better part of a decade to get anyone to take a second glance at *The Chieftain's Son*.

I feel truly fired for the first time. After the way I acted on the ship last night with Dash and his omission of not consulting me about my cast and the panel, it's obvious my termination is official. The clench in my throat warns that tears are close. They're not my cast anymore. Jack, Niks, Sir Kevin...They all belong to Cian.

"Cian Malley has balls of steel to submit that proposal behind your back," says Bobby, eyeing one of Deidre's mini-Jamesons.

"Who now?" says Deidre, returning to her seat next to Doolin.

I down the rest of my whiskey-laced coffee. My opinions on day drinking shift from resistance to appreciation. Fitting the cup to its saucer, I meet her eyes. "Mr. Cian Malley, your new head of publicity for *The Chieftain's Son*.

The only way to describe Deidre's exclamation is a snarl. "Flip a couple of letters in that name, and you have yourself a Cain."

CHAPTER 20
AN INVITE

Banging on my hotel room door pauses and then resumes. Blackout curtains prevent me from knowing if it's day or night. I don't care which it is.

A deep, masculine voice rumbles through the door. "Meg, are you alive?"

I rise onto an elbow as I register the source of reverberating thunder. Why is Jack O'Leary pounding on my door? My immediate thought is that something is terribly wrong. Right on its heels is the reality whatever's brewing is no longer my problem.

"He won't stop until you answer," calls Gilly.

Being the expert on Jack's stubborn side, her warning confirms my hiding-under-my-covers strategy is ruined. I move the curtain of hair off my face. "I'm alive. Go on with you."

Honestly, alive is an overstatement. I touch the tender skin beneath my eyes. Och, my face feels twice its normal size from a record-setting, prolonged post-pub cry before I fell into the sleep of the dead. I catch illuminated numbers on the bedside clock. It's half-six. I've been underground for eight hours.

"Glad of it." Jack's voice booms. "But we're going to need a bit of proof."

Realization is a brick to my temple. "Holy damn." My star knows I've been sacked. Bobby or Deidre is the likely leak. My money's on Deidre. She and Gilly are thick. Of course, Gilly told Jack. My eight-hour grace period to disintegrate alone is over.

I grab my phone from the bedside table. Text after text from Bobby, a collection of Maureens, a Taryn, and fuck all, a fair amount from Cian. None from Dash. My money is on Maureen putting Jack and Gilly up to this raid.

Of all the people my scenarios wronged, it's the two outside my door that've suffered most. Yet here they are, demanding a face-to-face. Sneaky Maureen knows I'd not turn the pair of 'em away.

Gilly pitches her voice lower, but it penetrates my fortress of self-pity. "We know, Meg. Please talk to us."

I want to ask her why they bother, but I know the answer. It's always been about team for them, the show, and its people. I've given the concept lip service but never truly ingested it. Meg McGrath is a one-woman show existing inside something larger. I set myself apart, and it's gotten me exactly here in a dark room with a bloated face.

"Can I wish the pair of you away?"

"No, ma'am," says Jack.

"Fine," I extricate my limbs from the tangle of covers pinning my legs together and pull aside the blackout curtains. Mulberry clouds stretch over the distant horizon, warning everyone sunset is not far off. My eyes pulse, resenting the onslaught of light. I don't want to see or talk to anybody, but I owe Mr. and Mrs. Jack O'Leary a debt of gratitude for their generosity—a kindness I don't feel entitled to.

A renewed wave of sadness washes over my heart. I promised the two a wonderful wedding out on the Skelligs during our filming of season three. If they still want the public ceremony in addition to their previous private one, I'll pin Cian to a wall with knives until he swears to follow through with that plan.

Cian. I will be forced to talk to the man. The transition of power makes chatting unavoidable. God willing, it'll be back home where I'll be fortified with a sense of security from the land beneath my feet.

I wrap the hotel robe around my yoga pants and T-shirt. After twisting my rat's nest of hair into a knot on my head, I shuffle to the door. The plan is to open it a crack, tell the pair of fools how much I appreciate their caring, and go back to sleep until my plane leaves Monday morning.

The moment I slide the security locks and turn the handle, a gleaming silver, six-foot-four star trooper muscles his way into my room. Right behind him is a princess in head-to-toe, form-fitting armor covered in metallic lace. Her majesty holds out a small, brown, handled bag to me.

"This was outside your door," says Gilly, inviting herself into the room.

I set the bag down next to the television and cross my arms. "Here I am."

Jack peels off the helmet and sets it on a chair as Gilly closes the door. "The head bucket is misery," he says. Sweat plasters his hair to his forehead. One long butter-colored braid flops over his shoulder.

"It did the trick, though," says Gilly. "No one recognized Jack on the convention floor."

He looks flustered. "Sorry to complain. Thanks for suiting us up, Meg."

I wave him away and purposefully fail to give Cian credit. "Glad to do it." I perch on the edge of my bed. "You've heard?"

They look at each other and then back at me. I see twin expressions of concern that I appreciate, not pity.

"I can't believe Bobby will let this stand," says Jack. "When he puts a team together, he means it to stay together."

I arrange my robe to limit the view of what lies beneath. "You understand if I'd rather not speak about this." I can't discuss my situation without fragmenting again. I haven't wrapped my own psyche around it. "As you see, I'm not stepping out on my balcony for a jump, so go on with you now."

"Come out with us," says Jack. "We're going to the Costume Contest."

Gilly nods with enthusiasm. "We watched video of last year's competition online. It's crazy amazing."

I snort. "You're both mad." I make a shooing motion with my hands. "I'm in for the night." I've no desire to see a parade of characters on display no matter how jaw-unhinging the costumes are supposed to be. Truth be told, the energy of a crowd may crush me. I need solace and space to be miserable.

"We insist." Jack sticks his bum out toward the smallish, rolling office chair tucked against a desk area built into the long counter with the television and coffeemaker. I've never been especially gifted in the spatial department, but even my untrained eye can see the chair is not going to be a friendly fit for Jack's bulk, especially in his contraption of a costume.

Gilly senses the same and grabs to stop him a beat too late. The back of his thighs hit the chair, sending it into a collision course with the counter. Jack, all disjointed star trooper limbs, lists dangerous to one side. A panic flash of the star of *The Chieftain's Son* dashing his head on the corner of a hotel desk sends me diving for him as well. The joint effort of Gilly and me manage to aim Jack's silver-armored ass on a collision course with the bed instead of the carpet. He flails on the way down, costume rattling, and misses the mattress.

"The fuck, I'm wedged here."

A man who sits a horse as a magnificent knight of old and wields a monstrous sword like a butter knife flips and twists, a turtle on its back. Jack O'Leary is utterly ridiculous.

"Either of you ladies planning to lend a hand here?"

Laughter pours out of me in such a mighty burst, I'm hard pressed to breathe. Gilly is as useless as I am. Together, we haul Jack up on the bed and collapse on either side of him, clutching our middles in a full force belly laugh. Poor Jack continues to flap his arms, straining to sit upright. It's a sight to see.

A welcome variety of silly tears roll down my cheeks. "Rethinking your choice of costume, Mr. O'Leary?"

Gilly takes pity on her man. "Stop wiggling." She helps him sit.

Jack's face is the color of Mommy's favorite red rose, but he draws himself to his feet as a good star trooper should. Poised and proper, he bows to me. "We'll come for you at seven."

"Thanks to the both of you for the giggle, but stepping out is a no-go for me."

With a quick swipe, Jack steals the keycard to my room from the table. "I disagree." He waves it in the air. "Now there'll be no need to knock when we come a-calling."

Gilly retrieves a plastic bag I didn't notice from the corner by the door. "We brought you stuff to wear since I'm betting you're not the costume type." She pulls out a superhero hoodie and a pair of red runners dappled with white stars. "Maureen said these are your size."

Jack aims a black-and-silver gloved finger at me. "None of your proper business clothes. Tonight, we play."

Here's a new dynamic, Jack and Gilly painting a scenario I'm to follow. "What are the two of you doing to me?"

Gilly lays clothes on the bed next to me and then attacks me with a hug. "We're caring about you." She ends the hug but keeps her fingers wrapped around my arms. "Let us."

She fades to Jack's side. He slides a hand around his princess's waist. "There's fun to be had, Meg," says Jack. "Grab some with us, will you?"

I take in the sight of this lovely man holding my keycard. The warmth running through me is better than any shot of whiskey. Jack was the first of the talent brought on board. We've been on *The Chieftain's Son* journey together since the beginning. We shared a yoke, tugging the show down the road to a place that surpassed our grandest hopes for it. He and I had our rough patches, to be sure. I've set his personal life on fire by insisting he fit into a public image of my design, yet here he is, picking me up off the floor. Only a devasting ingrate would turn him down now.

"If I say yes, will you give me my keycard back?"

Jack cocks his head to one side. "Naw." He waves the card in the air. "Insurance." He catches the time on the bedside clock as Gilly pulls the door open. "Get to it, Superhero Woman. My armored beauty and I will be back in twenty."

I don't want to go out with them. My hotel room makes a fine cocoon, but wanting and doing don't always partner up the way you hope. I'll go out with the fools. Their gesture is too sweet and genuine to turn down.

The small, brown, handled bag Jack set near the television catches my eye. It's from Bobby, no doubt, leaving me a sugary treat to cheer up, or maybe Deidre's set me up with some of her Jameson junior bottles. I peek inside. There's a paperback book. *Odd.* I pull out *"The Importance of Being Earnest,"* and immediately drop it.

The one person in the city of San Diego who knows *Earnest* is near and dear to me is Cian Malley.

The book hits the carpet with a thump. Between the pages, a neon green sticky note marks a page. Huffing at the paperback, I walk past and head for the shower. I'd better be quick about putting myself together before Jack and Gilly barge in. I don't make it three steps past before my resolve evaporates. I turn to grab the book. A single line on the neon green sticky note page is bolded. It's the last line in the play.

"I've now realized for the first time in my life the vital Importance of Being Earnest."

Damn you, Cian Malley. Whatever he means by his confession is late to the party. He's been deceiving me since the day we met. If this is a plea for absolution, he can kiss my ass.

My cell buzzes on the nightstand with a text. As my gran used to warn, *"Think of the devil, summon the devil."* It's another message from Cian.

I catch sight of the message before it joins the tower of Cian's previous texts.

I've left something outside your door.

A wise woman would delete Cian's messages unread, but curse the man, he's blurred my wisdom into a shape I don't recognize. God help me, I want to know what his messages say. I open the blasted things one at a time in order.

There are things I need to say.

You are completely justified to hate me.

I'd say I'm sorry, but I won't be shallow and cliché with you. I'm also not stupid enough to believe a simple apology atones for what I've done.

As a person who puts words in other people's mouths, I find I have none that fit. Tell me what words work for our situation, and I'll say them. I swear I will mean every one of them.

If you call me, I won't pick up. Use the message to rage at me. Give me the truth of what you think of me. You'll be right.

Is there any chance, any at all, you see a way not to cut me loose? Can we find a way to work through this? To work through it together?

The man has no right to set my head spinning. The pleading tone of his text plays a note or two in my heart I wish I couldn't hear. But the last one...Work together. Bollocks. Say what you mean, Cian Malley. Work for you, not with you.

Oh, please, Meg. Anything. Give me anything.

I will my heart to harden, but there's something in his last message that won't allow it.

I've left you something outside your door.

Does he think me a priest, waiting to hear his confession? *"I've now realized for the first time in my life the vital Importance of Being Earnest."*

I toss the paperback play onto my bed. What I can't work out is why he didn't come clean from the start about our dynamic. If he'd already won, where's the point in winning me over? All I can figure is he posed as a benevolent mentor to pull my strings and groom me to accept the position of his number two.

"Och, you do need me, you goddamned thief." It's the transition he wants me for, not my inventiveness, skills, or drive. Once Cian Malley drains my brain of all things *Chieftain's Son*, I'll lose the last droplets of my worth to him and his True Time overlords.

I shudder as the reality of Cian's well-orchestrated insincerity rains down on me like an icy winter cloudburst and head for a hot shower to warm the chill in my heart.

CHAPTER 21

THE IMPORTANCE OF BEING EARNEST

The Cali Con Costume Contest is quite the craic. We're back in The Grand Ballroom, the scene of our triumphant panel. True Time snapped up a row near the front, but as far as I can tell, it's not occupied by any of their A-listers, save Jack, who's hidden in silver, molded plastic. His bulk takes up the better part of two seats, causing Gilly and me to snug thigh to thigh. Every time he shifts position, all three of us realign.

I'd normally tap out of such a close-quarters situation, but the competition is mesmerizing. Folks in brilliant costumes perform mini scenes to music or recorded narrations to showcase their creations. If Bobby was on the lookout for a costume designer instead of a production designer, this party would be the perfect hunting ground. The craftsmanship in these cosplay costumes is slap-me-to-silence impressive.

"Who's that fellow?" I speak directly into Gilly's ear as a seven-foot-tall living sculpture dancing to the beat of tribal music appears. The performer is decked from top to bottom in a collage of silver and blue metallic pieces, an impression of Picasso's cubism come to life. He twirls about the stage, affording us a 360-degree view of a bloody masterpiece.

Gilly names the character, but it rings no bells for me. My lack of knowledge in the realms of video game and anime characters is blatantly on display. I lean into Gilly to ask what she and Maureen cooked up for the scavenger hunt today. I bowed out of writing riddles to lick my wounds. The two of them and my secretary back at The Clan set the next meet up in motion.

The sight of the couple kills my wondering. Jack's fingers are twined with Gilly's, and she gravitates toward him, a flower to sunlight. The two share a laugh, and their joined hands slide to her knee. Their synchronicity is a dance. They whisper, the motion of one effortlessly complimenting the other. Even in the middle of a boisterous crowd, Jack and Gilly are clearly enchanted with each other's company.

It hurts damn bad to watch them. Not because I begrudge their intimacy, but because I'd dared to entertain the notion I might find such a thing with Cian.

"Did you say something?" says Gilly.

I startle at her question.

"You're staring at us."

"I'm seeing you." Her brow wrinkles, and a pot inside me boils over. "You and Jack are a beautiful thing. I've been a villain to you both, shoving him at Niks while hiding you in the shadows. All the while, I knew it hurt you, but I didn't stop." I close my eyes for a long beat. "I am truly sorry." I feel a world class shit.

Gilly squeezes my hand. "You were thinking of the show."

I squeeze back. "The show isn't everything."

The next vignette is shrouded in sidelight with yards of silk twisting and writhing across the stage to a new age musical piece. Its floaty notes return me to a state of melancholy. The distraction of the contest loses its power, and I land smack in the puddle of loss my life has become.

Gilly squeezes my hand again. "For what it's worth, I know Cian lied to you over the job dynamic, but I don't believe he was dishonest about being into you." She tugs at my hand when I try to turn away. "You weren't playing a game with him either, were you?"

I glance at Jack, who bobbles his helmet to the new upbeat tune splashing over the audience. Convinced he can't hear me, I allow St.

Gilly to hear my confession. "I fell too hard and too fast for sweet that turned sour. The notion of a lightning bolt when it comes to attraction is bad business. I should know better."

Gilly turns her whole body to face me. "Do you think Jack and I are bad business?"

"God, no." I'm mortified she thinks I'm lumping her grand relationship with Jack in with the disaster of Cian and me.

"I knew in my gut Jack was more than a flirtation by the second day I knew him. When he transformed at the table read into Donal Cam, I recognized him as the artistic partner I'd always longed for. Don't get me wrong, I fought it hard. Told myself I was a loon, landing in the same sort of secret relationship situation I'd just escaped at home." Gilly leans so she's touching Jack as if breaking contact with him violates a covenant. It's so natural, I'm sure she's not even aware she's doing it. "What if I'd run? What if I'd rationalized the speed of our attraction as proof it was not legit?" Her eyes fill with tears.

Those tears jolt me to my core. How many times in the last few days did I attempt to discount the pull between Cian and me as a lark, a fling, an empty, lust-filled escapade? My own gut resonates with the same surety Gilly is voicing. The connection to Cian is an experience that opened my heart in a way it's never been opened before. With Cian, the concept of "*we*" began to shred the layers of "*me*" I'd mummified myself in.

Until he stabbed me in the back

"What do you want in life, Meg?"

I know what she's about. The writer in Gilly mines my layers. She's digging in to figure out what makes me tick. Usually, I'd resent it and put her off, but there's caring and hopefulness in her eyes that touch my heart. My own eyes fill. I fan a finger between Jack and her. "This. What you two have. The partnership. The respect."

Love took Gilly straight into a dream marriage and a Crystal Award nomination. If she'd walked away from Jack, would the incredible season finale she wrote even exist? Love made her fight. It made her strong, not weak.

I try to blink away a new damn burst of tears and fail. "I'd decided such a thing was impossible for me, until that bloody Cian Malley showed up."

Gilly pats my shoulder as I drop my head into my hands. "Impossible is defeat talking. Defeat and Meg McGrath do not mesh."

She's too right. Defeat is the enemy. Defeat is handing my position over to Cian without a whimper. I've got a horse in this race, my time and expertise on the show. One of Cian's texts burns in my brain.

Is there any chance, any at all, where you can see a way not to cut me loose? Can we find a way to work through this? To work through it together?

Jack and Gilly's relationship shows me the way. Partnership. Equal power. Cian and I share the top spot.

Pride is a tall stone wall. I've built mine strong and unassailable. The thing about walls is they do protect you, but they also keep out what might be wondrous to let in.

Jack hovers over both Gilly and me, his helmet switching back and forth between the pair of weeping females next to him. "What's wrong then?"

I don't want the sweetness of Jack O'Leary and Gilly out of my life. I don't want to step away from the show or Bobby, Maureen, the exquisite sets that transport me to times past, or the marvelous stories Deidre LaRochelle's spun into gold. I'm not willing to give up the rush of pride experiencing the monumental fan support for my people that I've helped build. *The Chieftain's Son* is my world and my life's blood, and damn if I'm not fighting hard enough to remain a part of it. My bottom line is as clear as a picture window. Staying with my tribe is the only choice that makes a lick of sense. Pride be damned.

"It's a chick thing," says Gilly. The girl has my back. It's time I have hers as well.

Jack digs a hand under his helmet to scratch.

It's a rare thing for perspective to shift so thoroughly in the space of a heartbeat. Trusting the wisdom threaded through one's emotion is terrifying. Yet here I sit with a pair who told logic to fuck off and took the gamble on their heartbeats. When I was offered such a leap, I didn't know quite how to deal with it. Cian didn't make matters any clearer by withholding fundamental truths from me.

I've a conclusion to draw. If I plan to push for equal billing with Cian, is the *"we"* Cian and I started worth trying to fix, or is Meg McGrath as a *"me"* the smarter choice going forward?

Gilly nudges me. "It's okay not to keep everything to yourself, Meg."

Is it her writer's proclivity for sniffing out truths or Gilly's easy caring for others that allows her to read my knotted emotions? Whichever it is, she's got me. The woman is a life lesson in herself. She's proof love adds to success. It doesn't weaken your drive to achieve, it fortifies you.

I dip my mouth as close as I can to Gilly's ear without giving her a kiss. "I need your take on something, writers being keen on subtext and all."

Her eyes widen and she gives a teeny *"go on with you"* nod.

Before I chicken out, I tap on the thread of Cian's messages and hand her my phone. My heart races as she skims over his words.

"Someone's groveling hard," says Jack.

Gilly and I whip our heads to face him. My cheeks flame as hot as one of the propane-driven Tiki torches on Dash's ridiculous boat party. The man's helmet seemed to face away while the eyes inside locked on my texts.

I fight the instinct to hide my head in my hands. "Groveling, you say?"

Gilly chews her bottom lip. "There's a definite build to his intention and a plea woven in."

"But do you get the sense he's genuine or is it more bumbering?"

Gilly's face squinches up. "Bumbering?"

"Messing about with the truth. Deceiving. Pulling a fast one," says Jack. "It's from the play, '*The Importance of Being Earnest.*' I played Earnest in Dublin before *Randy in 6B.*"

"Please tell me there's video." She nudges him, then faces me. "Given the shit Cian pulled on you, it could go either way," she says, handing me the cell. "Which way do you want it to go?"

There's the question. I want Cian to have been straight with me. I want the nightmare of losing the show erased. I want to believe the connection between Cian and me was mutual and equally unsettling to both of us because it happened too fast. How can real materialize over days rather than weeks, or in our case, hours? I look between Jack and Gilly. Sometimes real shines brighter than time.

"Don't discount the groveling," says Jack. "It doesn't top of our list of manly choices."

"Which means," I spin my hands in circles for him to elaborate.

"If Cian's belly crawling, I'm betting he's got something to say you might want to hear."

Gears in my head that misery ground to a halt moan as they take the first precious turn toward full movement. Soon they're back, spinning at full power.

Gilly grabs my hand. "I say talk to him, but trust your instinct to walk away if your bullshit meter hits red."

"True enough." Jack lifts his helmet far enough to give Gilly a quick kiss. He's incognito again before anyone is the wiser of the star trooper's identity.

They're right. In a bizarre way, I've got the upper hand. Cian wants to talk to me, and I have an earful for the man. I will not accept a demotion and fade silently to the number two position, but I am willing to entertain the notion of an equal partnership. Cian's experience is nothing to be scoffed at and tossed away, but neither is my investment in the show. The only way Cian Malley can redeem himself to me and not nullify what's happened between us is for him to support my idea of a shared job title and responsibilities.

In creating the *Ship of Dreams*, the two of us proved to be a successful "*we*."

Is "*we*" the same for him?

If it is, Dash Everett will need to be convinced Cian Malley should be by my side, not blocking me from view.

I press fingers into my temples. Can my ego and trust bear the idea of sharing?

Like two halves of a deck of cards shuffled into one neat stack, my time with Cian plays through my mind. When I tease each moment away from the rest, there is no stink of sabotage. His advice and support made me shine brighter. In retrospect, it feels not as if he were preparing me to take a fall but building me up to avoid a plunge.

"Two more minutes in this plastic hell and I'll start throwing punches," mutters Jack.

A trio of masked characters prance across the stage. Masks. Masquerade. Hidden truths. I'll never discover why Cian didn't come out with the truth from our start if I avoid a showdown with him. He owes me solid truths about the game he's been playing with me. As daunting as a face-to-face with him feels, I see no alternate means of a path to keep me with the show.

Gilly threads her arm through Jack's armor and rests her head on his shoulder. The silver bucket on his head rests against the top of her white metallic tiara.

What do I want in life, Gilly? I want to remain a part of *The Chieftain's Son* for its entire run.

I reread Cian's texts with the fresh perspective supplied by Jack and Gilly. Do I dare trust him? Do I risk playing the fool to try for what I want as my future? I'm sacrificing a massive slice of security to offer Cian a way back in. To open to the rare possibility of seeing if I could one day let the man into my life terrifies me, but my gut tells me to give it a go.

This massive risk I'm taking hinges on the Cian Malley I thought I'd come to know to be real.

"I've now realized for the first time in my life the vital Importance of Being Earnest."

I'll be holding you to that, Mr. Malley.

CHAPTER 22

SHIP OF DREAMS

ozens of times throughout the night, my finger twitches to text or call Cian. I stay my course to face him in person at the *Ship of Dreams* panel. I need the chance to read his raw reaction to my plan of sharing the number one P.R. spot.

"You need me, Cian Malley. You need me, Dashell Everett." I chant my new mantra on the way to the pre-panel gathering.

Security is double-teamed for the confluence of two massive shows. For a fleeting second when I flash my I.D. badge, I worry Dash slapped me on a banned list. Thankfully, I pass muster, receive a wristband, and enter the small gathering room from which we'll be escorted under guard into Harborside Hall.

Deidre, Bobby, Jack, and Niks are hob-knobbing with the *Star's Shadow* crowd. My gaze flicks from them over to the gaggle of True Time Network execs. I spot Dash. One of Cian's assistants reviews info on a tablet with Sala Singh. Chip works the room, handing everyone a paddle with Jack and Niks on one side and Sala and Malachi, the couple from *Star's Shadow*, on the other. Despite her ire at the panel being pulled out from under me, Deidre didn't back out of moderator duties. Her devotion to the show and the characters she created won out in the end.

She is the perfect pick to guide fans on the quest to decide who True Times's quintessential love couple will be.

Bobby waves me over. I take a circuitous route through the crowd to troll for Cian. The man is a phantom. My element-of-surprise plan will be a bust if the object of the surprise is missing in action. There's no logical scenario for why he isn't here. I'll bet he's already in Harborside Hall, waiting to pounce on the name tags so his people land the most desirable positions on the dais, a Malley move I'm familiar with.

An arm threads through mine, and for a heart-stopping moment, I imagine it to be Cian. A full body flush rises from my toes to the top of my scalp. Gilly's California accent brings me back to reality.

"Did you get a load of Doolin?" She jerks a chin to the corner of the room where he's planted himself.

I bray out a laugh akin to one of Doolin's adopted donkeys back at The Clan. "Have mercy." Our resident Irish teacher/curmudgeon is decked out in a garish pink and purple Hawaiian shirt, khaki shorts, slip-on sandals he won't get a lick of use out of back home, and an electric blue baseball cap with San Diego splashed across the front. I wonder if Deidre dressed him while he was asleep. I've never seen the man in anything but a dozen shades of dignified brown or gray.

Doolin's getup takes a nibble out of my tension level. Since Gilly is well-versed in my Cian dilemma, I'm not shy to ask, "Have you seen Cian?"

Gilly does a rapid scan of the group and crinkles her nose. "He must be here." She bumps my shoulder. "Maybe he's scared of your right hook."

Before the two of us shuffle over to *The Chieftain's Son* folks, the call rings out it's time to move the party into Harborside Hall. Adrenaline fountains through my core. Whatever my future with the show, I want to remember this moment. I own the triumph. I conceived this brilliant panel. Cian and I teamed up to flesh out details, but my beloved show wouldn't be headed for Harborside Hall, the Mecca of Cali Con, without Meg McGrath. I have every right to be proud.

"Pictures, Meg," says Gilly.

Too right she is. I take a series of shots with my phone of our march to glory. Gilly grabs my cell to include me in the photo spread.

We flow into Harborview Hall surrounded by security. Deidre and the two couples hover offstage of the dais while the rest of my team and the True Time contingent grab reserved seats in the first row.

I grab Gilly's arm. "Sit with me." If anyone had told me a week ago I'd cling to Gilly for support, I would've laughed them off.

Event center folks set out name tags on the dais. Niks and Jack claim the first two positions next to the moderator podium, the power seats. Is the placement our consolation prize from Cian?

I scan the first row, the base of the dais, and the True Time offstage throng. Cian is nowhere in sight. It's then the rumble of the crowd resonates in my bones. I turn to take in the massive cathedral that is Harborside Hall. The seats fade so far into the darkness, there's no spotting the end of them. Jumbo screens are placed at intervals from the dais to perch over the audience. Energy in the room sets my blood singing a victory tune. My darling show soared above the clouds in its first season.

Bobby sidles up next to me. "Well done, bringing us to the winner's circle, Meg. Thank you." My dear friend kisses my hand. "There's an insane amount of people in line outside, hoping for seats. However high Dash set your bar, you've soared far above it. Don't forget that."

"Thank you, Bobby, for..." Words stick in my throat for a moment. "All of it." He treats me to one of those Bobby Provost smiles that make you believe you're top of the heap. What brilliant luck a small town Cahersiveen girl was granted passage on this journey. It's glorious, and God willing, not over for me yet, even if I do have a bit of pride to swallow with my plan to share the reins with Cian.

Bobby's eyes dart to Dash, who's holding court with a cadre of men in ties. "Speak his name and the devil appears."

I bump shoulder with him. "You sound more like my Gran every day."

He laughs and leans close. "Heads up. Something's brewing with the big boss in the form of a very large bee up his ass."

"No ideas?"

Bobby shakes his head. "If he tries to rain any more shit on you, I've got your back."

"Then I'm as safe as I can be. I think the Everett shitestorm has already done its worst to me," I say, smiling. Dash knocked me down. The question is, will he accept my terms of getting back on my feet?

My moment of comradery with Bobby is overshadowed as pandemonium shakes the walls of Harborside Hall. Our two power couples and *The Chieftain's Son* North Star, Deidre LaRochelle, are introduced and take their place on the dais. A trio of serious movie cameras capture every moment. My mind races with the publicity opportunities this panel will spawn, then stops with an abrupt halt, a runaway car colliding with a brick wall.

None of these ideas will matter if I can't find Cian and set the wheels in motion for me to stay with the show.

Deidre's got the crowd eating from her hand before she's done with her preamble. She takes off, posing the series of questions Cian and I wrote to pit Donal Cam and Nieve against Starry Night and Event Horizon. A tally chart appears in the lower right corner of the screens. So far, the couples are in a dead heat. A draft flutters across my skin as fans behind me raise paddles en masse to answer Deidre's latest "best" question. I swivel to see the smiling faces of Niks and Jack on a stick inches from my nose.

"And *The Chieftain's Son* scores another win for most swoonworthy male lead," Deidre announces. A chant of "*Donal Cam. Donal Cam,*" breaks out on the left side of the hall, quickly answered by "*Event Horizon. Event Horizon,*" in a pocket near the center. The crowd is as completely sucked into the competition between the True Time power couples as I knew they would be. My *Ship of Dreams* panel claims the heart of every romantic and, dare I say, skeptic in the room.

"And now," says Deidre. "Let's talk kissing."

The floor vibrates beneath my feet as stomping provides percussion to the chorus of hoots and cheers behind me. Deidre prompts the couples for their input on the topic.

Niks waves her hands. "Oh, no, Deidre. I never kiss and tell." She rests her head on Jack's shoulder, gazing up at him with those huge, round, blue Scandinavian eyes. Thank goodness Gilly laughs.

"Oh, but we do," chirps Sala Singh as she pulls Malakai Bono into a kiss that would curl anyone's toes.

Pockets of both boos and hurrahs erupt in geysers throughout the hall.

Deidre, master of the game, salutes the *Star's Shadow* couple. "Fine acting, you two." She deftly negates their PDA and refocuses the crowd to our team. "Now Jack and Niks, back to"—she plays to her audience— "How do you folks say it, IRL?" She winks. "Rumor has it, Jack, there's a certain special *event* on your *horizon* with a lovely lady."

Gilly isn't laughing now. Neither am I, despite Deidre's clever name play of *Star's Shadow* leading man, she's gone too far off book. *Oh, God no. Do not mention Jack's slip of the lip about having a fiancé.* Social media's already splattered with the false lead.

To my surprise, it's Niks who waves her hands wildly as if to ward off Deidre's insinuation. She pushes Jack away. "No, no. Don't put my horse in the cart."

The audience roars at her misuse of the phrase.

Niks looks puzzled. "No? My horse isn't in the cart." She turns to Deidre. "Who's in the cart?"

I thoroughly enjoy Niks's deflection of the fiancé issue until a hand rests on my shoulder.

Dashell Everett looms over me, blocking my view of the dais. "A word, Meghan." He nods toward the side of the room near the door we came in.

Holy God. Has the hour of my sentencing come? Did Cian confirm I said to fuck off his offer of the number two position? My mind races to our confrontation at the True Time party. Did I say anything irreparable?

Damn Cian for not being here. He's turned coward, unable to watch Dash give me the boot. Damn the man for not giving me the chance to paint a different scenario for our future than the one dictated by Dashell Everett. Damn me for playing the fool and not calling Cian as soon as I came up with my new plan.

I do a decent acting job as I casually stroll with Dash into the shadows near the wall. Anger crosses Bobby's face, and he rises from his seat as we pass. With a curt shake of my head, I keep him from following. This is my battle to win or lose. If I hide behind Bobby, any power I may gain will bear the taint of dependence. Such a chink in my armor spells potential to be exploited by the likes of Dashell Everett in the future.

Dash can't keep from fidgeting when we reach the edge of the room. He runs a hand through his hair as he shifts from foot to foot. I've never seen the cool exec display nerves. It's bloody unsettling.

"Meghan," he says, then clears his throat as if he swallowed down the wrong pipe.

I play the counterpoint to his unease and feign nonchalance as if I haven't a care in the world. I'm on the brink of making a play to push my way into a role on the show I can live with, working by Cian Malley's side, not under him. Bless the darkness of Harborview Hall for hiding my face when I imagine being under Cian.

Dash appears to compose himself, but his rapid-fire speech tells a different story. "I'm here to eat a healthy portion of crow. It's come to my attention the inception of this impressive offering is your brainchild and not Cian Malley's."

His admission widens my eyes for half a second.

He fiddles with his tie before continuing. "You understand how I misconstrued the credit for your concept since the proposal came from Cian's email before he clarified the situation. So, well done, Meghan."

Clarified? What did Cian say to Dash? And why did he submit *Ship of Dreams* instead of his Plan B?

"The original idea was mine. Cian and I partnered up for fine-tuning."

Dash waves his arms as if my statement is unnecessary. My gut clenches at the dismissal. Is this all I get from the man, a weak apology and then a boot to the backside?

Creases along his forehead and down his cheeks shift Dash's resting smug face into a portrait of tension. "I gave you a false lead, making you believe a strong Cali Con debut would change the dynamic of *The Chieftain's Son* publicity department."

Now it's my turn to sprout face creases. What is he on about? Surely not a compliment. Is this more buttering up for me to accept the number two position?

"A dynamic you'd already achieved," he mutters and then clears his throat. "My decision was in error, given your accomplishments. I'll need to you stay on in your position at *The Chieftain's Son*."

His statement corresponds to an explosion from the audience. I'm certain I've not heard the fool correctly. I lean in. "Pardon." I wave a hand at the crowd and point to my ear.

His fluster rapidly sours to irritation. "True Time will not be making a change in the publicity department of *The Chieftain's Son*."

I stare at Dash. No change? I'm still number one? What should be elation is colored with suspicion. There's a catch here. A trap. A gigantic pile of mess he's not showing me.

"So, to be clear. I am the head of publicity and marketing for *The Chieftain's Son*, not Cian Malley."

I expect his lips to crack, they're so tightly pushed together. A quick "Um-hum," is the stingy reply.

Everything stripped away is handed back to me in the space of a shallow conversation. I don't trust the ease of his turnabout. "And why is that?"

"Cian Malley is no longer with the True Time Network. He resigned this morning."

Resigned.

Gone.

Disappeared.

The flurry of Cian's text messages pours through my mind. While I was engineering the vision of a partnership at my end, he was bowing out. Why? The answer comes as swift and true as an arrow to the chest. Cian is giving me my dream. Did the thief succumb to conscience, or did his motivation go deeper? Instead of crawling away from Cali Con as the victim of a backstabbing, the future I've striven for spills out before me thanks to Cian's defection.

Or does it? I can't stomach subsisting in the same professional vulnerability I've been subjected to. My eyes narrow. "Tell me truthfully,

Dash. Are you putting me in as a placeholder until you find the next True Time candidate to supplant me? Because if that's your intention—"

Dash's throat ripples like a fat snake swallowing a frog. "Consider this my admission that I've underestimated you, Meghan. Your position with the show remains yours with the caveat you can count on more mentoring support from my end." He pretends to be captivated with something Deidre says. His gaze darts back to me when I don't answer immediately. "Are we good here?"

I stare past his shoulder, my mind on the down loop of a roller coaster. Scenarios fly off the end of my mental paintbrush. Of course, I want the position, but I'm not showing my unguarded belly to this fickle, game-playing man again. Cian would never give an immediate smile and thumbs up to an offer born of Dash's plan gone sour. He'd outthink Dash, outplay him. Cian would see a bubble of opportunity floating in the air and pop it to see what treasures lay inside.

Forget Cian. I won't project what he might do. It's about what Meg McGrath will do.

"I have conditions."

Dash's expression is what I hoped for, arrogance barely masking the sweet shine of surprise. The fool expected me to bow and scrape. Has he ever really seen me at all? Dashell Everett needs me, and he knows I know it.

No doubt he considered handing the show over to one of his L.A. stable boys, but they'd have to relocate to Kerry and start from zero without me. I'm the one with established relationships, a damn fine record of success, and blueprints past, present, and future for the show. *The Chieftain's Son* is a language I speak. Faith in myself that withered when Dash handed my show over to Cian bursts back into the sunlight.

Dash pretends to be focused on Deidre's next volley. "Let's hash out the details after the panel. Shall we?"

"I think now is a fine time," I say, crossing my arms. I revel in the fit of my new suit of confidence. Before he can argue, I launch into the list newly formulated in my brain. "I want a budget increase to allow for at least two more assistants in Ireland to handle the show's uptick in popularity."

He raises an eyebrow as a new *Donal Cam/Nieve* chant ripples through the audience. It's as if I cued the chorus as background music to emphasize my case.

"Besides support in Ireland, I'll also need someone on the ground at the L.A. office that answers to me."

He raises a hand. "Done."

"Grand." I nearly ask for an end to our weekly calls that seem more evaluation than communication but decide I'll finesse his tether as we go. Healthy communication with L.A. is in the best interest of the show. "And you'll name me as publicity lead for Jack O'Leary's spin off show '*My Ireland*.'"

This unsettles him. The man who didn't trust me enough to hold on to one show is being asked to add another to my duties.

"I will consider it with a detailed proposal and commitment from Jack."

I've got a whopper of a proposal bubbling. I want Jack O'Leary to introduce his American bride to his love of Ireland. There's a romantic twist ole Hollywood Dash won't see coming.

"Fair enough." I'm happy to concede the point to make the man feel a modicum of power in our negotiation, especially since I'm set to brain him with my biggest get.

"And I'll be needing a run of show contract."

I hold my breath. An extended contract with clauses to give me stability is my guarantee True Time can't put my head on a spike without cause. I'm through being tested. I need to be trusted. From the bitty dance his jaw does, I'm certain the man grinds his teeth. There's no telling for sure with the roar behind me in the room.

"Will that make this happen, Meghan?"

Here it is, the moment to determine my future. I've always feared the outcome of spontaneity over careful planning. Cian's praise of my thinking on my feet buoys me. It's time to speak from my heart and market Meg McGrath.

"Yes. I've proven my devotion to the show as well as my ability to navigate its success. Every flaming hoop you held up for me to jump through, I soared beyond. I bear enough humility to admit I've got a learning curve. My strengths lie in my vision for the show's future. I'm not a sort to settle into cocky confidence. I swear, I will ask for your guidance and advice when I need it. The question is, can you trust me to continue the momentum I've begun?"

As Dash studies my face, I set my jaw and look him square in the eye to say, *"The job belongs to me, so give over."*

"You make a convincing argument, Ms. McGrath." He offers me his hand, and I shake it.

Harborview Hall bursts at the seams with adoration for *The Chieftain's Son* as Deidre proclaims our couple as the hands-down winner of the *Ship of Dreams* and MetaMeme takes the stage.

I swim in a delicious soup of joy, pride, and dreams of my own, but there's one dream floating out of my grasp.

Cian.

Reality thumps my temple with a painful wake up call.

Cian quit. He didn't only refuse to step into my shoes at *The Chieftain's Son*, he left True Time.

I grab my cell and, with shaky fingers, hit his contact. As promised, he doesn't pick up my call.

"Cian, despite your fine offer of last night, I'm not calling to rage at you. Are you still here, in San Diego? Meet me. Call me." I pause, formulating a proper ending to the call. My mind replays his series of texts to me.

There are things I need to say.

You are completely justified to hate me.

I'd say I'm sorry, but I won't be shallow and cliché with you. I'm also not fool enough to believe a simple apology atones for what I've done.

What Cian did by stepping away is plenty of atonement. He forfeited something he loves very deeply to restore what I'd lost. It's more than a kindness. It's a treasure.

"There are things I need to say. Don't take another step. I'm coming to your room."

As a rapidly cut-together montage of lovey moments from both *Star's Shadow* and *The Chieftain's Son* fill the massive screens to the music of MetaMeme, security ushers our group out of Harborview Hall. Bobby arranges a final get-together with *The Chieftain's Son* crew before we all head off for L.A. or home. I clutch my phone in anticipation of the vibration of an incoming call or text.

Deidre snatches me into a lung-squeezing hug. "This is one for the record books, Meg. Well done."

"Well done, you," I say. I nearly spill my news about staying on with the show, but she'll know soon enough.

I spot Bobby and Dash off a ways with their heads together. They both look at me, and I throw a salute. Bobby says something to Dash that makes the True Time boss raise his hands in surrender.

This should be my moment, and it is, but at the center of it is pain. A hollow ache reaches for the true loss today brought.

Cian.

I slink off to a corner to call him again when my eye catches a tiny red number one on my text message icon. When my fingertip makes contact, a single message with a single word fills my screen. It is from Cian with a time stamp well before I called him.

Goodbye.

Oh no you don't, Cian Malley. Without a word to anyone, I fly from the room. Thankfully, our hotel is a short sprint from Harborside Hall. I'm up the lift and running to Cian's room.

I'm finished calling what we started nothing more than a grand weekend. I want to give *"we"* a go. Jack and Gilly showed me a beautiful romantic tangle can be real no matter how quickly it begins. I want the same with Cian. I have it with Cian. I truly believe anyone who's willing to do what he did for me is as much in the thick of it as I am.

A buzz of anger at my own stubbornness makes my heart race. I should have called him, texted him, made some form of contact after his tower of texts. I pant like a woman who's never swam a lap in her life as I skid up to Cian's room. The housekeeping cart blocks the open door.

"Cian."

No answer. I slip inside and startle a woman with an armful of bedding. There's nothing of Cian in the room. No messenger bag, no computer, not a stitch of clothing in the closet. He's gone.

I slump onto a chair. He reached out, and I cut him off, never giving him a chance.

I swipe my phone screen, hoping for a message, but there's nothing. Cian's done what he's done.

My eyes skate over the sparkles covering the water of the bay. Am I romanticizing Cian's gesture because of a few brilliant nights in his embrace?

I drop my head to my hands.

"Ma'am, whoever you're looking for checked out."

I nod and slip out of the deserted room and away from the bed Cian and I called ours.

Romanticized, my ass. I met someone who fit. He kindled feelings in me I'd written off as unnecessary. His intellect and humor knocked me flat. I like the Meg McGrath who connected with Cian Malley. I don't want to lose her either.

I head down the hall to my own room. If the only way I can talk to Cian is to leave a message on his damn cell, then I'll do it.

I pace, attempting to squeeze the right words out of my head. To hell with planning. Whatever comes out, comes out.

"Cian. It's Meg. What you did for me is extraordinary. You're extraordinary. This weekend with you was not just brief jolly days to me. It was a fucking shift in my reality. I need you to know that."

I pinch the bridge of my nose.

"I'm not going to lie, I wish you'd told me the truth, but I've gained some perspective on the fiery pit Dash controls. It's all part of the game. As you said, the whole P.R. business is bumbering." I choke as truth surrounds my heart in a sweet blanket of heat. "Cian, you've showed me what you're made of, leaving *The Chieftain's Son* to me. I want to see what we can be together. Is there a chance?"

I've no clue how this will work. Ireland. Hollywood.

I keep going. "There it is. Damn it, man. I don't want you gone from my life."

I hit the end call button in near panic. The old Meg shell quavers at what I admitted to the man who gifted me the shift in my reality. Fear shatters as quickly as it came. I see so clearly the security I've always found in being a *"me"* was my end game. It's the *"we"* with Cian I want now. *"We"* opened a window for me. I see possibilities of not believing everything must be pre-planned and orchestrated to be successful. I've let past disappointments in others close me off. Fearing to trust anyone but myself made me small. It's terrifying to change my rigid life philosophy, but God help me, I'm ready for big.

There's nothing weak or wrong in what I admitted to Cian. I meant every word.

It's a damn shame I had to say them to a phone. One that's not ringing me back.

CHAPTER 23
BACK IN THE SWIM

I'll be forever in my sister, Taryn's, and her husband, Roy's, debt for buying the *Swim and Gym*. Even more grateful Roy dragged his arse out of bed to be on hand so I can get my laps in before my first day back at work since Cali Con. The laps I swim are meditation. God knows I need a Zen experience to quell the bloody sadness streaming from the empty spot in my heart that won't feck off—the void I orchestrated by not returning Cian's messages one awful night at Cali Con.

Was it only three days ago? It feels as if I've been in mourning for a month. I'm exhausted from checking my phone for texts or emails from Cian. Taryn thinks I'm mad not to keep at Cian from my end. She hounded me the whole two-hour-plus drive from Shannon Airport to Cahersiveen to reach out to him.

"*Elaborate*," she says. That's my sister's way of telling me to poke him relentlessly with details about my new situation until I wear him down and get a call back.

If he wanted to respond, he would have. I did reach out, and Cian broke with me, clear and simple. No looking back. I've got no complaints about his parting gift of my job. Bobby, bless the man, set

Dash on a hot seat to fashion me a contract so bright and shiny one won't be able to look directly at it without eye damage.

Cian's done with me, but my bruises from losing him are too painful to touch. Another lap, and another, and another. I'll swim him out of my heart. Where are endorphins when you need them?

Water leaks into my goggles. As I near the wall, the sting of chlorine begins to blur my vision. I've got to get a new pair with a better seal.

I see well enough to catch sight of a pair of hairy legs swishing over the edge of the pool just in time to pull off the aquatic version of a skid and avoid planting my nose onto a furry kneecap. I stand, ripping off the useless goggles and run a hand down my drippy face.

"Damn it, Roy. Don't dangle yourself in my lane."

"I'd do more than dangle, but I'm not dressed for it," says the last voice I expect to hear in the *Swim and Gym*.

The endorphins I wished for mid-lap surge through me. The rise in my body heat will surely start the pool water bubbling.

Cian nods to the *Proper Swim Attire Required* sign on the tile wall. "I don't want to get on your family's bad side by breaking rules."

Thanks be, I've got water to hold me up. "Cian?" The sound of his name bouncing off the tile walls adds to the altered reality of the moment.

He leans elbows on knees, bringing his gorgeous face closer to the water. "Hi, M-Squared."

"You're in Ireland." A statement of the obvious to be sure, but it's all I can dredge up.

He laughs his wonderful laugh that tells me he enjoys everything about me.

"A last minute, criminally over-priced plane ticket agrees with you."

Goose bumps blossom along my skin like a field of dandelions after the rain. I cross my arms to fight off the dual chill of cold air and surprise. "How is it you're at my sister's *Swim and Gym* at the crack of dawn?"

His hands dabble in and out of the surface of the water. "A very nice fellow named Roy let me in after another very nice fellow named Bobby told me where I'd find you at the crack of dawn."

I take a single step closer to those darling, dangling legs. My dependable, rational mind pinwheels aside, reducing my intellect to a nest of twisted, electrified, emotional threads. The very threads this man pulled out of hiding. The woman who prides herself on her cloak of rationality doesn't fit on my bones anymore, not when Cian Malley opened a window, treating me to a view of something bigger. Something with infinitely more possibilities than a solo life.

So fast. I've fallen so fast for Cian. The moment logic tries to weasel its way in, I remember what Gilly said about almost not letting Jack into her life. Wisdom of the mind says not to trust the lightning bolt, but wisdom of the heart is where the stuff of poetry and song dwells.

"You vanished..." I catch myself before I say *and hollowed out my heart with your silence.* "And now you appear in the morning mist like a faerie from an enchanted well." I drift toward him just beyond the reach of those long, floating fingers. "What do you have to say for yourself?" I need this moment to be what it seems to be. A moment that drove a man across an ocean to find me. I need this moment to be everything.

Cian stretches his arms out to me, hands waiting for mine. "I got your message."

"Did you now?" My fingertips brush against his.

"Finely worded and very effective, as you see."

I slide my fingers between his until our hands lock together. "You didn't ring me back."

With a swift tug, Cian pulls my body between his knees and wraps those wet hairy legs around me. He dips his head down to mine and whispers against my lips. "There are answers better given in person."

The contact brings every moment, every touch that's happened between us roaring back to life. His breath warms my skin. We're both still, savoring the anticipation of what may come next. Lightly dancing my lips across his, I murmur, "Such as?"

Cian captures me in a kiss the likes of which I've been aching for. A kiss I thought I'd never have a chance at again. His hands thread through my wet hair as he pulls me closer. The kiss deepens as his tongue tastes and claims. My grab at the front of his shirt, to better kiss the life out of him, is too enthusiastic. He plunges forward into the water with a smack, non-appropriate pool attire and all.

Our laugher bounces off tile walls to fill the air. We clutch each other until there's no space between us. I wrap my legs around his waist and continue the thorough kissing of Cian Malley. I relearn the softness of his mouth, the solid definition of his chest under the sodden shirt. He runs his hands down the sides of my body and then to curves better left ignored in a public pool. If it weren't for the threat of Roy or Taryn walking in on us, our water ballet would quickly turn into quite the randy dip.

It's a miracle Cian is here.

He twirls me through the water and then rests his drippy forehead against mine. "Meg, I'm gutted about the way everything went down in San Diego. I was dead wrong not to come clean with you on that first day. Dash was going to tell you straight away, but I asked him to let me break it to you. Idiot me thought I could ease you into the concept of being my number two."

I lay a finger on his lips to stop him. "Let's agree you took a massive wrong turn, but since..." My finger slides down to rest on his chin. "Your messages...What you've done..." I train a soggy lock of hair out of his eyes. "I hear you, Cian Malley. All I ask is to be worthy of the truth from now on."

"O'Malley."

"O'Malley?"

"Your first taste of truth. O'Malley is legally my last name. I shortened it to Malley for my Hollywood persona, but since I'm here now, the real thing'll do fine."

I drop my hands from around his neck and break contact. There's a question I don't want to ask, but I need to know the answer. What scenario does Cian intend to paint?

"And what does 'I'm here' mean?" It's a fair question for a man who shows up as fast as the flick of a lamb's tail with no warning. Is this an apology trip—a sweeter way to end things between us? Is he here for a visit with his grandparents and a bit of fun with me? Heaven help me, it's going to hurt worse to get more of him and then let go again, even if it is on a better note than the hell that went down in San Diego.

Cian's lips twitch into a smile. "I think you put it best when you said, 'a fucking shift in my reality.'" My heart pounds hard enough to start ripples in the pool. "I understand there may be an opening for an assistant in the McGrath P.R. and marketing empire."

I drop my hands and shake my head. "No, Cian. If you're on the show with me, I'll always sense True Time is waiting for me to misstep."

His hand glides through the water, finding mine. "I'm finished with True Time, Meg." Cian kisses me gently. "That's not the assistant spot I'm gunning for."

I'm feeling a chill from being still in the water. "Please no riddles."

There's his smile again. For me. About me. Designed for no one else.

"I've been fixated on the notion you shared with me back in California of boosting the visibility of local artists. Irish artists. Meg, there's something big there. I feel it the way I did with MetaMeme. What if artists and musicians like my father didn't have to leave Ireland to get the recognition they crave?"

"I thought your father was a doctor."

Cian's smile is sad. "He is, but that wasn't his first dream."

A knot forms in my chest. "My deal with Dash is for a run of series contract. I'm not pissing that away to give in to what my parents think I should be doing, even for someone as wonderful as you, Cian."

He spins me 'round, pulling my back against his chest. Arm muscles flex as he fans the air in front of me. "Not their scenario. I see you and me developing our own PR/Marketing business for the artists. You, my darling M-Squared, will of course be an integral part of the brains and the vision, but I intend to do the legwork while you stay with *The Chieftain's Son* until it's final curtain call."

Cian tightens his grip as a shiver runs through me. "You're mad to step away from a ripping career to tuck into Kerry."

He kisses my cheek. "I'm the opposite of mad. Ambition stunted my perspective. That night we commiserated over the lies we fabricate to feed the publicity beast, something snapped. I remembered the rush, the thrill when I worked with MetaMeme to put them on the map. It was personal. We were a team. That's what I love about my job. Helping talent be seen. Not the bullshit. Not the over-the-top spins on reality. It scares me, Meg, how easily I inhabited the Hollywood construct of make-believe to make myself look good." His fingers find mine. "I adore the way you shout to the world *The Chieftain's Son* is brilliant. Your plans, your scenarios," he chuckles as he borrows my phrase. "They're never about you."

"I'm not giving up my ambition." My gaze trickles over the water. "The way I mucked about in Jack and Gilly's life was forcing that construct on real people. It was wrong."

"True Time dictated the image they wanted Jack to project—their make-believe, not yours." Cian shakes his head. "You did your job, and he did his. Your ambition is the right kind. Meg McGrath is incapable of anything less than devotion to her people, to her show. That's what drives you. Your loyalty to the projects you commit to will take you wherever you choose to go."

"What if Hollywood is the end of my road?"

"Then so be it." He digs his chin into my shoulder so we're cheek to cheek. "Meg, you've reminded me of who I was. The me I want to be again. My trajectory stopped focusing on the shows or the groups I represented and became only about Cian Malley." He tightens his grip on me. "You knocked me off that path. I'm not just here for you. I'm here to find me."

Here we are, two intelligent people shifting our reality together. What could be grander?

He nuzzles my neck. "That, Meghan McGrath, is one of the many reasons I'm in danger of falling in love with you."

I spin in his arms to look in his eyes. He says words I'd only dare hoped might rise between us. "Cian, we could tally up the hours we've know each other without a calculator." Damn me for being too cowardly to assure him I'm alongside him, falling.

"Is this your way of telling me I'm crazy?" Cian's confidence wavers.

I lay a hand on his cheek. The contact sloughs off the last of my coward's shell. Fear of *"we"* bobbles away on the surface of the pool. "It is, and I'm right there with you."

He crushes his lips to mine with such force we slip on the tile stripe beneath us marking a swim lane. Even underwater, we don't break the kiss. When we come up for air, I smooth hair out of my eyes. "*The Chieftain's Son* potentially runs for nine or ten years, more if Deidre keeps writing."

"And what a glorious decade we can make it." He takes my hands again. "If you'll have me, Meghan McGrath."

He tries to drop to his knee in the pool, but I pull him to his feet. "Slow it down there. It's definitely too soon for any one-knee business."

Cian drags me toward the steps and manages a knee-drop position despite my protests. "I do have a proposal for you, M-Squared."

I lay a hand on his chest. "Oh, no, you don't. If you ever have a *proposal* for me, there are a thousand places more romantic in Ireland than a *Swim and Gym*."

He laughs. "Aha, more proof my Meg McGrath is made of softer stuff than she shows the world." His expression shifts to serious. "Here me out. I propose we open a business together here in Cahersiveen with a goal of expanding to Dublin. I propose you clear out a closet for me in your townhouse. I propose to open my eyes each morning before you wake for the pleasure of watching you greet the day in my arms. I propose you give us a shot." Cian takes both my hands in his. "And I repeat—if you'll have me, my darling, M-Squared."

The most life-changing decisions I've made lately happened in this pool where my head is always clear. My heart joins my head in glorious agreement. "I'll have you, Cian *O*'Malley." Emphasizing the "O," I slide my arms across his shoulders until my body presses against every inch of his drenched clothes. I smile against his lips. "I'll have you just fine."

EPILOGUE

Cian O'Malley could charm a wish out of a faerie. In his few months in Ireland, my man won over the family. Taryn bellyaches in a loop that Mommy and Dad prefer him to Roy. I forgive her beautiful belly since it's holding my first niece or nephew.

After a long day at The Clan, including the first production meeting of Jack's new show, working title, "*To You Beloved, My Ireland,*" I slip into the storage room of my parents' art gallery we've turned into the headquarters of M-Squared Marketing. Splattered across one wall like a battle plan are the particulars for Gilly and Jack's public wedding, our first project. The Chieftain's Son is on the brink of starting to shoot season three, "*Skies of Mist and Wind.*" We've nailed down permissions to shoot on Skellig Michael in late June, early July, limiting the number of shoes that'll walk onto the island. I've gotten nice and cozy with the particulars of booking helicopters.

The culminating day of production will in fact be the second wedding of our star and our Crystal-Award-winning writer. I get teary every time I read the press release set for the nuptials of my friends. Teary and a bit guilty for forcing the O'Learys to keep to the shadows for so long about their love.

Cian's bent over my dad's old drafting table. I lean across him and kiss his cheek. "Hello, my lovely."

He swivels his office chair to pull me into his lap. The "M" of my name starts as a purr and ends in a kiss that kicks fatigue from the day out the window.

I can't get enough of the man. He's become a wonderful mentor for my work on the show, upping my game rung after rung, along with my confidence. He's my Cyrano, whispering tips and advice into my ear with no one the wiser. My working relationship with Dash and True Time has taken on a whole different timbre since Cali Con. The green girl Bobby went to bat for is coming into her own.

I worry Cian misses the Hollywood life. It's my head game, not his. My man's sights are on our company.

"How was your meeting?" His naughty hand strays down my thigh to the knee, then doubles back on its journey under my skirt.

I slap his hand. "Daddy's on the other side of the door, you sneaky fool."

"But you've made the package so easy to unwrap." He succeeds in an indecent grab that sends me to my feet.

"Have you noticed the frown on my father's face? He's quite aware you're unwrapping this package."

Cian laughs. I love it when Cian laughs. "Unwrapping aside, your father likes me."

I straighten my skirt. "The meeting was brilliant. Gilly's nervous the new show will get tongues wagging before their second wedding, but I promised we'll keep the premise under wraps until she and Jack go public."

"And let me guess, Jack is saying fuck all."

I laugh. "Yep. Our resident bull in a China shop is of that mind. I thought his eyes were going to fry me like a rasher of bacon when I reminded him the breakup with Niks has to hit first before our Gilly steps into the light."

"A ticking bomb for another few weeks, yeah?"

I click on my phone to a draft of the press release I drew up before leaving work today and hand it to him. He skims the doc and looks up at me, startled. "This Friday?"

I nod. "It'll be brilliant. Niks and Jack will appear at the TVUK awards as a couple. They'll make nice, then announce their amicable split with a kiss. By the way, you'll need a tux."

He scratches his hair, a sign I've come to know signals racing thoughts. His eyes circle as he plays out the scenario. The corner of his lip rises. "Well played." He frowns. "Dash?"

I whip out my terrible Dashell Everett impression. "Agreed, Meghan. Time to bury the drama deep in the vault."

He laughs. "You're a bad audition tape for a crime drama." He presses his lips together. "What prompted the timeline escalation?" His eyes widen. "Oh shit, is Gilly pregnant?"

I take his hands and pull him to his feet so I can snatch him up in a proper embrace. "Nothing so urgent. If Niks and Jack split now, the fans will be ready to see their boy happy in love by Christmastime."

"The sentimental play. Damn, you're good." He kisses my nose. "And it'll get you a much bigger Christmas gift from Jack." He chuckles. "Niks and Marisa will probably buy you a pony."

I swat his adorable backside. "Och, you've seen right through me again, O'Malley." I'm about to pull the door closed and grab more of my favorite backside when Daddy calls from the gallery.

"Meggers, you lock up. I'm off home."

I dot a quick kiss on Cian's soft and eager mouth and catch up with my dad. The relationship between my parents and I warmed considerably since Cian and I started our business in their backroom.

"Sure, Daddy." I give him a hug and prepare to lock the front door behind him when Cian joins us.

"We're leaving, too, Mr. Mac." Cian's got his coat on, and keys jingle in his hand. "Remember, love, we're going to check out the gallery space for the October art show in Killarney."

"Tonight?"

"Sure, and then I'm craving the cocktails and duck at the Stoney Bistro." He threads an arm around my back. "Have I sufficiently tempted you with a walk through an artist's space and dinner?"

I'm dying to kick my shoes off so Cian can work his magic thumbs over my feet, but he's so bouncy at the prospect of a night out, I can't say no.

"Sounds like the sort of proper date you might have had before you shared an address." Daddy's grumble is for show—and probably the priest. He's all in on Cian. Daddy's also got a standing golf date with Cian's grandfather. I'm not the only one who fell for this particular O'Malley in record time.

I begin to sink into a lovely doze as Cian navigates the curving roads of the Ring of Kerry. My plans crumble when the tires groan over the gravel of a car-park.

"What's wrong? Is it the car?" My car is sturdy, but it's nearing the time when trading it in is looking better and better. I sit up and see we're at the Glenbeigh lookout.

Cian opens my door and extends a hand. "Join me." We walk to the fern border overlooking a perfect arc of dark teal water that forms the bay below. Splashed across the sky above the Atlantic, crimson reds bleed into a stripe of light melon.

Cian pulls me against his chest as we lose ourselves in the beauty of the dying day.

I rest my arms on his, leaning on my new swimming partner. I love beginning and ending my days with Cian. We're sunset clouds, one color melting into the other to create the perfect blend of something new.

"Meghan, I have a new proposal for you."

My mind plays the ideas we've batted around over the past weeks, like relocating in Killarney even though it would more than double my commute to Waterville and The Clan. I'm not selling my place in Cahersiveen, but I'm maybe willing to convert it to an Airbnb for a stretch. To my surprise, Cian has dual American and Irish citizenship since his dad was born here. Our talk of buying a place together works out fine given I've got myself an Irish lad.

I chuckle. "Is our date a ruse to show me real estate?"

"You were too right. It's much lovelier here than the inside of the *Swim and Gym*. Thank you, Ireland." Cian guides my hand into the pocket of his coat. He wraps my fingers around a tiny box with a velvety feel to it. My heart pounds as a sizzle sings through my body.

Cian frees the bitty box and my fingers clamped around it from his pocket.

"Meghan, there's a promise inside the box I'm ready to make to you." He drops light kisses behind my ear. "We happened fast, but everyday I'm with you makes me want a thousand more." His lips find the corner of my mouth. "My promise will wait until you're ready to hear it."

Oh, so gently, he slips our hands and the velvet box back in his pocket. Cian removes his hand, but mine continues to grasp the tiny promise. Not a tiny promise, the promise of a life with a man I love. A partner who honors my intelligence, my ambition, and my heart. No one has influenced my life and my dreams like Cian O'Malley.

Are we fools for falling through the sunset hand in hand? Could be, but then again, maybe not.

I bring the box free of his pocket and hand it to him. "What do you propose, Mr. O'Malley?"

He takes his velvet promise from my hand and opens it. Inside, a delicate gold ring dotted with tiny chips of diamond, emerald, and an aqua gem pick up the last of the sunlight. "It was my great grandmother's. Grandad's been keeping it for the day I came to my senses and found the perfect woman to share my life with." Cian drops to one knee. "An Irish treasure for my beautiful Irish dream. Will you spend your life with me, M-Squared? *I bring you with reverent hands the book of my numberless dreams.*"

"You've got me at a disadvantage, Sir. What self-respecting Irish girl could ever say no to a proposal using words from Mr. W.B. Yeats?" I sit on his knee and throw my arms around him. "And by the way, that's a yes."

As the sky darkens enough to welcome the stars, I kiss my way into the beginning of my forever *"we."*

Thank you for reading! Did you enjoy? Please add your review because nothing helps an author more and encourages readers to take a chance on a book than a review.

And don't miss book three in the *Behind the Scenes* series, <u>NOT TO SCALE</u>, available now. Turn the page for a sneak peek!

Also be sure to sign up for the City Owl Press newsletter to receive notice of all book releases!

SNEAK PEEK OF NOT TO SCALE

The tall blond Irishman on the morning shift behind the rent-a-car counter at Shannon Airport pins me with a knowing stare. "Ms. Pettipas, are you certain a stick shift is the way to go? It'll be your off-hand doing the work."

I treat him to a casual wave while my insides organize an uprising. Twirling the silver birthstone ring on my right ring finger with my thumb calms the insurgence. "I'm always up for a challenge."

Five minutes later, I'm loath to admit tall, blond, and Irish was right. I should have opted for an automatic rental. It's been ten years since I last drove a stick, and that was with my right "on-hand." There's a serious communication breakdown at present between my brain and left extremity as I attempt to work the gear shift. I'm not even close to leaving the rent-a-car parking lot when sticky third gear growls an unhealthy grinding noise. I half expect the cheery rental car attendant to throw himself in my path, waving his arms to insist I stop torturing his car. Adding to the miserable experience, I look over my right shoulder instead of my left to back up and stare at the car door.

A wise woman would head inside to the counter and insist on an automatic with a backup camera. Stubborn and determined me refuses to give in to my perpetual fear of failure until I stall for the third time in a row. Crawling back to the original parking place in second gear, I kill the engine and drop my head onto the steering wheel. Seeds of panic sprout in my chest.

I can't do this.

I punch my thighs. "Stop it, Elodie. You're thirty-two. At your age, panic is a choice."

At far too many points in my life, in my career, I've let anxiety drive me into hiding. It's set me back and made it harder on the next job to convince myself I'm not a fraud. Today it will not be anxiety for the win. I've landed my dream job, heading the art department of a crazy popular TV show with resources that would make most production designers moan with contentment. Even better, *The Chieftain's Son* is a time-hopping period piece begging for the very research deep-dives that set me on the road to my career in the first place.

I point a finger between my eyes. "You will not cocoon because of a stick shift." Determination to seize the gift of reconstructing history my new job promises bubbles inside me.

After fourteen hours in the air and a lost suitcase, I wish this moment was history. Years of travel working in film taught me to pack my carry-on as if I'll be stranded on a deserted island with only the contents of two zipper compartments for survival. My current deserted island is Ireland.

"Elodie Pettipas, you are a self-sufficient and capable woman."

My therapist, Kevin, is a huge proponent of positive self-talk. Still, the vise constricting my chest converts breaths into gasps.

"Correction, you are a self-sufficient and capable hot mess."

The bright yellow sticker on the sun visor screams at me to drive on the left side of the road. My whole life has veered onto the left side of the road. I will be living in Ireland for the foreseeable future. I barely know the sum total of one person here, Bobby Provost, the showrunner who hired me from video chats and phone calls. Rich and Amethyst Bettencourt, the angel mentors who took me under their wings in my early days of TV art direction, plunked me onto Bobby's radar and vetted me to the showrunner. I respect their faith in my talent more than my waning confidence. The Bettencourts would never recommend me if they doubted I could handle this monumental opportunity. Screw imposter syndrome, I will not let them down.

Their daughter, Gillian, is a writer on *The Chieftain's Son* and married to its star Jack O'Leary, a union I've sworn not to blab about. I suppose that increases my total to knowing one person virtually and two others by association. Three people in Ireland I almost know.

The cell buzzes in my pocket. It's Bobby Provost. "Hey Bobby."

"Welcome to Ireland, Elodie. Are you still at Shannon? The airline said your plane landed an hour ago."

I'm surprised how quickly his voice grounds me. We've already planted the seeds of our working relationship long distance. Bobby is easy to laugh with. We're both guilty of bird walking off work topics, then stretching conversations by sharing the horror stories from previous shows we worked on, disagreements over movies and other TV shows, and regaling each other with theater major shenanigans from our mutual but separate days at the same Hollywood adjacent college. I enjoyed talking to Bobby at the end of his days when mine were just beginning in LA and felt a little guilty keeping him chatting into his wee hours. Not guilty enough to end the call. I wonder how much opportunity we'll have for these talks when we're both buried in the demands of a brutal production schedule.

"It did. The short customs line was the stuff of dreams."

"Our driver, Patrick, can't find you."

"You sent me a driver for a three-hour trip?" Am I offended he discounted my ability to drive from County Clare to Kerry or touched at the gesture? I settle on relieved I'll dodge baptism by fire on Irish highways while jet lagged.

"Didn't you get my text?"

I scan my phone screen. "No text."

He's quiet for a second. "Damn, I emailed. Sorry, meant to text." Bobby pauses. "I wish I'd had time to call before you took off, but my schedule was nuts today." There's a definite charm running through the scattered tone of his voice, reminding me why I'm always eager for his calls. "Anyway, Patrick's camped out at baggage claim."

Judging from the small crowd at the single terminal airport, Patrick's probably the only person still at baggage claim.

"Look for a retired footballer type in a *Chieftain's Son* baseball cap."

The long trip and lost luggage tip my attitude from *relieved* to *touched* by Bobby's gesture. "A guy who will save me from driving an off-hand stick shift on the left side of the road? Yes, I'll go find St. Patrick in a baseball cap."

Bobby laughs. A surge of warmth dissolves my rising panic. I'm getting very used to that laugh. I wouldn't mind getting even more used to it.

My phone buzzes with an incoming call from the airline. "I've got another call. Talk with you soon, Bobby."

"Looking forward to it, Elodie Pettipas."

The man's voice is the sunny equivalent of a smile. I answer with my own smile as I click over. My heretofore jumpy stomach is infused with a dose of Bobby Provost honey for a moment before my nerves fire up again. Am I leaning too far into the connection I've forged with Bobby over our transatlantic chats? Damn, I know my therapist would push play on his familiar tune that I tend to attach to authority figures and hunger for their approval. Bobby probably already has an Irish girlfriend. The good ones usually do. I hard swallow the lump of disappointment taking up residence in my throat as my phone pesters me with a reminder someone is waiting for me to answer. "Elodie Pettipas here."

"Ms. Pettipas, good news, we've found your luggage. It should be arriving at Shannon Airport within the hour."

Luggage, a driver, and only a few hours until I meet Bobby face-to-face. Looks like Ireland is not my deserted island after all.

Don't stop now. Keep reading with your copy of NOT TO SCALE

And find more from Leslie O'Sullivan at
www.leslieosullivanwrites.com

Don't miss book three of the *Behind the Scenes* series, NOT TO SCALE, available now, and be sure to discover all the details on Sullivan's website at www.leslieosullivanwrites.com

Elodie Pettipas is reeling from landing her dream job, the coveted production designer position on the hit Irish TV show, *The Chieftain's Son*. Even though her talent and excellent track record of bringing history to life on screen has allowed her to soar past much more experienced competitors, Elodie battles with anxiety and the self-doubt of being able to handle the demands of the mega-show.

After months of virtual meetings, Elodie arrives on set in Ireland finally meeting cinnamon roll showrunner, Bobby Provost, face-to-face. As Elodie struggles to win over her new crew, Bobby's generous support and belief in her talents boost her confidence. What began as an easy online friendship in virtual meetings deepens into a steamier collaboration.

Just as Elodie succeeds in winning over her team and allows herself to embrace the budding romance with Bobby, a career-making offer from Hollywood intrudes on her idyllic vision of the future.

Will the lure to rise in the Hollywood hierarchy destroy Elodie's path to happiness?

Please sign up for the City Owl Press newsletter for chances to win special subscriber-only contests and giveaways as well as receiving information on upcoming releases and special excerpts.

All reviews are **welcome** and **appreciated**. Please consider leaving one on your favorite social media and book buying sites.

For books in the world of romance and speculative fiction that embody Innovation, Creativity, and Affordability, check out City Owl Press at www.cityowlpress.com.

ACKNOWLEDGMENTS

Hooray for my fellow Comic Con super fans: Melissa, Cameron, Tiffany, Robert, Gwynneth, Trillian, and Tab. May we always meet success when facing the spinning blue wheel of doom for tickets and the line at Hall H. Special shout out to Rob and Chris Desmond who took me to my first Comic Con.

Shannon K., squeezy hugs for your endless supply of support and kindness. Beware: We'll get you to Comic Con one of these days.

Thank you to everyone at City Owl Press for being dream makers. Huge gratitude to my editor, Theresa Cole, for championing this series and giving my story sparkle.

Dearest family, your belief in me as an author is priceless. X to Cameron, Melissa, Rich, John, Elizabeth, and Sidney. Wonderful friends, Diane, Laurie, Flo, Lisa, Julie, Sarah, Katharyn, and Shona, your talents and sweet encouragements are a constant source of inspiration.

A huge whoo hoo to the Booktokers and Bookstagrammers who shower the world with love for books and stories. Maximum gratitude to the readers who've come along with the cast and crew of *The Chieftain's Son* on their San Diego Adventure. Thank you so much.

ABOUT THE AUTHOR

LESLIE O'SULLIVAN is the award-winning author of the adult romantasy *Rockin' Fairy Tales* series of fairy tale retellings set against the backdrop of a fictional Hollywood music scene and the contemporary romantic comedy series, *Behind the Scenes,* that peeks into the off-camera sizzle of a wildly popular Irish television drama. She's a UCLA Bruin with a BA and MFA from their Department of Theater where she also taught for years on the design faculty. Her tenure in the world of television was as the assistant art director on "It's Garry Shandling's Show." Leslie loves to indulge her fangirl side at Cons.

www.leslieosullivanwrites.com

facebook.com/leslie.osullivanauthor

instagram.com/leslieosullivanwrites

x.com/LeslieSulliRose

tiktok.com/@leslieosullivanwrites

ABOUT THE PUBLISHER

City Owl Press is a cutting edge indie publishing company, bringing the world of romance and speculative fiction to discerning readers.

Escape Your World. Get Lost in Ours!

www.cityowlpress.com

f facebook.com/YourCityOwlPress
X x.com/cityowlpress
instagram.com/cityowlbooks
pinterest.com/cityowlpress